LONG WAY
HOME

J. B. TURNER

LONG WAY HOME

THOMAS & MERCER

Published by Thomas & Mercer, Seattle

www.apub.com

Amazon, the Amazon logo, and Thomas & Mercer are trademarks of Amazon.com, Inc., or its affiliates.

ISBN-13: 9781542039772

eISBN: 9781542039789

Cover design by @blacksheep-uk.com

Cover image: © Gorloff-KV / Shutterstock; © Miguel Sobreira / ArcAngel;
© Nico De Pasquale Photography © Xinzheng / Getty Images

Printed in the United States of America

LONG WAY
HOME

Corpses fell from a black sky.

Hundreds of them.

He stared through the windows at the ghostly faces as they passed. Their bone-white skin. Down below on the street, the bodies piled up.

Jack McNeal awoke and sat bolt upright in his bed, bathed in a cold sweat. He breathed hard, heart pounding. He got his bearings. He waited for the fear to subside. He was safe. It was just another bad dream.

He closed his eyes for a moment. Terrifying nightmares had plagued him for nearly three years. He hadn't told anyone besides his psychologist. He couldn't tell her why he was experiencing such terrors. But he knew why they had begun.

McNeal groaned as he got out of bed. He shuffled to the bathroom, splashed cold water on his face. He stared at his reflection in the mirror. Haunted eyes, ashen face.

He went to the living room and opened the blinds.

The late afternoon sun streamed in through the floor-to-ceiling windows. Outside, snow covered the New York City streets. He was alive. Thank God he was still alive. Then he thought of the bodies *again. Not the corpses in his dreams. But the bodies of the men he had killed. They existed in the darkest recesses of his mind.*

One day, they would be found. He knew that.

It was just a matter of time . . .

One

Three minutes after midnight.

Jack McNeal sat hunched at his desk with his headphones on as he watched surveillance footage of a corrupt New York City cop. He felt numb. The man under investigation was a ten-year veteran. His name was Jesus Ramos. A bike cop with three kids and a wife at home in Staten Island. But here he was, filmed by undercover Internal Affairs investigators, cycling from the station house in Brooklyn to the brothel in Park Slope. The brothel was located inside a four-story building. They'd bugged it with audio and video cameras as part of a plea deal with the owner. Ramos was brazen. The shameless bastard was wearing his NYPD uniform. He didn't conceal his badge or his identity. It was almost as if he wanted to get caught.

Jack turned up the volume and listened carefully. The madam, a Haitian national, told a Nigerian prostitute to have sex with Ramos. Then the madam gave instructions that the officer wasn't to be charged. *It's on the house, honey.*

McNeal took verbatim notes of the verbal exchange. The notes would go into his final report. The video footage told its own story. It had been weeks since the initial complaint had been lodged anonymously against the officer. McNeal had requested authorization for the premises to be bugged. It had taken nearly a week to get the authorization from not only his superiors but also the court. But now, he finally had compelling and conclusive proof that the officer was indeed corrupt.

He felt soiled, but he watched and listened to it all. The years he had been doing the work had taken their toll. He felt sleazy, immoral, and downright debased. He wondered how long he could stand it. His one saving grace was that he didn't need the money. His one saving grace.

McNeal took off his headphones. He switched off the monitor and leaned back in his seat. He took in the third-floor office, a handful of investigators taking calls coming into the Command Center of the NYPD Internal Affairs Bureau. Sergeant Aisha Williams grimaced as she fielded an irate call. It might be a distressed wife making allegations about an errant spouse. John Q. Public witnessing a cop attacking a panhandler in broad daylight. Or roughing up a Bronx kid down a back alley. Or taking a bribe from a bar owner. Or kickbacks from neighborhood mobsters. Or bottles of whiskey from a bodega owner in exchange for turning a blind eye to the sale of cigarettes to kids.

The more Jack thought about it, the more he wondered why the hell he was still doing this job. It was killing his soul. Eroding whatever what was left of his humanity. The lowlifes he investigated. Day after day. Night after night. No end in sight.

He had options. He didn't have to do this job anymore. His brother and father thought he was nuts for still working. He had money. A lot of money.

McNeal stared at the photo of his late wife on his desk. A brilliant and successful journalist. The wife who had left him before her death—her murder. He had never stopped loving her, though he had felt the distance grow between them over the years. He knew he wasn't the easiest person in the world to get along with. Not by a long shot. His dark moods and brooding nature had worn her down.

Jack's world had collapsed after her death. The waste of life was too much to bear. She'd had so much to offer the world. She was supersmart. An acclaimed political journalist. She had written books. She investigated stories. She authored *New York Times* bestsellers. She knew the movers and shakers in Washington. Her father had left her a fortune when he died. And when she was tragically taken from this earth, her will explicitly said that he, Jack McNeal, her husband, albeit separated, was to receive everything from her estate. He felt guilty for inheriting millions of dollars under such tragic circumstances. More than thirty million dollars in assets, including bank accounts and stocks from her late father.

He didn't have to be here. He didn't need this shit. He should be down in Florida enjoying the sun like his Internal Affairs pal Dave Franzen. He could do with some warm rays. The blue skies. Not a care in the world. He had thought about it. A lot. He imagined buying a place in Boca Raton.

Despite everything, he still loved his job.

He figured that if he retired early, the days would be long, stretching out before him, nothing to do. It would be fine for a few weeks. Outside estimate could be as long as a few months. He would need to find a hobby. Would he take up golf? He couldn't imagine himself striding down the fairways under a blistering sun, hacking his way around a golf course. He didn't know the first thing about it. It wasn't really him. The chances were that if he retired, he would inevitably head to a bar to pass the time. That would be his daily life, replacing his work in the NYPD. The job gave him purpose in the world. A focus. A reason to live, even.

That didn't take away the emptiness inside, though. Gnawing away at him. He had been hollowed out by his deeds. He still found it difficult to reconcile his job with what he'd done.

McNeal had played with the idea of getting a one-way ticket to a place where no one would ever find him. He had figured a country without an extradition treaty was the way to go. But he hadn't done it so far.

His cell phone rang, snapping him out of his morose thoughts. McNeal checked the caller ID. It was his brother, Peter.

"Jack, you working?" His brother's voice sounded tense.

"Yeah. I'm on nights. You okay?"

"Turn on Fox."

"Why?"

"Turn it on!"

McNeal put his headphones back on and pointed the remote at the TV. He switched to Fox News.

"You got it?"

"Yeah, I got it."

McNeal stared at the TV. A female reporter stood, cloaked in virtual darkness. A glittering stretch of water behind her. A police patrol boat edged into view in the background. He could make out the silhouettes of frogmen with searchlights. And on the screen it said simply, *Body Found in Maryland Reservoir.*

"You watching this, man?"

"I'm watching."

The reporter spoke excitedly. "Today, a strange story out of rural Maryland. While working on the Liberty Reservoir, divers found a body encased in cement. Police are currently investigating, and Chief Sonia Reinhold told Fox News that she has a few leads on identifying the remains."

McNeal's blood ran cold. It was happening. Just as he feared.

Two

The psychologist Belinda Katz consulted from her swanky Greenwich Village prewar apartment. High ceilings, modern art on the whitewashed walls. It had been three years since he had been referred to her by his boss at Internal Affairs. The reasons? Anger issues, hostility, and increasing isolation stemming from the tragic accidental death of his son five years before his referral at a backyard family party. Jack's partner, Juan Gomez, in a drunken stupor and wanting to kill himself, had waved his gun around and fired at a wall, but the bullet ricocheted and killed Jack's son, Patrick. His world collapsed. He had blamed himself. He still did. But Caroline's death, only a short while after he'd started therapy, sent his precarious mental state into a hellish tailspin.

Katz wore an impeccably cut black suit, her signature look. Dark red nail polish, matching lipstick. She brushed her stylish bob behind her ears. Then she tilted her head forward and peered over her glasses. "You look tired."

McNeal took a deep breath and exhaled slowly. "I feel tired."

"We've talked about this before, haven't we? Is this work-related? Stress?"

"What can I tell you? I'm busy. Busy is good. It keeps my mind off things."

"I've met a lot of workaholics. Work is important. But so is taking care of ourselves. Mind, body, and soul."

McNeal shrugged. He'd never found much time for himself.

"Let's talk again about hobbies."

McNeal said nothing.

"Why don't you have any outside interests?"

"I don't know."

The psychologist took a few notes. "What does that mean?"

"I mean I don't have outside interests."

Katz pinched the bridge of her nose as if she was facing a stubborn toddler. "I've talked to two clients today similar to you. But they both have outside interests."

"I don't really have time for outside interests."

Katz leaned back in her seat. "I've been seeing you, off and on, more off than on, for nearly three years, right?".

McNeal agreed.

"I'm not buying it."

"Not buying what?"

"That you don't have any interests outside work."

McNeal shrugged. He couldn't really see the point of what she was doing. He was getting bored by the sessions. He thought they were unduly intrusive. He liked his personal space. His personal headspace. He was a private person who preferred to keep his moods and emotions to himself.

"I'd like to explore that area, just to get a better picture of what makes you tick. All we've ever really talked about is work. We've spoken about your problems at work. We've spoken about how you define yourself by your work."

"I go to the gym."

"Okay, that's good. Endorphins are very good for raising mood. I'm curious, do you socialize?"

"Are we going out on a date already?"

The psychologist's stare lingered a second too long for McNeal's liking. "Humor can mask our true feelings, Jack. The underlying condition. Clinical depression, anxiety, maybe self-loathing."

"What's your point?"

"You mentioned your sleeping patterns . . . You said . . ." Katz flicked through her notes. "On November third you said you barely sleep. A couple of hours, maximum, which points to either an individual who doesn't need normal amounts of sleep or perhaps a borderline insomniac. That's not a great thing to be. I know, I've been there. Many years back."

"What can I say, I'm wired. Really wired. I find it hard to relax. I go to the gym. I get rid of my energy. But my mind is always racing."

"Which brings me to my next point. Your dreams. Bad dreams. Nightmares. This element seems to have become quite profound. Terrifying. But it's only in the last three years."

McNeal's mind flashed back to waking earlier in a cold sweat. The falling corpses. The terror.

"Tell me about these nightmares. You mentioned previously about having vivid dreams. Awful dreams. You imagine bodies falling past your office window. The same recurring dream . . ."

McNeal sighed. "I know it makes me sounds crazy."

The psychologist scribbled some notes. "Three years is a long time to experience such disturbances. The mind is a powerful thing. Do you know anything about repressed emotions?"

"Not my area of expertise."

"Let me help you out here. Something that we've done or witnessed of a violent nature, for example, can trigger subconscious thoughts. Recurring nightmares. Terrifying bad dreams."

McNeal crossed his legs. "I watch surveillance footage of cops stomping on kids, killing people on the subway. You name it, I've seen it. The death of my son too. A lot of stuff. Stuff I can't unsee."

"That's true, very true. But I believe, and this is just because I've come to know you much better, that these nightmares are symptomatic of something that happened to you. The nightmares only began in the last three years. Your son's tragic death at the hands of your colleague was years before that."

McNeal closed his eyes. His mind replayed dropping Nicoletti down the mine shaft buried deep underground.

"Do you remember when we first met? You had what appeared to be a psychotic reaction. You were in the middle of a breakdown."

McNeal cleared his throat. "It was tough. But I somehow managed to work through that period."

"You went missing for a few days. No one could contact you. Can you think back to that time, Jack?"

"Sure."

"I remember that you seemed—and don't take this the wrong way—paranoid. Full of acute anxiety."

McNeal sat in silence.

"Shortly after you had been referred, your wife died under tragic circumstances. I remember you missed an appointment or two. You said people might be out to harm you. I found that quite a striking comment."

"It was a bad time I was going through."

"Do you remember you told me a name? You called me. And I wrote the name down on a scrap of paper."

Jack could hear the sound of his heart thumping through his chest.

Katz checked her notes, found what she was looking for. "I remember you said that if something happened to you, you would deem one man responsible. You were very specific."

McNeal wondered where she was going with this.

"You see, the reason I ask is that this morning I turned on my TV, and there was a reporter talking about a missing man. Henry Graff."

McNeal shifted in his seat. He felt his anxiety levels rise.

"The same name you told me. I'd scribbled it down so I wouldn't forget."

McNeal remained quiet.

The psychologist looked at him. "It's a bit of a coincidence, isn't it?"

"I don't know. Sounds plausible."

"I watched the report. It mentioned the man had been missing for just over three years."

McNeal groaned.

"Do you want to talk about that?"

"I've got a lot of things on my mind. I can't remember much about that episode. Three years is a long time."

Katz just looked at him and jotted down some notes. "That's our session for today."

McNeal was pleased to step outside and feel the cold air on East Tenth Street. His breath turned to vapor in the January chill. Out of the corner of his eye, he saw two guys wearing suits approach.

"Jack McNeal?" The first guy was wearing a heavy navy overcoat.

"Who are you?"

He flashed an FBI ID. "We've got a few questions. You mind coming with us?"

Three

It was a short drive to the FBI's field office in Lower Manhattan.

McNeal and the two Feds rode the elevator in silence to the twenty-third floor. A sense of foreboding washed over him. He stared as the numbers of the floors changed. He felt disconnected. This was something he had long expected to happen.

McNeal checked his expression in the elevator's mirror. His sunken eyes stared back at him. He halfheartedly checked if the elevator had hidden cameras monitoring him. It was the FBI, after all. Had things really changed since the Hoover days? In some ways they had. He knew many agents who were by-the-book investigators. But he got the impression from the agents he knew that a different mindset was in place among the highest echelons of the organization.

"You're not under arrest, Jack," one agent said.

McNeal remained silent.

The Feds escorted him down a series of long corridors to an interview room.

Tony Contini, the Special Agent in Charge of the FBI in New York, was seated behind a table. "Can I get you a coffee? Water?"

"Coffee would be good, thank you."

"Take a seat."

McNeal did as he was told.

"Lot to take in, huh?"

McNeal said nothing.

Contini scribbled a few notes. "We don't record interviews. We don't find that helpful. If it's okay with you, I'll take a few notes. We just want to ask you some questions. You know how these things work, don't you?"

McNeal knew very well the FBI didn't record interviews. At least not officially. It was a very convenient way for them to distill the interview into an "official" summary. Their summary. Their version of events. Instead of an audio and visual record of an interview, the Feds held the cards. It might have been the twenty-first century, but the analog methods, such as eschewing the recording of interviews, were not fit for purpose in a modern law enforcement sense. They were a relic of the Hoover era.

McNeal sipped the lukewarm black coffee he was handed. He thought about how he was going to play it. As he lifted the cup to his lips, he noticed a tremor in his hand. He was still in shock. He needed to pull himself together. He knew full well that the Feds would be scrutinizing his every move.

Contini slowly opened a manila folder. "You're probably wondering what this is all about."

The FBI would have checked their database. That would show he had been interviewed before with regard to Graff.

"I just want to reiterate," Contini said, "this is an informal chat. We're carrying out inquiries related to an ongoing investigation."

McNeal knew where this was going.

"It's a missing person inquiry. A guy named Henry Graff. Is that name familiar to you?"

McNeal took another sip of his coffee. "Graff, you say?"

Contini repeated himself. "Correct. Henry Graff."

McNeal judged how much the Feds really knew. He sensed they knew a hell of a lot more than they were letting on. But that was to be expected. They were following a well-trodden path. They asked questions they already knew the answers to. They would have already established that he had previously visited Henry Graff's office. But if he lied and denied knowing Graff, he would have dug a deeper hole for himself. He knew how it worked. If he said he had visited, they could lead him down the road of *Did you have anything to do with his disappearance?* or *Can you account for your whereabouts on the dates that Mr. Graff went missing?* He would slowly get boxed into the place where they wanted him. And then they would pull out that he was a person of interest. He knew the way it worked.

Jack felt all eyes on him. It was already time to pull up the drawbridge, so to speak. "I'd like to speak to a lawyer."

"This is purely informal."

"I understand."

"So, what's the problem answering the questions?"

"No problem at all. Can I speak to my lawyer?"

"We were hoping you could help us with this inquiry."

"I am. So, you have no problems with me having a lawyer here with me?"

Contini checked his notes as he tried to regain the upper hand. "There is nothing formal here."

"You said that before. I understand that. So, with all due respect, I would like to speak to a lawyer, and have them here with me. That shouldn't be a problem."

"We were hoping you would be more forthcoming."

"I'm here. I'm very forthcoming. I'm more than happy to help as much as I can, but I'd like a lawyer of my choosing to be present."

"I don't understand, Jack."

"What don't you understand?"

"Why the need for a lawyer at this stage? We're just asking a few simple questions."

McNeal knew they were trying to rile him. He took a sip of coffee. "Of course, and I understand that."

"Let's forget about the lawyers for now. We would like you to give us an answer. Did you know a Henry Graff? Is that name familiar to you?"

McNeal leaned back in his seat, and Contini leaned a bit closer. McNeal caught a whiff of cologne. "You see, we believe that Henry Graff is not only familiar to you, but to your late wife."

McNeal remained impassive. He sensed Contini was trying to pick at a raw nerve. He figured Contini was hoping that by dropping his late wife into the conversation, he could get McNeal to respond, perhaps emotionally. Lash out in anger. He was tempted to. He was in turmoil. But he couldn't lose his control.

"We know you reached out to the FBI field office in Bridgeport just over three years ago." He scanned his notes. "In connection with some files allegedly belonging to your late wife. Files which may or may not be classified in nature. We believe those files were stolen by your late wife."

McNeal remained impassive.

"To do with a *Washington Post* investigation, apparently." Contini scribbled some notes. "I didn't expect you to be taking the Fifth."

McNeal said nothing.

"I'm going to ask you. Are you taking the Fifth?"

"That's correct. I'm taking the Fifth. Until I see a lawyer."

Contini looked slightly downcast. He leaned back in his seat. "You know Mr. Graff, don't you, Jack? You not only know him, you visited him. So, surely it's far better if you just come clean."

McNeal wondered if the session was being covertly filmed, like through a one-way mirror on the wall behind him. He kept his expression neutral.

"We know quite a lot about you, Jack." Contini flicked through a few pages in the folder. "We've been doing some research on you. There was a period more than three years ago in particular when you were seeing a lot of a psychologist in New York. Still are."

"What's your point?"

"It's not unusual. Stress, mental collapse, pressures at work. I get it, trust me, seen it many times. It's nothing to be ashamed of."

"What exactly are you getting at?"

"There was a period, as I said, three years ago, almost to the day, when you reached out to the FBI in Bridgeport."

McNeal shrugged.

"But here's the thing that intrigued me. According to some of your colleagues, you disappeared for a while. You couldn't be contacted for a couple of days. Dropped off the grid, so to speak. The problem is, Jack, we need to know your whereabouts at that time. Just to eliminate you from our inquiries."

McNeal remained silent.

"I'm trying to put myself in your shoes, Jack. What would I do? And I've got to say I'd be a hell of a lot more forthcoming. You have nothing to hide, right?"

McNeal stared at Contini, who averted his eyes quickly.

"It would make sense that, if your wife had died, you would be traumatized. I get it. If you can't account for some of that time. But it's really important for our investigation that you clarify what happened. Maybe you blacked out. It happens."

"This is all very intriguing. But I'm still waiting to know when I can get a lawyer. I've been incredibly patient so far."

"And I appreciate that. The problem is, there are unanswered questions. Time gaps. You could clear it all up if you let us know what happened. I mean what really happened."

McNeal's gaze wandered around the room. He turned and stared at the mirror on the wall. "Are we being filmed?"

"Are we being filmed?"

"Could you answer the question?"

Contini exchanged glances with the special agent sitting beside him. "I'm asking the questions, Jack. Got another one for you. I believe you also made contact with your wife's psychologist in DC shortly after your wife died. Three years and three months ago. Not your psychologist in New York, but another one. Why was that?"

McNeal didn't respond.

"It could all be perfectly innocent. I'm sure it is. But it is important to our investigation that you clarify the points we're raising."

"I'm curious why I'm still having to ask for my lawyer."

"Plenty of time for that. Here's an interesting aspect from events of three years ago. We have been led to believe that you made contact with a well-known Mafia captain in New Jersey. Can you tell me if this was pertinent to an Internal Affairs investigation?"

McNeal sat in silence, allowing the questions to wash over him.

"Could be a perfectly rational explanation. Was he a man whose name had been linked to a corrupt cop, and you were carrying out an investigation? That would be understandable, in that context. The problem is . . . the man you contacted is known to us. We believe he is involved with murder and extortion across the tri-state area. He has connections in Atlantic City, Vegas, and Los Angeles."

McNeal's gaze skittered around the room.

"You seem distracted. Are you okay? I can imagine it's a bit of a shock."

McNeal fixed his glare back on Contini. "Let's recap. I've asked repeatedly for a lawyer, and I haven't received confirmation that I can call an attorney. I've also asked if these proceedings are being filmed behind the mirror. Why can't you answer that, Contini?"

Contini flushed. "I'm very disappointed in you, Jack."

"I'm very disappointed in *you*. Do you want to cut the bull-shit, Contini? Disappointed? Give me a break. Is this how you treat law-abiding citizens? I would have expected to be afforded the courtesy and have my legal rights as an American citizen respected."

"We're simply asking questions."

"I'm still trying to figure out why I can't see a lawyer. And to determine if there are cameras filming this. Is that too much to ask?"

"My point is, taken together, all these different elements point to a man having a breakdown. If you need help, we want to help you get that care, if that is indeed what the problem is. We know you visited Henry Graff in person. It might've been for something perfectly innocent. But it is important you clarify what your relationship with him was."

McNeal said, "I respectfully invoke my rights under the Fifth Amendment of the US Constitution on the grounds that answering questions may incriminate me."

Contini bowed his head and scribbled some more notes. "Very well. I'd like to thank you for coming in. But it would be remiss of me not to inform you that we might want to speak to you again."

"Am I free to go?"

"You're free to go."

Four

The cold, deserted beach was only yards from McNeal's house in Westport, Connecticut. It overlooked the slate-gray waters of Long Island Sound. No one around. Not a soul within earshot.

McNeal wore a thick puffer jacket against the biting wind as he walked on the sand, accompanied by his brother, Peter. They didn't say a word as they headed down to the shoreline. He stopped and looked around. "I'm assuming you have no electronic devices?"

"None," Peter said, hands deep in his overcoat. "Left them at home."

"This is very important. You don't have any cell phones, iPads, pagers on you right now?"

Peter shrugged. "I told you, I left them at home. What's wrong with you?"

"What's wrong with me? I'll tell you what's wrong with me. They're onto us."

"I know."

"We need to be careful."

"You don't have to tell me. I was watching TV before I left. Fox is still running coverage at the reservoir. But I also saw it on *Good Morning America* too. There's no mention of the name. But the cops and Feds will know it's Graff."

"That's why I want to talk."

"What do you mean?"

"I got hauled in by the Feds."

"Are you kidding me?"

Jack shook his head. "They wanted to know if I knew Henry Graff."

"And?"

"I said nothing, obviously. Gave them the *I'm taking the Fifth* spiel."

"They're fishing."

"I know that. But I sense they know a lot already. That's what my gut is telling me."

Peter grimaced as he rubbed his hands together in the bitter cold.

Jack elaborated. "I contacted Graff a few days before he disappeared, and we reached out to the Feds in Bridgeport about my wife's death all around the same time. Diplomatic Security was speaking to me about the hard pass Caroline had for the White House, and I think they pieced together our movements."

"Hard pass?"

"You know, Caroline was one of those journalists who had the highest level of access at the White House. They call it a hard pass. That's why Diplomatic Security spoke to me. I imagine the FBI has now taken charge of this from the Secret Service."

"It's been nearly three fucking years, Jack."

"I know. Consider this: they might have tracked my car's GPS signals or have surveillance footage from the interstate of us driving in Maryland."

"Which took us past the reservoir." Peter closed his eyes, shaking his head. "Fuck. This isn't good."

"I figured it might take decades to find the bones, not years. But they caught a break."

"So, what are we going to do?"

"Listen to me. This is what's going to happen. I'm going to own this. This is my problem. And I'll deal with it. I want you to let me handle it my way."

Peter eyeballed him. "That's not going to happen. They come after you, they come after me."

McNeal had to resist the urge to grab his brother by the scruff of the neck. "We did what we had to do. That was then. Now? I will deal with it."

"I will never walk away. That was the deal we made. Did we or did we not agree?"

"I'm not asking you, I'm telling you. I'm on my own. If we stick together, we will fall together. I'm going to take the rap if the shit hits the fan. But I'm taking the Fifth, so they need more than circumstantial evidence."

"We both did it."

Jack stared down the full length of the empty beach. They began to walk again. "Let's put aside who's going to take the fall for now. We need to think of the basics before we have the luxury of guessing who's going to take the fall. All you have to know for now is if they come for you and haul you in for questions, you stick to our agreed playbook, as we discussed."

"I know. I take the Fifth."

"Exactly. I'm not going to get into whether we should or shouldn't hang together, worst-case scenario."

Peter rubbed his face as if trying to wake himself up from a bad dream. "How did it get so crazy?"

"Who the hell knows? It's a mess."

"I can't believe the Feds brought you in."

McNeal's mind began to race. He had originally tried to do the right thing by contacting the FBI about Caroline's file and her suspicious death. But when he didn't hear back from them, McNeal knew he couldn't just forget about it. His wife had been murdered.

21

He had thought he was doing the right thing. But vengeance was going to come at a high price.

"You really do look like shit, Jack."

"Thanks for the pep talk. I'm not sleeping too good."

"You too? Doctor suggested I needed sleeping pills. You believe that?"

"What did you tell him?"

"I told him I wasn't going to become a fucking zombie pill head. There's enough wandering the streets of New Jersey as it is."

Jack nodded in agreement.

"You know what's been bothering me for a while?" Peter asked. "Since . . . you know?"

"What's that?"

"The names we were given. I keep on running the two other names over in my head again and again."

"What names?"

Peter shrugged. "You know, the names."

"What exactly are you getting at? The Feds have me in their sights, and you're talking about names."

"Remember, the names! The names that fucker Nicoletti gave us. The names? Karen Feinstein, right? And Woodcutter. Two of the people involved. The people who probably organized Caroline's death."

Jack shook his head. "I'm not going there. What we did was crazy. Insane. The last thing we need to do now is think about those two. I've got enough on my plate without going down that road. We need to forget about that and focus on the present."

His brother stared at the water. "So, we should forget about it?"

"I can't face it. Going down that road again."

Peter shook his head. "I want to know more."

"So do I. But I don't want to hunt the fuckers down. I don't want to have things play out like last time. I want us to draw a line on this."

22

Peter closed his eyes and exhaled. "Agreed."

"Keep one thing in mind. What happened to me? This is only the beginning."

"You think they have something on us?"

"Even if they prove that we went that route, and I'm assuming that's what's brought me into their investigation, they still have nothing. It's purely circumstantial."

Peter was quiet, contemplating their fate.

"There is nothing linking the body to us. You think there'll be anything left for forensics?"

"Highly unlikely."

"Let's not panic. Let's stay alert. Stay aware of what is going on. And not say a goddamn word. We deal with this in-house. We say nothing. But in the meantime, I want to revisit what Caroline knew."

"The dossier?"

"Precisely. I'll go and get it from the safe-deposit box, and I'll reexamine in detail what she's got."

"Is that a good idea?"

"They're searching the reservoir. They know it's Graff. And they will come for us. Either the Feds or the cops or Feinstein's people. It might be worth having a second look at the dossier."

"We didn't find anything about the identity. There was no mention of the name in the dossier. Just the video of her talking, right before she died."

"I think we missed something the first time. Nico gave us the name Woodcutter. But we need to know more. Who the hell is he?"

Peter shook his head. He turned to face the water. "We know too much, Jack. We both know too much. I don't think it's going to end here."

"I think you're right. But we need to be prepared. We need to be ready for them."

Five

The operative scanned Compo Beach with military-grade binoculars, watching the McNeal brothers deep in conversation. He was lying flat on his stomach in an attic room at the far end of the beach alongside his sidekick, Ramirez, a dead-eyed Hispanic woman he had never worked with before. The location had a perfect line of sight. Their one-month Airbnb "beach" rental had been perfect for their needs. It was close enough to Jack McNeal's home. It gave them a base nearby when the Internal Affairs investigator returned from working in the city.

Ramirez watched the brothers through a high-powered telephoto lens, occasionally taking shots of the two NYPD detectives. "No fucking audio," Ramirez said.

The operative pursed his lips. "I know."

"So, what do we do?"

"Give the boss what we have."

"We don't know what they're saying."

"Yeah, no shit." The operative knew his boss wouldn't be happy. He had worked with FeinSolutions for the last five years. He was ex-CIA and had worked with Karen Feinstein in Iraq and Afghanistan. He was a covert specialist. But he was also a trained killer.

He was part of a two-person team, alongside Ramirez, tasked with keeping an eye on the brothers' movements.

Steele would be pissed off that he hadn't gotten audio on the beach. It was vital to the operation. The operative was closer to Steele than anyone. He had been broke when he left the Agency. He had spent all his money on alimony and child support and booze. He had been asked to head back to Iraq for big money. But his stomach wasn't in that anymore. He wanted to stay in America, no matter what. This job had given him that ability. Financial security, great perks, and Tom Steele as his boss. A guy who inspired undying loyalty. He exuded quiet, Southern charm. But the guy was as ruthless as they came.

The operative knew Steele would be getting the flak for this. The microphones on Jack and Peter's cell phones had been activated remotely. But without any results. It meant that the brothers were one step ahead.

He pressed his finger to the miniature listening device in his ear. "Still waiting on audio. I repeat: still waiting on audio. Do a further systems check."

Ramirez groaned as she tapped away at the laptop by her side. "Same as before. The GPS is showing the cell phone in New Jersey. Jack McNeal's cell phone is in his house. They went onto the beach without their phones."

The operative had figured as much. "Cute."

"The boss is going to be real pissed."

The operative scanned the brothers on the beach. "Why didn't you bring a long-range microphone?"

"I'll get one sent over."

"Don't let this happen again. You don't get another chance."

Six

The gated community was situated on the outskirts of the affluent town of McLean, Virginia, a short drive from the headquarters of the CIA. Woods surrounded the enclave and protected it from prying eyes.

Karen Feinstein's car pulled up to the gatehouse, security cameras high up on poles watching her approach.

A uniformed guard holding an iPad bent down. "We've been expecting you, ma'am. Need some ID."

Feinstein showed her driver's license, and the guard scanned in the details. "You know where the house is, ma'am?"

"Far end, right?"

"You got it. Nice and slow."

The metal gates opened, and Feinstein headed through. She pulled slowly away and drove through the deathly quiet streets. Mansions with neat front lawns, ornate streetlights, nothing out of place.

Feinstein spotted his home. A modest colonial located on a quiet cul-de-sac. The house belonged to William Garner, former deputy director of operations for the CIA before he retired three years earlier.

She reversed into the gravel driveway. The front door opened. Annette Garner, an attractive, middle-aged, Midwestern woman, smiled at Feinstein's approach. She wore a floral dress, expensive pearls around her neck.

Feinstein walked up the path. "Appreciate William being able to see me on such short notice," she said.

Annette beamed. "He just got back from a trip to Doha. So, apologies if he appears a little jet-lagged."

Feinstein knew Garner had other clients, mostly foreign governments. She was shown into the study.

Garner sat behind his desk, leafing through some papers.

Feinstein cleared her throat. She always felt slightly nervous in his presence. She didn't know why that was. "Thank you for making the time to see me, William."

Garner didn't look up. "This is becoming more problematic than any of us had imagined."

"Very true. Do you mind if I sit down?"

Garner pointed to the worn brown leather chair opposite his mahogany desk. He looked up from the papers. He wore a pale blue shirt, one button open at the neck, black flannel trousers, and tan boaters. "Of course, my dear."

Feinstein sat down, her gaze analyzing the room. Floor-to-ceiling bookshelves. Historical biographies: Roosevelt. Rockefeller. Carnegie. Churchill. Thatcher. Reagan. Gandhi. Military books on Vietnam. Military strategy. Counterterrorism books. Counterintelligence. And interestingly, *The Devil's Chessboard: Allen Dulles, the CIA, and the Rise of America's Secret Government.* She had a copy herself, a gift from Henry Graff. "How are you, William? Annette mentioned you just got back from the Middle East. How was it?"

Garner grimaced. "Too damn hot."

Feinstein laughed.

"I slept well on the way back. I'm in good health. Bad hip, but I'm lucky. Church. Family. Hours of peace and quiet when I want. Works for grouchy old men like me."

Feinstein rolled her eyes. She had known Garner from the day she first joined the CIA. He had been one of Henry Graff's closest friends. Cut from the same cloth. They worked in the shadows. They advised. They plotted. They schemed. They talked in private to select individuals and corporations. And governments. And politicians. They had a worldview rooted in American exceptionalism. She had that same view. But those two were old-school Cold War warriors. Indoctrinated from a young age.

They had a long list of things they hated. In particular, they held a visceral hatred of Russia, Communism, China, liberals, and American colleges and universities, because they thought they were breeding grounds for Marxists, especially cultural Marxists. If Garner had his way, he would reorder America. But Feinstein could see that America had changed since she had grown up. America was more diverse now than ever. Political correctness, which had started when she was in college in the 1980s, had taken root. At the time it hadn't seemed like much of a threat to the established order. But the country was changing.

Garner and his ilk could only watch as his country transformed. Tearing down statues of American heroes seemed like barbarism. White liberal elites in the media, politics, and the entertainment world had seeded their quiet revolution, either willingly or unwillingly. The problem was there was nothing anyone could do to reverse the moves. The genie was out of the bottle. It was too late.

Feinstein accepted this. Graff and people like William Garner never would. It was a generational thing. They wanted to have a clean-out of "indoctrination facilities." Garner and Graff were astonished at the lack of dissent. The lack of discussion. The lack of questioning.

Feinstein encouraged dissent in her board members. She wanted them to question her decisions and judgments. It was sometimes uncomfortable. But it produced better-informed decision-making.

Garner leaned back in his seat as he leafed through the latest briefing she had sent him on Jack McNeal. She knew that Garner wouldn't sugarcoat what needed to be done to eliminate the threat McNeal posed.

Feinstein had hired Garner for his impeccable and far-reaching connections throughout the intelligence and political establishment. He was a man of strong opinions. But he was also her most trusted confidant.

He had joined the board of her company as nonexecutive chairman. He advised her and the rest of the board, in no uncertain terms, on the direction they should follow. She had appointed him within a month of starting up her new firm. His contacts in government, on Capitol Hill, at the Pentagon, and even in the White House had secured hundreds of millions in contracts. He received a payment of one hundred thousand dollars each month for his services. He had proven himself very good value for the money.

She remembered Henry Graff mentioning that Garner was among a group of powerful men who had wanted Reagan to be replaced by George H. W. Bush. He had considered Reagan a degenerate social liberal at heart. Permissive of abortion, homosexuality, and any number of aberrations, as Garner viewed it. Some said Garner had deep ties with the Saudi royal family, going back three generations. Others said he was one of the prime movers to instigate cooperation between the CIA and Pakistan's Inter-Services Intelligence. It was his idea to funnel covert funding and weapons to the Mujahadeen to help the insurgency against the Soviet regime in Afghanistan. He was an original member of the Trilateral Commission. But his name never appeared in any memos or documentation of meetings. It always freaked Feinstein out when she thought about that. No one knew much about him. But Graff had known everything there was to know about Garner, and he had told Feinstein, usually when he was inebriated. He had also warned her once, eyes heavy, that not a soul must know. Feinstein had been sworn to secrecy.

Garner put down the papers on the desk and steepled his fingers. "You believe it's Henry's body?"

"Sources within the FBI have confirmed that to Tom Steele."

"You believe Jack McNeal, along with his brother, killed him?"

"That's correct."

Garner stared at her with his cold eyes. "Forgive me for being blunt, but why haven't they been neutralized before now?"

Feinstein felt herself flush. She was embarrassed that she had taken such a risk-averse approach. The end result had been a disaster. "The problem is that there are no good options."

"But you do have options."

Feinstein considered this.

"Jack McNeal is clearly very resourceful," Garner continued. "This situation could be dealt with in a heartbeat. So, why haven't you?"

Feinstein sat in silence. It was tough to hear such criticism. But it was important that she listen to his views. He knew what he was talking about.

"You have allowed this to fester. Why haven't they been killed? Car accidents happen, do they not? Falls in subways?"

"William, you know as well as I do that if Jack McNeal or his brother is suddenly killed, and there are any suspicions, it might inadvertently fall on my company. My links to Graff are well known. There is also the small matter of the potential multimillion-dollar contract with the Pentagon. I take it you have heard of due diligence."

"Indeed I have."

"They're going through our audited accounts, our personnel records, our subcontractors, all security clearances, facility security clearance for contractors—the list is extensive."

Garner scribbled a few notes on a pad in front of him.

"They need proof that our contractors are in compliance with the National Industrial Security Program operating manual. Have you read that recently?"

"I don't think so."

"Contractors working for my firm or associates working at my firm can't be implicated in criminality. I can't have any attention or suspicion falling on the firm right now. This DoD contract has been too long in the making. Your high-level contacts have been invaluable. So, to answer your question, I am not going to jeopardize the financial security and stability of my company with rash decisions."

"I understand your rationale. But with the FBI and cops investigating the discovery of Graff's body in the reservoir, all they have to do is check cell phone records and messages, and you are right incriminated. They probably already have. My view? Deal with them now, or God knows where this could lead. If you require, I will speak to a foreign government. They can do the operation. No trace. In and out."

Feinstein felt deflated. "I thought you would be more understanding. I'm looking at the big picture. The substantial contracts will span not only North America but Africa and Asia as well over the coming decade. I can't jeopardize those for operatives or employees of my firm acting illegally. At least not now."

"So, what's your plan for Jack McNeal and his brother? I'm assuming there is a plan."

"I've put them under surveillance. It's a watch-and-wait, just to keep an eye and an ear on them. Bottom line? I don't want anyone rocking the boat. Not right now."

"What does Steele think?"

"Tom thinks we should shoot first and ask questions later."

"I'm sorry to say he has a point."

"I understand your frustration with how long this is taking, William, but I can't give the green light because of the scrutiny from Pentagon committees, intelligence committees, et cetera."

"I know all that. So, where are we at? Watch and wait for the cops to charge McNeal and his brother?"

"That's the main idea. But we are ready to neutralize, whatever it takes, rest assured."

Garner was contemplative. "I'm glad to hear that. I've had time to read your file on the McNeals and what you believe happened at the reservoir. Interesting pair. The other one, Peter. He's also NYPD?"

Feinstein clicked her tongue. "Correct. We know, from several people, including FBI and police sources, that Jack and Peter McNeal are persons of interest with regard to the disappearance of Henry and Nicoletti. That has been confirmed. I am quietly confident that the McNeals will be arrested for Henry's murder. And that will take care of them."

"Are the police aware that the McNeals are wanted by the Feds? It's a bit of a mess, Karen. My view? You shouldn't rely on government to do what needs to be done. You need a different playbook."

"As I explained, we need to fight smart."

"These bastards need to pay."

"Trust me, they will. I would prefer to pick them off at a time and place of our choosing, but the Feds are closing in on them."

"Henry was a good friend. Great patriot. I knew his father well. Talk about backbone. Those men had backbone."

Feinstein shifted in her seat. "I will fix this."

"How? When?"

"Jack McNeal's position is getting more and more precarious. As I've said, the Feds and the Secret Service both have him in their sights, as do the Maryland cops. It's simply a matter of time."

"I'm not so sure. Sometimes neutralizing the targets when the opportunity arises is best. In broad daylight if need be."

Feinstein sighed.

"There's a simple beauty in just killing them. Hire a crazy, give him a gun, ply him with drugs and ten thousand dollars, and he'll blow anyone's head off."

"I know that. But don't forget our client on this job . . ."

"Woodcutter?"

"That's right. He's terrified there's going to be blowback if we go too direct on this. So, that's a second element. First, oversight of our firm. The procurement people want ethical businesses to deal with. Second, the client doesn't want to make more waves. Meyer was neutralized by our operatives. The journalist investigating was neutralized as well. So, now the client just wants to move on."

"What the hell is it to him how we do our job? He's not an expert on our world, is he?"

"No, he's not, but he's a tougher cookie than I gave him credit for."

"Woodcutter is out in the real world, right?"

"That's right."

"Know what a little bird told me?"

"What?"

"A little bird told me that some New York publishers are interested in his life story. Big seven-figure advance has been dangled for his diaries. Did you know he kept a diary?"

"I did not."

"Listen to me and listen good. The guy's a charmer. A complete narcissist. He might tell tales. Embellish. I don't like that. Andrew Forbes sure as hell doesn't need the money."

"So, why is he doing it? It doesn't make sense."

Garner rubbed his hands together. "Karen, he's been cocooned in privilege his whole life. He's looking to the future."

"You heard something?"

"That's why you have me as a consultant, Karen. I know things. I make it my business to know about people. He has secrets. Just like Jack McNeal."

"You want to explain what you mean?"

"First, I think your carefully calibrated and nuanced way of dealing with Jack McNeal has, with all due respect, come up short. It's failed. With hindsight we should have just shot him in Graff's parking lot three years ago. Or broken into his home. However, there may be merit to what you say. I believe the chain of events that are underway, starting with the police searching the reservoir where they thought Henry's body was, McNeal being incriminated, but also what we have in store for Jack McNeal further down the line, means your slow burn method will win, eventually, albeit at a terribly high price."

"I don't disagree with that. We've got some serious lessons to learn."

"We all make mistakes, Karen. It's about learning from them, not allowing them to happen again. That's for you to figure out. But I want to focus, if I may, on an overlooked aspect of all this."

"What overlooked aspect?"

"I want to talk about Woodcutter."

"He's not my main concern."

"He should be. I've talked to a few people who know about these things too. They say he knows too much. Way, way too much."

Feinstein shifted in her seat. She felt uncomfortable with Garner's tone. "What do you mean?"

"I'm going to be very careful how I say this so there is no misunderstanding. He is a threat so long as he lives."

"You want us to kill the client, Andrew Forbes?"

"He is a real and present threat."

Feinstein hadn't expected to hear that. She had come here to get insight from Garner on Jack McNeal. She meditated on whether Garner was right. Andrew Forbes had blindsided everyone. Woodcutter had proven himself her Achilles' heel.

The upcoming book deal was brilliant for raising Andrew Forbes's media profile. He might go on the talk show circuit, regaling hosts with tales from the White House. But he might also inadvertently compromise the operation by being in the spotlight. Craving the media attention. Would the media start digging for stories on him?

She was angry that she had allowed Forbes to make such an impression on her. It was true, she had been intensely focused on slowly neutralizing the threat posed by Jack McNeal. Her company could be at risk. They had been paid millions to kill the President's mistress. Then the journalist who was investigating her death. But it had unleashed consequences that threatened not only to destroy her but also to bring down the American president.

"You see, Karen, I've worked with you for a long time, as did Henry, and he knew you were the best. Scrupulous. But I'm wondering whether you're telling me the full story about this Woodcutter."

Feinstein felt her cheeks flush. "I'm not sure what you're getting at?"

"Let me enlighten you. When was the last time you spoke to him? Woodcutter, I mean."

"Three years ago."

Garner fixed his icy look on her like a disappointed father. "Has he contacted you since?"

Feinstein shook her head.

"You sure?"

"Yeah, quite sure."

"I'm going to tell you something. Something very few people know. I have it on good authority that the Secret Service is conducting an investigation into Andrew Forbes. Did you know that?"

"I don't believe you."

"It's true. Do you know why Woodcutter is a person of interest to the Secret Service?"

"I do not."

"I have been shown documents that link him to the sudden suspicious death of the President's chief of staff."

Feinstein felt as if she had been crushed. She sat transfixed, in shock. She composed herself. "That's not possible."

Garner shook his head. "It's true."

"How can you be so sure?"

"The Deputy Director of the Secret Service is an old personal friend. Known him for over twenty years."

"Are we talking about the same person? Andrew Forbes? Are we absolutely sure?"

"Trust me, this is the same person."

"Did the Deputy Director indicate how Woodcutter might have been involved in the death of the chief of staff?"

"The opioid pain relief medication Woodcutter takes for an old skiing injury is believed to have been the substance that contributed to the death of the chief of staff. The only problem for the Secret Service is that there is no proof. Woodcutter and the chief of staff were together, in a private meeting, shortly before they both got on Air Force One. It's believed that Forbes might have drugged the chief of staff prior to the flight."

Feinstein felt as if she had slipped into a parallel universe.

"It doesn't end there. The former chief of staff is believed to have been passed photos that showed you and Woodcutter in—how can I put this? In a compromising position."

Feinstein felt herself flush again. "I don't know what to say."

"I'll tell you what I'll say. You've got a problem. A major problem. The question is, how the hell do you tackle it?"

"What do you suggest?"

"It depends if you have the stomach for it."

"Trust me, I've got what it takes. I didn't build my company by luck. I know how to be ruthless."

Garner tipped an imaginary hat to her.

"Any final thoughts, William?" Feinstein said.

"You need to kill him. Pure and simple."

Seven

The following morning, McNeal drove down from Westport and headed straight for a sketchy back street in the Bushwick neighborhood of Brooklyn. He parked his car and headed into a nondescript brick building surrounded by low-rise houses. The facility was home to five hundred safe-deposit boxes. The building had previously been owned by Wells Fargo but had since been bought by a storage company.

The vault was protected by a foot-thick steel door. Inside sat hundreds of metal boxes. Two keys were required to open each box. The storage company had one, McNeal the other. He had registered the safe-deposit box under a false name and paid five years' cash in advance.

McNeal was paranoid the Feds would clean out the contents of the dossier he had originally left in a safe-deposit box in Rockefeller Center. This low-key facility was perfect for his needs. The box he had stored contained hundreds of pages of his late wife's research into the death of Sophie Meyer.

McNeal followed a storage guy, keys hanging around his neck, into the vault. The two keys opened the metal box. He looked inside. The contents were there. He took the box over to a private viewing booth, setting the box on the table.

"Do you need anything else?" the storage guy asked.

"I'm fine. Appreciate your help."

The guy left McNeal alone, shutting the door behind him.

McNeal pulled out the half-foot-thick pile of documents. He sighed. Hundreds of pages, a combination of classified Pentagon intelligence documents and classified diplomatic cables. The latter—about Meyer, who was under surveillance wherever she went abroad—had been sent to the State Department by embassies and diplomatic missions across the world, but then was sent by a whistleblower to WikiLeaks. The data haul covered social functions overseas which Sophie Meyer had attended, most notably the Cannes and Venice Film Festivals. A high-profile affair with an Italian film director, viewed as a "Communist sympathizer" by the CIA's station chief in Rome, was a "red flag" incident.

What was also clear from the cables was that Meyer's relationship with the President and her numerous affairs across Europe and South America were noted as "problematic," and Meyer could be a "potential blackmail target," in their eyes. The documents also contained typed pages of Caroline's thoughts on Sophie Meyer. Her background. Education. Friends. Social circle. Within the huge dossier were black-and-white photographs of the socialite, including numerous newspaper clippings of Sophie Meyer attending glittering balls and social events.

He pictured Caroline typing up the notes on her computer in her DC apartment. Maybe consulting Post-its and scribbled notes. It was hard to believe that here he was, reading the same typed pages. He thought of Caroline's last hours, then of her gasping for breath as Nicoletti drowned her. He was glad he had dropped that fucker to his death down a mine shaft. He deserved to die.

McNeal felt the weight of responsibility. He wanted to unlock the secrets of what Caroline had already unearthed. He also wanted justice, but he knew the time for justice had come and gone.

He stared at the pile of papers in front of him. It was the second time he had perused the documents. More than three years earlier, shortly after his wife died, McNeal and his brother had worked through the file as they uncovered the details of the astonishing investigation. His wife had wanted to find out how Sophie Meyer had died. She didn't believe that Meyer had committed suicide. It became clear in her investigative notes and documents that there had been a conspiracy to "neutralize" her. Meyer had been married to Henry Graff. Graff might be implicated in some way. But McNeal knew there was more. Hidden within the documents, he believed, were clues to further avenues his wife had explored.

He read and read until his eyes were strained from the poor lighting. The more he searched the documents over the passing hours, the more it brought back all the painful memories. A terrifying picture of shadowy forces at work to crush Meyer, a mistress to the President, reemerged. It was all coming back as if it was yesterday.

McNeal marveled at how Caroline had dug up such an explosive and compelling collection of documents, but what he was most interested in was the identity of Woodcutter. Shortly before Nicoletti had been dropped to his death, he had revealed that Woodcutter was the Secret Service code name for someone who worked at the White House. A person loyal to the President. A person who wanted to protect the President. Nicoletti had revealed that there were compromising photos of the President and his longtime mistress, Sophie Meyer. And it was Woodcutter who began the top-secret operation to kill Meyer. A crucial cog in the operational planning was Meyer's husband, Henry Graff—a close friend of the President. Meyer's death had been made to look like a tragic drug overdose. But when Caroline, in her role as a journalist, began to investigate the suspicious death, Woodcutter had given the order to kill Caroline. She drowned in the Potomac, and it was made to look like an accident. It was Nicoletti who drowned her. But it was Woodcutter who was behind it all.

Jack thought back to the night when he had nearly become the victim of a classic honey trap. He wondered if that had been organized by the same people that had killed his wife. A young woman in a bar in DC began hitting on him, saying she was from Staten Island. She invited herself back to his room. But he could see it was a trap. The woman, Francesca Luca, was a prostitute. It was all a plan to blackmail an NYPD Internal Affairs detective. A plan to drug him and photograph him naked with the prostitute. A plan to undermine his credibility and destroy his career and investigation.

It had been a close call.

He read on. He scanned more and more documents, looking for clues. He was sure he must have missed something.

McNeal picked up a photo. It showed Sophie Meyer, a glass of champagne in her hand, chatting to a man in a tuxedo. He scanned the picture. In the background, New York's elite danced and partied. He picked up another photo. It had been taken in Beverly Hills at an Oscars party. She had her arm around a French film director who was holding a joint. The next photo was of Meyer on a yacht in St. Barts, kissing a member of the British royal family.

She certainly got around.

McNeal's cell phone rang.

"How you getting on, bro?" It was Peter.

"Well, the dossier is still here, so that's something."

"That was a smart play moving it. Any progress?"

"Not at all." He checked his watch. "I need to grab a bite to eat. I've been here for a couple hours."

"You on the late shift?"

"Yeah."

"I don't think you'll find what you're looking for. It's a needle in a haystack, Jack."

"Maybe. But I'm convinced we've overlooked something."

"Whatever. You take care."

"Will do. And . . . be careful."

"You got it."

McNeal was famished and drove from Brooklyn back into the city. It had been a frustrating couple of hours, looking over the huge dossier. His brother might have been right. It might have been a waste of time.

Back at his apartment, he showered and changed. Then he headed over to a diner in Lower Manhattan. He wore his usual work attire: navy suit, white shirt, and blue silk tie, ready for the start of a new week in Internal Affairs. It was important he keep up appearances. He knew he might be watched.

McNeal checked for any new emails on his cell phone as he waited for the waitress to bring his order. There were a couple from Bob Buckley looking for updates on his cases. He put his cell phone away as he looked around at other diners. He was the only one nicely dressed. Everyone else was casual. A few workmen from a nearby construction site in paint-splattered jumpsuits talked loudly about how much the Yankees and their supporters "suck." A Black couple at the next booth argued about Beyoncé. The wife liked her, the husband thought she was fake. A white girl with impossibly long nails talked loudly into her cell phone with what sounded like her latest boyfriend.

He sent an email back to Bob Buckley saying he would give him an update when he got into the office. The waitress returned with his food and coffee. He ate at a leisurely pace, knowing he had plenty of time.

He wondered what else lay in store for him. He sensed the FBI had a lot more up their sleeve. Their initial questioning might have been a fishing expedition to find out exactly what he knew or didn't know. A tentative attempt to coax him into talking. A way to lure him into incriminating himself.

A different waitress filled his coffee cup for a third time. "How are you today, honey?"

"I've been better."

"Trust me, you don't want to have the kind of day I'm having."

McNeal looked at the girl. "Rough day?"

"Every day's rough now. My mom got laid off. So did my dad."

"Sorry to hear that."

"It ain't easy."

McNeal quietly pressed two fifty-dollar bills into her hand.

"I can't accept that, I'm sorry."

"Take it."

"Are you serious?"

"I had a win at the track," he lied.

The girl stared him. "I don't know what to say."

He smiled at the girl. "Look after yourself."

The waitress dabbed her eyes. She thanked him again and made herself scarce, perhaps thinking if she stuck around, he might change his mind. McNeal stared out the window as a car pulled up outside. A guy got out and headed inside. He walked in and sat down at a booth adjacent to him. The guy was wearing a nice button-down shirt, jeans, sneakers, leather jacket. He was unshaven. Hair short. McNeal sensed the guy hadn't sat down there by accident.

The man turned and gestured. "You mind if I join you?"

Was he FBI? He sure didn't look like any Feds he knew. "Free country."

The man sat down opposite McNeal. He ordered a black coffee. He sat silently until the waitress returned to drop off his drink.

"Do I know you?" McNeal said.

The man took a gulp of his coffee. "We certainly know you."

"What's that supposed to mean?"

"It means I'm going to be in your life for the foreseeable future."

"Are we going on a date?"

The man stared at the pedestrians walking by on Leonard. "They say you're a smart guy."

"Do you want to get to the point?"

The man leaned in closer. "The FBI believes you are a person of interest. You might remember the case. Missing man. Three years ago. We're following this case as well."

"I'm assuming you're going to get to the point soon."

"We know what you did. And we know what you know. The problem for you is we know everything there is to know about you. We know all about your family."

McNeal felt a knot forming in his gut. "Are you threatening me?"

"Just giving you a little advice. You might decide you want to talk to the Feds. Let them know the full story. You see, that might be a problem. What I'm telling you, and let's be clear, this is a warning—you talk to the Feds about what happened, try a plea deal, mitigating circumstances, and your world will come crashing down one more time."

McNeal felt an anger burn deep within him.

"The smart move is you keep your mouth shut, the way you have so far." The man gulped down the rest of his coffee and left a ten-dollar bill under his cup. "You think you got away with all this. Trust me, we never forget. Keep that in mind."

"Or what?"

The man leaned closer. A whiff of cologne. "Let's not go there. Just know that we are watching your every move. All the time."

McNeal shrugged.

"You don't believe me? Let me change your mind." He reached into his jacket pocket and slid three black-and-white photos across the table.

McNeal stared at the photos. They showed him walking with Peter on the beach. "You're an amateur photographer. Good for you."

"Don't be a smartass. I took those photographs. We were watching you. We still are."

McNeal said nothing.

"We are serious people. And you need to know that. Important to remember in the coming days. Be a good boy, and we can forget everything you've done."

"What are you insinuating?"

"I'm not insinuating anything. Be a bad boy, and things are going to go downhill for you in ways you can't even imagine."

McNeal's stomach tightened.

The man got up slowly from his seat. He stared down at McNeal. "Don't forget." He smiled and walked out of the diner, not looking back or making eye contact with any of the other diners. He walked toward the car, quickly glancing back at McNeal through the window.

McNeal held up his cell phone and took a photo of the man.

The man stopped in his tracks for what seemed like an eternity. Then he got in the car, which pulled slowly away into traffic.

Eight

McNeal scanned the photograph he had taken of the man. He zoomed in on the guy's face. The photo was pin sharp. High resolution. Thirtysomething white guy, piercing blue eyes. He thought about the right move to make. He pulled up a number on his cell phone. A private investigator in Florida who had helped him out before. A guy who had found out everything he needed to know about Henry Graff. The guy could be trusted.

He called the number.

"O'Brien Investigations Agency." The raspy voice of Finn O'Brien, a former NYPD cop, like McNeal's father.

"Finn, Jack McNeal. You okay to talk?"

"Anytime, son. What's happening in New York?"

"It's January. Slush and cold. What can I tell you?"

O'Brien chortled. "I don't miss all that, trust me."

"Tell me about it."

"What can I do for you, son?"

"A quick question: Does your company have access to advanced facial recognition software?"

"We certainly do."

"I'm talking high-level software, not off the shelf."

"I employ some of the best people in the business. There's a lot of money down in Florida. Some of my clients require identifying all sorts of people to make sure they will be suitable partners for their daughters or sons. Businessmen, you know. Government records, passports, crucial for us. We have one of the best databases held by a private company in Florida."

"Sounds impressive. But I don't just need run-of-the-mill police records, I'm talking best in class."

"The guy who is in charge of that area for me used to work for the FBI, believe it or not."

"Seriously?"

"Doubled his wages, and he's doing great work for us."

"If I send down a photo, you think you might be able to identify the individual?"

"Can't promise anything. Encrypt it and send it by email."

"The guy I've asked you to identify might be difficult to identify."

"Listen, son, if anyone can ID the guy, we can."

"I owe you one."

"Where your family is concerned, it's on the house."

McNeal sent the photograph via encrypted email. He left the diner. He walked along Leonard and turned up Hudson toward Internal Affairs HQ. The encounter had rattled him. He searched his mind for who could have sent the man. Friends of Henry Graff? Karen Feinstein?

He knew the fuckers were playing with his head. Trying to force him to make a move. A wrong move. He knew that. Were they following him now? Watching him from afar? He saw a white van with dark windows parked on the opposite side of the street. Were they watching him from there? What was stopping them from killing him right here and now?

The more he thought about it, the more he realized they had him in their sights. They were toying with him. He knew they could take him out whenever and wherever they wanted. They were letting him know that. He knew too much. Way too much. He could see they were worried he was going to tell the FBI everything. He saw that clearly. They were putting the squeeze on him. Slowly suffocating him. Intimidating him.

McNeal knew that he could cut a deal with the Feds, confess everything, keep Peter out of it, and he'd spend a few years in a low-level facility. But he also knew that the people who wanted him dead could reach whoever they wanted, no matter if they were protected. He had seen it before. Accountants who had swindled clients and squirreled away millions and were serving an easy five-year stretch in a minimum-security prison, who got shanked on the inside. It was easy.

He ran the scenarios to figure out who was responsible. The name that made the most sense to him was Karen Feinstein. Nicoletti, the man who had killed his wife, had mentioned her name. Just seconds before McNeal and his brother had dropped the poor fucker hundreds of feet into the dark abyss. Was the guy in the diner one of hers? Was he a friend of Nicoletti's? A fellow hired killer?

McNeal sidestepped a panhandler who was foaming at the mouth, hands outstretched for money. He had thought, incorrectly, that it was all over. He naively thought that he had eliminated the people who had killed his beautiful wife and that it would all end. He had begun to quietly get on with his life. But that wasn't to be. Not now. Not ever.

He swiped his ID card as he entered Internal Affairs. He rode the elevator to the third floor, trying to shove the events to the back of his mind.

McNeal scanned his card again and headed through the secure doors to his desk.

"Hey, Jack, you catch the game?" Detective Steve Arquez grinned.

"Too busy."

"The Rangers were awful."

"The Rangers are always awful. No change, huh?"

"You look like shit."

"I feel like shit."

"You need a vacation."

"I'm working on it. How's the family?"

"The wife is nagging me nonstop to head down to see her mother in Florida."

"Sounds good."

"You haven't met my mother-in-law."

McNeal chuckled. "Take it easy."

"I'll catch you around. Bob is looking for you."

"I'm meeting with him soon."

McNeal slumped down in his seat. Files were piled up on his desk. A few yellow Post-its to return calls to lawyers of cops he was investigating. He checked his watch. He was fifteen minutes early for his shift. But he realized he was breathing fast. He took a few minutes to compose himself. He wanted to call his brother to tell him about the little visit at the diner. But it was probably not the right time. Later, when the office had thinned out a bit.

He got up and fixed himself a cup of coffee, then he sat back down and turned on his computer.

"You got a minute, Jack?"

McNeal spun around. His boss, Bob Buckley, stood in the doorway. "Sure thing. Do you want me to bring in the files?"

"That won't be necessary. It's not about your cases."

McNeal thought Buckley's tone sounded unduly officious. It was very unlike his boss. He could chalk it up to the stresses of the job. He got up from his seat and walked into Buckley's office, shutting the door behind him.

He sat down across from Buckley. "Good weekend?"

Buckley stared long and hard at Jack. "Effective immediately, you are suspended. You will be on full pay. But you cannot access this building, your files, or your locker while this investigation is ongoing."

McNeal swallowed hard and caught his breath. He needed to be careful what he said. "I'm sorry. What investigation, Bob?"

"The FBI has been in contact. They say you're the subject of an investigation. Person of interest with regard to a missing man."

"Are you serious?"

"Are you denying the FBI has interviewed you? When were you going to let me know?"

"I need to find a lawyer before I can talk about this."

"The Feds say you visited a man by the name of Graff down in Arlington just over three years ago. I'm led to believe that Graff was a close personal friend of the President. The fucking President!"

McNeal sat in silence. He didn't want to rile Buckley.

"Do you want to comment on this? Feel free. Were you involved in this guy's disappearance?"

McNeal composed himself. He couldn't say anything rash. "This is way out of left field, Bob."

Buckley shook his head. "We can't have an Internal Affairs investigator, no matter how good he is, being the subject of an FBI investigation while carrying out Internal Affairs business. We just can't have it."

"And that's it?"

"I'm afraid so. The official letter has been sent to your home in Westport and your apartment here."

"Bob, this is all a terrible misunderstanding. That's all I can think of."

"I'm sure it is. But my advice, for what it's worth?"

"What?"

"Let this blow over. Take a vacation. A long vacation."

Nine

The thick-paned windows of the publishing company's offices overlooked Fifth Avenue.

Andrew Forbes felt all eyes on him, but he zoned out. His boredom set in as he judged those sitting around the oval-shaped table while they talked about his forthcoming book. The fresh-faced liberal arts graduates. He listened intently as they discussed the merits of his book proposal. It was all bullshit. He sat and lapped it up.

The editorial director, Guy, a fortysomething wearing a cheap, ill-fitting suit, awful, crumpled white shirt, and brown polyester tie, droned on about how he "fell in love" with Andrew's narrative style and the "insanely compelling story" he had to tell.

Forbes giggled to himself. He hadn't written it. It was a former *New York Times* journalist-turned-ghostwriter who specialized in turning nonfiction books into bestsellers. And it had been a friend of his father, a literary agent in Manhattan, who had secured his services.

"Let me tell you, Andrew," Guy gushed like a coy teenager, "we all fell completely in love with your book proposal. And that's why we outbid five other publishing houses for the North American rights. I can't wait to get started."

Forbes reveled in the heady praise. He was in his element. He took perverse pleasure in listening to politically correct, vacuous drivel. It was one thing listening to the President pontificate about everything from the buzzing in his right ear to why he couldn't get a pair of decent Oxford shoes in Montana. But this was an altogether different level of inane talk. Warm words, cajoling, stroking egos. It was pathetic. But, as a raging narcissist, part of him loved it.

Forbes adjusted his Hermès tie. He felt superior in every way. Guy looked like he had gone to bed in his cheap suit. By contrast, Andrew prided himself on his appearance. He wore a white Turnbull & Asser shirt, a bespoke navy suit he had bought on a recent trip to Savile Row, and black Cleverley shoes. He lingered on the editorial director's attire. He felt sorry for him. He figured that if Guy was making $120,000 a year, he really should make an effort to look the part. Then again, the publishing world, from what he'd heard, was a world unto itself. Whey-faced and anxious white girls saddled with six-figure student debts from liberal art colleges, working twelve-hour days for next to nothing. "Really looking forward to working with you and everyone," Andrew said. "Very excited to get to work and make this book the best it can be. I want to hit this out of the park!"

Guy had tears in his eyes, as if overcome by emotion. "What can I say? Music to my ears!"

Forbes grinned. "Whatever it takes, right?"

Guy grinned at Forbes. They were now the best of friends. What a crock of shit. "You see, that's what I'm talking about. You know what it takes, don't you? You've got to work and work to produce the best possible book. And what an explosive story. Your revelations about the President watching as his chief of staff did lines of cocaine on a vanity mirror in a bathroom, at the American Embassy in Beijing of all places, is priceless."

"You had to be there to believe it."

Guy held up the black desktop diary Forbes had kept throughout his four years as body man for the President. "What a testament to your journal-keeping. Bravo!"

Forbes soaked up the admiring looks from Marketing and Editorial. He appreciated how he had made it out of that nuthouse in Washington. The beating heart of America. Tumultuous years. The long hours and incessant demands of the President for everything from supplying some gum to getting someone to shine his shoes, buying a proper suit, fetching him a toothbrush, or finding a place he could get a burger at three in the morning in Nashville. The guy never let up. Was his hair too gray? Was his wife neglecting him? Was he eating too much junk food? Do the South Koreans really have faster broadband than the United States? Who allowed that to happen? Should we send monkeys to Mars? Is Bruce Springsteen a grandfather? Has Bruce Springsteen had an operation on his vocal cords? Why doesn't America host the world snooker championships?

"These are some of the most vivid contemporaneous political diaries I've read. And I've read a lot. I particularly liked the section where the President talked at length about Lee Van Cleef! What the hell? Talk about obsessive. I didn't know he liked spaghetti Westerns. It's trivia like this that makes this so compelling."

"He loves spaghetti Westerns. The outsider and all that. I believe he also wanted to erect a huge statue in New Jersey, where Lee Van Cleef was born, and invite Hollywood producers to celebrate the day."

The editorial director beamed, as if transfixed. "We want to tease out all those nuggets. So much that a reader is going to go apeshit over it. I mean, Lee Van Cleef? Really?"

Forbes shrugged. "He had simple tastes."

"You know what one of my favorite sections is, Andrew?"

"What's that?"

"I love the bit where he's in the Situation Room eating instant noodles during a Navy SEAL kill mission in Iraq. That was hard to wrap my head around."

"The chief of staff confirmed it in his private diary too." Forbes's mind recollected the late chief of staff, who had tragically died aboard Air Force One. The man Andrew had poisoned. It was three years ago. He left a few months later, citing a chance to recharge his batteries and wanting a fresh challenge. But the memories of that period were still fresh.

The gasping for breath. The look of terror in the man's eyes. No one knew what had caused it, apart from Forbes.

"Great to be working on this with you, Andrew. It's going to be a tricky journey to make sure we get it into the best possible shape. But I'm confident it's going to do great. It better, as it cost us $5 million to tie up!"

Forbes and the fresh faces around the table laughed. When the meeting was finished, he posed for a few selfies with a couple of girls from Marketing.

Emily, who was probably months out of Sarah Lawrence, said, "We'll get this on our Instagram page. People will love this. It's a great teaser ahead of the book's publication."

Forbes thought Emily was a bit of a teaser as well. But he kept that to himself. He thanked everyone profusely and was relieved to get out of the room.

He rode the elevator alone down to the lobby. He was glad to be away from the cloying friendliness. It freaked him out.

Forbes headed toward the glass doors at the exit. He saw four men in dark suits.

One of the men stepped forward and showed Secret Service ID. "Andrew, we need to talk to you."

Forbes felt his gut clench. "What's this about?"

"I'm under orders to bring you in right now."

Forbes never thought the day would come. He thought he had gotten away with it. He needed to speak to his lawyer. "What's this regarding?"

"Let's talk back at the office."

It was a half-hour journey in the back of an SUV, across the Brooklyn Bridge, to the Secret Service office nearby. Forbes said nothing as he was escorted to an interview room. Two Secret Service agents sat at one end of a large table.

"Thanks for your cooperation, Andrew," the younger of the two said. "Take a load off."

Forbes sat down. He was sure he could hear his heart pounding. He brushed some imaginary fluff from his suit. "So, what's all this about? It's very unexpected. I was attending a business meeting Midtown, and you guys just show up."

"We are conducting an inquiry."

"What kind of inquiry?"

"Andrew, we want to ask you a series of questions about the late chief of staff."

Forbes shrugged. "I'm not sure how I can help with that. I was on Air Force One when he had his heart attack, but it was a long time ago."

"A lot of people were on Air Force One when he died."

"That's right. So, I'm asking why you want to talk to me about that. And why now?"

"With the President's term ending, we're finding it easier to have face-to-face time with both current and former members of his staff. Everyone has to find a new job anyway, so looser lips, right?"

"I suppose. Still, I'm not sure—"

The agent cut him off. "Shortly before you boarded the plane, you had a meeting with the chief of staff."

"I'm sorry, I don't see what relevance that has."

"It was the last meeting he had in the White House before the flight. It was in the chief of staff's office."

"Like I said, I'm not sure how I can help. And why now?"

"Three and a half months ago, the new director of the Secret Service ordered a review of our original investigation and the methods we used."

Forbes said nothing.

"We understand that you have been prescribed oxycodone in the past. Is that right?"

Forbes decided he needed to regain control of the situation. "I'm still unsure what you're getting at."

"Do you want us to spell it out?"

"Please do."

"We believe the chief of staff's coffee was spiked with an opioid. An opioid you had access to. You were the last person he spoke to in his office before the flight."

Forbes stared at the agent asking the questions. "That is completely outrageous."

"Are you denying that you had access to opioids?"

"I think I've heard quite enough. I'd like to speak to my attorney, Jason Iverson, before I answer any more questions."

"Andrew, you don't need an attorney to confirm what medication you were on. We know you had a bad skiing accident. And the drug is absolutely fine with us. It's just about establishing a few facts."

"I need to speak to Mr. Iverson before this goes any further. I'm sure you understand."

Ten

McNeal jolted awake as his flight landed in the bright Miami sunshine. The pilot announced it was a glorious seventy-one degrees. He was relieved to get out of the depressing New York winter. He needed to get away from his myriad problems as well.

The suspension from Internal Affairs, the FBI breathing down his neck, and the police finding Graff in the reservoir—it had all taken its toll.

McNeal picked up his checked luggage and walked out of the terminal building. The warm air hit him as soon as he stepped into the late-morning sunshine. He needed this. He needed the balmy weather to lift his mood. He needed to reset his life and gather his thoughts. But he also needed space. Space to breathe. Space to think.

He caught a cab to a fancy Art Deco hotel on Ocean Drive in South Beach.

The cab driver whistled. "Nice place, bud."

McNeal thought so too. He tipped the driver and took his case and overnight bag into the lobby. He checked into his room. He tipped the bellhop.

"Anything else, sir?"

"That'll be all."

McNeal stared out the windows at the blue skies and palm trees. White, wispy clouds in the sky. The bustle of Ocean Drive. He felt lighter. This was what he needed.

A place to hide out. A place to take refuge from events which seemed to be closing in on him from all directions.

McNeal unpacked his clothes and got himself settled in. He was glad he had taken Bob Buckley's advice to heart. He did need some time away. Time to recharge his batteries. But he also had another reason.

A face-to-face with Finn O'Brien.

McNeal hoped that O'Brien's firm had made progress in identifying the man from the Tribeca diner. He headed up to the hotel's rooftop pool. He swam countless laps. The more he swam, the better he felt. His mood lifted. Afterward, he lay back on a lounge chair, enjoying the hot sun on his body. He checked out the people lazing around the pool. One couple was immersed in their respective cell phones. It reminded him of his very last vacation with his late wife. A trip to the Lower Keys. Three months later, she left him. He had sensed something was wrong with her on the trip. She had seemed distracted. But so was he. He had kept checking his cell phone for messages from Bob Buckley or his colleagues within Internal Affairs on the progress of cases. He didn't really know how to switch off. The truth was he had been reluctant even to take a vacation. He had a month-long backlog of cases he was working his way through. But he had grudgingly set aside a week, and they flew down to Miami before driving down to Summerland Key and a beautiful cottage overlooking the turquoise waters.

Every day, he had been on his cell phone, sending emails, updating his boss on progress, and all the while he was supposed to be on vacation. His wife ended up doing the same, emailing her editor about her ongoing investigation into the death of Sophie Meyer, which McNeal, at the time, knew nothing about.

He rued his selfishness now. He was a workaholic. He loved his job. But it had come at a high price. The ultimate price.

McNeal called his lawyer, Leonard Schwartz. He updated him on the reasons for his suspension. Schwartz was shocked. But McNeal was more concerned with making sure his will had been revised as he had requested.

"That's all done, Jack. Don't worry about that. It's a prudent move. And don't worry about your estate, that's all handled."

"That's the most important thing."

"I'll put in a few calls and see what this FBI investigation is all about."

"It's three years ago, Leonard. My main concern is that my affairs are in order."

"They are indeed. You sure I can't reach out to the Feds for you on this matter? That's what we lawyers do."

"Not right now. We'll talk soon."

McNeal lay back on the lounger and stared at the brilliant blue sky. He ordered a cold Heineken and took a few large gulps.

His eyes felt heavier. The sun was growing stronger. Slowly he felt himself drifting away.

Everything turned black. It was night. He was floating far out on Biscayne Bay. All alone. He peered up at the stars. Then he turned to take in the lights of the glass towers of the Miami high-rise apartments in the distance. Luxury condos.

A split second, and he was up on a high floor. He stared through the window. Bodies began to fall. Corpses. Faceless. One by one. The sound of screams echoed from across the dark bay. Suddenly the water was lapping around his mouth.

The sound of his cell phone vibrating woke him from his bad dream.

McNeal's heart thundered. He gathered his bearings. He checked his watch. He had been asleep for a couple of hours.

He sat up on the lounger and reached over for his cell phone.

"Jack?" The voice of his psychologist, Belinda Katz, back in New York.

"Oh my God, sorry. I completely forgot."

"You're late. Again."

"Damn. Listen, things have been crazy. I'm out of town for a few days."

"I only agreed to see you on a monthly basis on the condition that you turn up, remember?"

McNeal questioned if he should tell her about being suspended. He didn't really want to get into the ins and outs right now. He decided it was more hassle than it was worth.

"I have an opening three days from now," she said. "I'll email you the details. How does that sound?"

"You got it."

A silence stretched between them. "Hope you are keeping well. What about the flashbacks? The bad dreams?"

"They haven't gone away. Not by a long shot."

"The mind can play tricks on us, Jack. It is vitally important that you take time to enjoy life if you can. Relax."

"I'm in Miami."

"Perfect. Sun is good. Have a beer. Do things you want to do. And really try and evaluate and take stock of things that have happened and learn to move forward, with plans for more vacation, seeing friends and family, you know. Be good to yourself."

"I hear what you're saying."

"You tend to beat yourself up. You're hard on yourself. You set yourself impossible targets at work. And you strive for perfection. It's important to remember that 'good enough' is often good enough. Take your foot off the gas, you hear me?"

"I hear you."

"Take care, Jack. But I really do need to see you in three days."

"I'll be there." McNeal ended the call. The conversation was a sharp reminder of his fragile psychological condition. She was worried about him, and she wasn't the only one. He did feel tremendous pressure from all sides. Now his suspension had left him at a breaking point.

He found it difficult to cope with his humiliating loss of status. He wondered if he would ever be able to face his colleagues at Internal Affairs again. But that was the least of his problems.

McNeal's head was full of dark thoughts, all of a sudden. The nightmare and the call had darkened his mood. The FBI was on his case. All the while, the demons in his head, swirling around, threatened to devour him.

Eleven

It was dark when McNeal's cab pulled up outside a soaring glass tower in Bal Harbour. He paid the cab driver, then walked into the huge, light-filled lobby.

McNeal approached the desk. "I'm visiting Finn O'Brien; he's expecting me."

The guy checked his computer. "Very good, sir." He pointed across to the elevators. "Eleventh floor. Turn right. It's two doors down, apartment 1103. Can't miss it."

"Appreciate that, thanks."

McNeal headed up to the eleventh floor and along the carpeted corridor, cameras watching his every move. He got to the huge wooden door and knocked three times. He waited. He guessed O'Brien was on a call. Or he was slow getting around. He knew his father had slowed down considerably in the last couple of years. He knocked again. Still no answer.

He knocked harder and turned the handle.

The door opened.

McNeal's senses came alive. "Mr. O'Brien . . ." He wondered if Finn, now in his seventies, had forgotten to lock up. It happened. But it didn't sound like the sort of thing a sharp guy like Finn

O'Brien would do. Unless he had had a couple of drinks at lunchtime. Now, that was a distinct possibility.

"Finn? It's Jack McNeal. Are you decent?"

McNeal headed down a hardwood-floor hallway. "Finn, I hope you don't mind me just walking in. Door wasn't locked."

He checked a bedroom. And a second bedroom.

The sound of water. Surely O'Brien wasn't having a goddamn bath.

"Finn, it's Jack McNeal."

McNeal saw steam spewing out from underneath the door. He knocked on the bathroom door. "Finn, it's Jack McNeal! The door was open, man."

No answer.

He knocked again. This time harder.

McNeal was starting to get concerned. Perhaps Finn had fallen asleep in the bath. He turned the handle. A steam-filled bathroom, water spilling onto the bathroom floor. Slowly the steam began to clear.

His brain struggled to process what he was seeing. Time seemed to stop. He stared, transfixed.

Sprawled in the bloodred water, gunshot to the head, brains splattered on the tiles, was the lifeless body of Finn O'Brien.

Twelve

The hours which followed were a waking, hellish nightmare. He had seen dead bodies many times as a cop in New York. Shootings. Stabbings. Beatings. He had thought he was immune to the shock. But his fractured mind was struggling to cope with this unexpected and violent death.

His dad's old pal, killed like a dog. A guy who used to visit them in Staten Island when Jack and Peter were kids.

McNeal wondered if this could really be the same people who had killed his wife. The same people who had threatened him in the diner.

The more he thought about it, the more he realized it couldn't be anyone else. Men like Finn O'Brien didn't kill themselves like that. Cops killed themselves when they felt they had nothing to live for. If their family life was a mess. If they had gambled away the family's life savings at the track. But O'Brien was a success story.

McNeal felt sick to his core. Numb at the events. Slowly it dawned on him that he might be a suspect. Of course. He was here, in the apartment, fingerprints everywhere. Captured on surveillance cameras.

McNeal breathed hard as he tried to compose himself. He got it together. His hand shook as he pressed the three digits, 9-1-1, on his cell phone. He stared at the body. He might be the prime suspect. Dammit, he was the *only* suspect. It was a diabolical plan. Did they plan for McNeal to discover the body? Had they hacked O'Brien's cell phone and learned of the meeting? He felt as if events were out of his control. Nothing he did could change the nightmare engulfing him. It was all happening again. They were shutting down the man who had helped him. The man who had unearthed classified information on Graff and his associates. O'Brien knew too much. That was on McNeal. That was his fault. No one else's.

The door opened, and cops with guns swarmed the apartment. McNeal got frisked and handcuffed. "What the hell are you doing? I called it in."

"Be quiet. This is a precautionary move."

Paramedics came in. But it was too late for them to help.

The cops hustled him away. He was whisked to a nearby police station next to the upscale Bal Harbour shops. The handcuffs were taken off before he was interviewed by local cops.

He gave a statement. It was like a bad dream, a dream that never ended. He dreaded never waking up.

Half an hour later, the FBI turned up. He mused grimly on what had taken them so long. He had been expecting them.

A thirtysomething guy flashed a badge. "Special Agent McEvoy. You need to come with us, McNeal."

McNeal bobbed his head meekly as he was ushered outside to a waiting SUV. He pressed his head against the window and focused on breathing all the way to the ultramodern FBI offices in Miramar, on the northern outskirts of the city. It was all glass, natural light, and chrome. A few miles from the Everglades. He was far from home. He needed to snap out of it. And quick. He needed to get his head straight.

He had already been interviewed by the FBI about his movements in Maryland around the time Graff disappeared. Now he was claiming to have discovered the body of a retired cop and private investigator, a friend of his father's, with his brains blown out in his fancy apartment. Clearly the two events were not a coincidence.

The Feds were going to exert pressure. That's what they did.

They escorted him to the fourth floor and left him in an interview room. A desk. Two chairs on one side, one chair on the other. He stared at his reflection in the glass. He knew they were watching his every move.

A female FBI agent came in and gave him a cup of coffee and a bottle of water. "You okay?"

McNeal sipped some water and gulped the coffee. He was grateful for the caffeine fix. "Thank you."

The female agent left, and he returned to his thoughts.

McNeal remembered what the man had warned him about in the diner in Tribeca. He had warned McNeal not to cut a deal with the FBI. It was the reason he had spoken to McNeal. Who was that guy? Had he been one of Feinstein's people? Had they intercepted a message received by O'Brien? Were they sent to kill O'Brien?

McNeal stared at his reflection. He had only just arrived in Miami. And now this? He was spiraling into the same hell he had gone through three years earlier. Vengeance. Bloody vengeance. Revenge. The same never-ending cycle once again.

Who was that man in the diner? He still didn't know. But the Feds would once they examined Finn O'Brien's computers and cell phones. They would have the cell phone photo McNeal had sent. It might take time to piece it all together. But he knew they would.

What a nightmare.

McNeal needed to get his game face on. He was in deep, deep trouble. The FBI wanted answers. They hadn't gotten them when they interviewed him about Henry Graff. He had already taken the Fifth. He couldn't incriminate himself, knowing he and his brother had killed Graff and disposed of the body in the reservoir. And he wasn't prepared for Peter to go to jail for the rest of his life. But what was he going to say now?

Think, goddamn it. Think.

He wondered how long it would be until they realized the second missing man, Nicoletti, Graff's henchman, had also been dispatched by the brothers. Was it just a matter of time? He and Peter had dropped Nico down a mine shaft, deep underground. He couldn't be sure of anything anymore.

Part of him wanted to cooperate on this case. He was a cop, after all, albeit suspended, but he was afraid that if he cracked, the floodgates would open.

Time dragged. Classic FBI tactics. He sometimes did the same thing with bad cops. He would watch and wait as they sweated. Fearful.

He watched the second hand on the clock on the wall. Eventually the clock ticked over to eleven p.m.

The door opened.

A couple of Feds sat down at the table opposite him. They had kept McNeal waiting for more than four hours.

"Jack, my name is Joseph Hernandez, special agent here in Miami, and this is my colleague, Gillian Hepworth. Sorry to keep you waiting."

McNeal took a sip of the now-cold coffee.

"I want to get straight to the point, Jack. Did you kill Finn O'Brien in his apartment, or is that where you dumped the body?"

"What kind of question is that?"

"I'll ask again. Did you kill Finn O'Brien? Simple question."

"Did I kill him? Are you serious?"

"What do you think?"

"I did not kill Finn O'Brien. Satisfied?"

"You were a person of interest three years ago after Henry Graff went missing. His body was retrieved from a reservoir in the last few days. Now you turn up in an apartment in Miami where a man is found dead, gunshot wound to the head. You call it in. And you're saying you have nothing to do with O'Brien's death?"

"That's right."

"Can you tell me why you were in town to visit Finn O'Brien?"

McNeal was quiet.

"This isn't a difficult question," Hernandez said. "We're just trying to establish why you were in town. And why you visited Finn O'Brien."

"I came down here for a short vacation and stopped in to visit a friend of the family."

Hernandez shrugged as if not expecting such a blasé response. "You visited the luxury apartment of a private investigator. He was a friend of your father's in their New York days, right?"

McNeal knew they already knew the answer. They were just trying to get him to either confirm that or lie. Either way, it established motive. "I hope you can understand that I'm still a bit shaken up."

Hernandez wrote on his legal pad. "I understand that. Do you want to see a doctor?"

McNeal brushed it off. "No, I don't want to see a doctor. Thanks for asking. I'll be fine."

"That's good to know. You only just arrived in Miami, didn't you?"

"That's right."

"And within a matter of hours, literally hours, the same day, you discover a body. Is that what you're saying?"

"That's correct."

"Let me ask you a second time: Can you explain the purpose of your visit to Finn O'Brien? Was it business or pleasure?"

"I'm concerned that you are implying that I was involved in some way. A friend of my father's is dead, and I found the body. I'm really upset about this."

"I understand that."

"Am I a suspect?"

Hepworth hesitated before speaking. "We're simply trying to establish why you were there."

"I had reasons."

"And they were?" Hepworth said.

McNeal cleared his throat. "My mind is not clear right now; I hope you can understand that."

"You said you didn't need to see a doctor," Hepworth reminded him. "I don't see why you can't answer a simple question. Were you looking for information on a cop you were investigating in New York? Doing some moonlighting for Mr. O'Brien?"

"Moonlighting? Listen. I know how this works. But I'm in shock. I don't feel ready to answer. My mind isn't clear."

Hernandez again scribbled in his notes. "Jack, let's cut to the chase. I believe this is connected to the disappearance of Henry Graff. You've had psychological problems. It all adds up to a lot of red flags. So, we'd appreciate it if you could stop this messing around. Answer the goddamn questions. Did you have anything to do with the death of Finn O'Brien? Did you kill him?"

McNeal thought it was time for some righteous indignation. "Are you serious? I just found the body of a beloved family friend, and you're treating me like I'm the perp? That's outrageous."

"I have to say I'm surprised by your attitude. If I was in your shoes . . ."

"But you're not, are you? It was me who discovered the body. You're coming at me with preconceived notions and ideas. I don't know if I trust you not to twist my words. This isn't being recorded, after all. At least I don't think it's being recorded. The FBI doesn't usually operate that way. So, under the circumstances, I'd like to see a lawyer."

"Jack, when the FBI interviewed you about the disappearance of Henry Graff, you took the Fifth. And now you're asking for a lawyer. The same playbook."

"I'm allowed to."

"That is technically correct."

"Don't the Feds believe in the American legal system?"

Hernandez laughed softly. "We can get you a lawyer."

"I don't want you to get me a lawyer. I'll get my own, thank you."

Hepworth stared at McNeal. "We would advise you against speaking to the press."

"I have no intentions of speaking to the press."

"This might be a long and complex inquiry."

"Well, if you've got no further questions, am I free to go? Unless you want to charge me with something."

Hernandez and Hepworth exchanged a knowing look.

Hernandez scribbled some more notes and stared at McNeal. "We know you've got a stellar record in the NYPD. Though it's true you're off your game, according to your colleagues, over the last few years . . ."

"My wife died."

"I understand that," Hepworth said.

"I don't know if you do. Do you know how that feels?" Hepworth averted her gaze. "I'm sorry for snapping. This whole thing has me shaken up."

Hepworth brushed that aside. "Have you ever been a client of Finn O'Brien?"

"He's a family friend, that's all."

"Do you know his client list?"

"How the hell would I know his client list?"

"He knows some interesting characters. Characters known for getting their way. He represented several powerful people here in Florida. Dangerous people."

"I don't know anything about that."

"Do you know his biggest client once served time for murder?"

"Like I said, I don't know anything about that."

"Were you working for one of his clients? Did they pay you?"

McNeal folded his arms. "Until I speak to a lawyer, I've got nothing further to say to you."

Hernandez picked up the thread. "The FBI will want to talk to you again about Mr. O'Brien's death."

"I called the damn thing in. What don't you understand?"

"So you keep saying."

"Am I free to go?"

"Yes, you're free to go. But I would advise you, Mr. McNeal, not to leave the country."

"Why the hell not?"

"Like I said: we're going to have more questions. Besides, we believe you know more than you're letting on."

Thirteen

The operative and Ramirez were in a Lexus rental three cars behind Jack McNeal's cab as he stopped off at his hotel in South Beach.

Ramirez trained the telephoto lens on McNeal and took a few shots as he disappeared into the Ocean Drive hotel. She looked at the pictures. "You want me to send them back to Steele in New York?"

"Right away."

Ramirez did as she was told. "So, what now?"

"Watch and wait. We know where he is. And that's good."

"Can't wait to get the hell out of here."

The operative scoffed. "Are you kidding me?"

Ramirez shook her head. "I grew up down here. Couldn't wait to leave."

"You don't like the beach?"

"I didn't grow up in South Beach. The place we passed a few miles back, Opa-locka, off 95, that's where I grew up."

"What the hell is Opa-locka?"

"You don't want to know."

"Bad memories?"

"It was all bad in Opa-locka. All bad. My dad worked like a dog all his life. Then he died broke and drunk and ready to check out. He was only thirty-nine."

"Tough part of town?"

"Back in the day, you could be shot for looking at a kid the wrong way. Knife fights just going to the corner store. Cops bustin' our heads. Gangs. Shootings. Drugs. It was bullshit. Never a fucking break."

"The Agency must've been a breeze after that."

Ramirez gave a rueful smile. "You got that right. Man, it was a rough place. My brother got shanked by our neighbor for playing his music too loud."

"What did you do?"

"I beat the fucker within an inch of his life and disappeared. This is the first time I've been back to Miami."

"I had no idea."

"Where you from?"

"Me?" The operative hesitated. "I moved around as a kid."

"Yeah, but where did you grow up? You got a hometown? Everyone has a hometown."

"I was an army brat. I was born in Germany. My father worked in intelligence."

Ramirez whistled. "Agency in the blood?"

"You could say that. He never talked about his work. Ever. He just said he worked for the American government. But I found out later what he did. He was a covert operative in Europe."

"So, you grew up in Germany?"

"Then we moved to the UK."

"Where?"

"The northwest of Scotland."

"What the hell was that like?"

"Pretty much what you would imagine. Wild and cold."

"Jesus."

"I liked it. No one to mess with you."

"And then?"

"Then, what?"

"Where did you go next?"

"What's this? A million and one questions?"

"Just curious. You know plenty about me, and I know next to nothing about you. I don't even know your name."

"Do you know anyone else's name on this operation?"

"Steele. Feinstein."

"That's probably two names more than you *should* know."

"Fair enough."

The operative gave a thin smile to show he had no hard feelings. "Where did I go next?"

Ramirez shrugged, looking at her chipped nails. "I've got plenty of time."

"My dad was posted back to the States. Pentagon. So, I grew up in DC, I guess."

"Very cosmopolitan."

The operative lingered in thought, peering at the hotel entrance. "It was shit. Boring."

"I've got a little place in Vermont. I want to move there when I'm finished with this."

"Too cold. I think this looks like the kind of place I'd like to retire to."

"No thanks. Miami's fucking crazy, man."

"It's nice here. By the beach. A few bars. Restaurants."

"Trust me, nothing's how it seems in Miami. It might look nice on the surface, but it's like a swamp. The people smiling at you would just as soon kill you."

"Where do you live now?"

"Me? New York."

"Whereabout?"

"Got a little apartment in Midtown. You?"

The operative raised an eyebrow. "I'm not far from you. Got a place in Montauk, far east end of Long Island."

"Fancy."

"It has its moments. You're probably thinking of East Hampton. Place full of celebrities and God knows who else in the summer. Montauk is a bit more laid back. Fishermen. Working people."

Ramirez's gaze fell on the Art Deco facade of the Ocean Drive hotel. "This Jack McNeal guy, is it true he killed Graff?"

"We're pretty sure it was him and his brother. Also took out Nico."

Ramirez shook her head. "This guy isn't what he seems, then, either. On the surface he's supposed to be NYPD Internal Affairs, investigating crooked cops, right?"

The operative nodded.

"And he does that?"

"Yup."

"We shouldn't underestimate this guy."

"Trust me, I don't."

Ramirez thought through her next question. "You think Karen underestimated him?"

The operative groaned. "I don't know. But the fact that the situation has escalated and he's still on the loose, talking to the FBI, is clearly not fucking good."

"We should've put a bullet in the guy's head on the beach. Both him and his brother."

The operative processed this.

"That's what I would've done," Ramirez said. "And I would have done it once he took his wife's files to the Feds. He was clearly a risk to the operation."

The operative said nothing. He didn't like bad-mouthing clients like Feinstein. He had worked with her in the past and knew she was very strategic, big on small details. She had obviously had her reasons. But the problem Ramirez highlighted was the down-side of undue caution. It was a classic case of overthinking. It had resulted in subsequent delays green-lighting a hit, missed opportunities, and ultimately failure. She was always looking for a zero-risk solution. But in their profession, that was impossible.

"Know what I'm saying? We're being reactive instead of proactive."

The operative sat quietly, immersed in his own thoughts, as Ramirez pontificated about the weaknesses of Feinstein. He wished she would just shut up. He had tried zoning out when she was talking. But it was no use.

He much preferred working by himself. But this job, every-one in little groups, was what Feinstein had deemed appropriate. Interestingly, Tom Steele hadn't advocated that. He had told the operative as much. But he had to roll with it when Feinstein made the call.

The operative saw McNeal emerge from the hotel with an over-night bag and a case. A concierge flagged a passing cab.

Ramirez eyed the taxi. "We could take him out now. We could take him out on the freeway."

"That's not your call to make. So, knock it off."

Ramirez went quiet.

"Let's just follow him discreetly. Tom will be in touch."

The car pulled away and Ramirez followed, mindful to keep a safe distance.

A few minutes later, as they headed to the airport, the opera-tive's cell phone rang.

"Our boy on the move yet?" The voice of Tom Steele, oper-ations director, and right-hand man of Karen Feinstein. He had been with Karen for years, through numerous operations overseas.

"Just left his hotel in South Beach a minute ago."

"Copy that. Got an update. He's headed to the airport. You're on the same flight to New York as McNeal."

The operative groaned. "I was just getting used to some warm weather."

"Get Ramirez to drop you off. Your bag is in a locker, number 4392, Concourse E, level 2. Documentation will be in the bag. Keep an eye on the fucker."

"Copy that. Do you want me to neutralize in-flight?"

"Negative. You enjoy the sun?"

"We were kinda busy."

"I hear you. Listen, don't lose him. We're putting a plan in place for when he arrives in New York. Things might be about to happen."

Fourteen

McNeal landed in New York after what seemed like an interminable flight. He had been dreading what he had to do now. He drove straight to his father's home on Staten Island. He delivered the terrible news about Finn O'Brien.

His father, who was stoic in nearly all things, slumped forward in his easy chair, head in his hands.

McNeal knelt down beside him and wrapped an arm around his bony shoulders. "Dad, I'm so sorry. This is my fault. It's all my fault."

His father wept like a child. "Finn was a good man. Decent as the day is long."

"He was helping me out. I think that got him killed."

His father blinked away tears from his rheumy eyes. "What was he doing for you?"

McNeal shook his head, not wanting to elaborate.

"How was he helping you out? Was it to do with Caroline's death?"

"Yes, indirectly. There's something else." McNeal felt reluctant to open up too much. "I was down in Miami because I got suspended."

"Suspended? In the name of God . . . Jack, what's going on?"

"Dad, I'm in trouble. Big trouble."

"What kind of trouble?"

"I reached out to O'Brien. Like I've done before. Remember he helped me when I was investigating Caroline's death?"

His father held his hand in a viselike grip. "What in God's name is going on? And don't give me any bullshit. I hate lies."

McNeal was conflicted. He had made a pact with his brother. A blood pact, to remain silent. Not a soul. That included their father. "Some things are better left unsaid, Dad."

"Did you go after the guy you believe is responsible for Caroline's death? Is that what this is about? Don't fucking lie to me, son." McNeal bowed his head low. "That's what happened, isn't it?"

"I don't want to talk about it."

"Jack, I deserve to know. You're my son, for Christ's sake."

McNeal looked around the old house. A photo on the mantelpiece of Jack graduating from the police academy. His father and his late mother standing proudly beside him. He saw his father's ten-year-old Nokia cell phone tucked away behind a pile of old boxing magazines on the coffee table. He couldn't risk talking about what he knew out loud in case his own father was bugged.

"Jack, talk to me, son."

McNeal leaned closer and whispered in his father's ear. "I love you, Dad. And I would never lie to you. That's why I can't say anything. I hope you understand."

His father sat motionless, tears in his eyes, still absorbing the news of the death of his closest friend on the force. Decades working in all conditions, through the sixties and seventies, when New York was notorious for muggings. Killings. Gang violence. Out-of-control boroughs. Cops at the front line. Always had been. It was always about upholding the law. The betrayal of that ethos is what probably hurt his father most.

His son had crossed a line and broken the law. The law was sacrosanct to him. His job was to defend it. His father had drummed that into him and Peter as boys.

"I've got things to do."

"Like what?"

"Things to take care of."

His father held McNeal's face in his old, shaking hands. "You need to think long and hard about this. Sometimes it's better just to walk away. And forget it all."

"It's too late for that, Dad."

His father closed his eyes. "I never imagined you heading down that road. Not you. Peter was always the wild one. Why, Jack?"

McNeal didn't have the words to explain it to his father. What had driven him to such madness? What had compelled him to kill, to avenge his dead wife?

"I understand if you don't want to see me again."

The tears filled his father's eyes. "You're my son. You'll always be my son. I know the sort of man you are. And I'll never turn my back on you. Don't ever forget that."

McNeal collapsed, mentally drained, when he arrived home at his apartment in Manhattan. The events of the last twenty-four hours had severely rattled him. He couldn't contain the anger inside him. He wasn't coping. He called Belinda Katz's office and asked for an emergency appointment.

McNeal was in luck. There had been a cancellation. He showered and changed into some fresh jeans and a T-shirt, a wool sweater, and an overcoat and caught a cab to the East Village.

He was shown into the home office of Belinda Katz.

"Appreciate you seeing me on such short notice."

Katz sat down, flicking through her notes. "This isn't like you to seek out help, Jack. What's wrong? You look terrible."

"I've had a rough few days. I thought I could bottle it up. I can't. I feel like I'm losing my mind."

Katz sat forward in her chair. "The last time we spoke, you said something came up. And you were down in Miami. You want to talk about that?" McNeal leaned his head back in the chair. "Just to let you know, I was also informed earlier today that you have been suspended."

"You no longer want to see me? Is that it?"

"Far from it. Under the circumstances, I think it's very important that we talk. How do you feel about this suspension?"

"How do you think I feel?"

"I'm asking you that."

"It's devastating. It's out of the blue."

Katz skimmed her notes. "I think you have far more on your mind than you've been telling me. I believe this suspension could be a tipping point for you. And I'm very worried."

McNeal closed his eyes, images of Graff's last moments seared into his brain. The sound of screams as Nicoletti plunged down the mine shaft.

"When we suppress our emotions, they can emerge in the dream state. Disturbing dreams. And I would suggest that something happened that triggered these recurring nightmares."

McNeal grimaced. "I wake up unable to breathe, fighting for air."

"So, there is acute anxiety at work, at the very least. We need to explore that. But first I want to talk, if I may, about Henry Graff."

"I'd rather not talk about that."

"You've said that before. Why is that?"

"It triggers me."

"His name triggers you?"

81

McNeal nodded.

"Why does it trigger you?"

"I don't know. Negative thoughts. Flashbacks."

"Flashbacks to what?"

McNeal felt his tongue go dry. It felt as if his mouth was running away with him. He needed to slow down. He was in danger of telling her what happened.

"My job is to explore your feelings, your psychological makeup, and try and help you overcome these negative and recurring dark thoughts. But it's important you open up to me."

"I can't say any more."

"Can't or won't?"

"I don't want to talk about that."

"You reached out to me. You need to tell me what's on your mind. I'm a psychologist. And I have a duty of confidentiality. So, that means whatever we say here remains private. Strictly confidential."

"No matter what?"

Katz grimaced. "Not necessarily."

"What do you mean?"

"It is a privileged relationship. It is built on trust. And my legal obligations are quite clear. I am under a duty of confidentiality if a patient declares they have murdered someone, for example. If you said to me, for example, 'I'm going to murder someone in the future,' then that changes things. Then I have a duty to inform the police. Or if you said you were suicidal and you were going to kill yourself. I need to let an appropriate doctor at a psychiatric facility know so we could get you treated."

McNeal was quiet as he took in what she'd said. He needed to tell her something. But what about the oath of silence he had agreed on with his brother?

"Tell me about Henry Graff."

"You've read that he disappeared. Until now."

"I'm not going to ask if you killed Henry Graff or were involved in any way in his death. Does that alleviate some of the pressure?"

McNeal acquiesced. "A bit."

"Go on. You were saying . . . How are you feeling? What are you thinking?"

"I don't know what I'm thinking anymore. I don't know the man I stare at in the mirror in the morning. I barely recognize myself."

Katz scribbled notes. "Tell me about your recent trip to Florida."

"I went down to Miami after I was suspended."

"Were you trying to get away from it all?"

"Sort of. It felt good to feel the sun on my face. Get away from the city. My job. But I also went to Miami . . . I asked a friend in Miami to help trace the identity of a man. A man who threatened me in a Tribeca diner."

"Interesting. So, you felt threatened? How did you get a picture of this man?"

"With my phone."

"Did you tell the police about being threatened? That's what I would have done."

"No, I didn't. I should have. But I wanted to deal with it my way."

"Most people would have contacted the police."

"Probably. I had my reasons. When I arrived at my friend's apartment in Miami, I hoped he could help me identify the guy in the diner."

"How could he have helped you?"

"He was a private investigator. I wanted him to identify the man through facial recognition."

Katz held her pen steady, waiting for him to go on.

"The private investigator . . . I discovered him. He was dead. He had been shot. It was a terrible mess."

The color drained from Katz's face. "Jack . . . I'm going to level with you. The police and Feds spoke to me. The Feds about Graff."

"The Feds have been here?"

"Yes. And the police."

McNeal's heart sank. "What did you say?"

"I cited client confidentiality."

"I appreciate that. Thank you."

Katz shrugged. "I feel like there is so much to explore . . . but I'm interested in whether the stresses of your job, the death of your wife, and your son a few years back, and the disappearance of Graff . . . That's enough to send anyone over the edge. But on top of that, you discovered this terrible scene. A dead body. I think my best advice is to take an extended vacation. Not in Miami. Try Europe. Really get away from it all. How does that sound?"

"I've been advised not to leave the country."

Katz grimaced. "I see. So, enjoy the peace and quiet of your house in Westport. Make it a refuge. A place of sanctuary."

"It's not as straightforward as that."

"Why not?"

"The man in the diner showed me photos. Photos of me walking on the beach in Westport with my brother. They know where I live. They know where I work. They know a lot about me."

"That's very worrying. Is there anywhere you can go?"

"There's places I can go, sure. But they know who I am, what I look like. They're on me."

"It's like you're trapped."

"In a way, I am. You see, for me, right now, there is no escape."

Fifteen

The Fifth Avenue law offices of Iverson, Walker & Faulkner took up the entire forty-second floor of a sixty-story Art Deco building. The floor-to-ceiling windows overlooked Bryant Park in Midtown Manhattan. It was the sort of place people with lots of money, who didn't mind getting fucked to the tune of $1,500 per hour, kept an attorney on retainer. Wood-paneled offices, hushed sounds in the corridors, legal tomes stacked to the ceiling, walls adorned with oil paintings of the founders. It all conveyed power, prestige, and impeccable discretion. It exuded a timelessness. But the firm was less than thirty years old.

Andrew Forbes sat patiently as Jason Iverson, senior partner and majority owner of the firm, speed-read notes from Andrew's meeting with the Secret Service. The lawyer had known Andrew since he was a boy. Iverson was the Forbes family attorney who dealt with everything. Andrew's father had used the firm shortly after they were formed. Business, personal, and everything in between.

If Iverson couldn't deal with something, he knew someone who could. He was discreet, with only select clients drawn from the world of commerce and entertainment. Hedge fund billionaires, property tycoons, a plethora of Hollywood actors and actresses, and a handful of overseas clients who were based mostly in Switzerland or the Cayman Islands for tax purposes. Andrew's father said there wasn't a problem in the world that Iverson or his firm couldn't solve or make disappear. He also said, half-jokingly, they could make people disappear as well.

"First things first," Iverson said, leaning back in his seat. "It says here that you politely asked for a lawyer to be present and wouldn't answer questions until I was there, is that right?"

"Correct."

Iverson gave a sly smirk. "Clever boy. Best thing you could have done in the circumstances. And here we are!"

Forbes cleared his throat. "Here we are indeed."

"Listen, what we say is confidential. Strictly confidential. I am unshockable. I've heard it all. Nothing fazes me. It doesn't matter what you've done or what hole you've found yourself in, I can help you. But you need to be honest with me. I can only do my job if you tell me what you know. And it's got to be the truth and nothing but the truth."

"What do you want to know?"

"Did you do it?"

"Do what?"

Iverson stared at him long and hard. "Did you do what they allege and infer that you did?"

Forbes was reluctant to spill his guts.

"Let me spell it out for you: Did you kill the chief of staff? Maybe it was a mistake. Maybe you didn't mean it to go so far."

Forbes shifted in his seat. "I feel awkward."

"Trust me, not half as awkward as you would be speaking to the Secret Service without legal representation. If you did what they say you did, I need to know." He leaned conspiratorially over his desk. "I won't say a goddamn word."

"How do I know none of the other partners get to hear about this? How do I know what I say isn't passed on to, say, your wife?"

"You kidding me? My wife? I love her. And she's a great mom. I'm lucky. But I do not divulge anything to her with regard to my clients. Never, ever. It's a rule I never break. Besides, she is only obsessed with what school our kids are in and what home furnishings we should buy."

Forbes chortled. He needed a bit more coaxing.

"Let me explain a bit about myself, Andrew. I've known you and your family for over twenty-five years. I represent your father. Your father is a big shot, money-wise. He is a smart man. He doesn't waste money on shitty lawyers. You know my background?"

Forbes shook his head.

"Eldest of a family of six, originally from a shitkicker town in the Florida Panhandle. I couldn't wait to escape. I got a scholarship to a boarding school in New Hampshire, where I began to work harder than I've ever worked. I read everything I could. I wanted to better myself. It was a fantastic school. After Yale, I gained a coveted place at Harvard Law School. Top of my class. Worked ten years, slaved as an associate. Then I was made partner at a big-name law firm just across the park from us. I stayed three more years and set up my own business. My business is built on discretion. Absolute and total discretion. I represent my clients in such a way that they don't have to worry about things. They can call me whenever they want, and they know that. Vacation? Not a problem. My cell phone, my iPad, and my computer I take with me everywhere. Anywhere in the world. I'm there for my clients, any time, any place. You know why?"

Forbes shook his head.

"Because I want to maintain my position as one of New York's most elite lawyers. My clients don't care if my vacation gets interrupted when I have to fly back from the Caribbean to speak to them, so I don't care either."

"I understand."

"I don't know if you do. You see, I'm not going back to that shitkicker town. Not now, not ever. This is where I belong. I represent the big shots in the big city, and sometimes, they come to me with big problems. You've got a problem; I will deal with it. You've just got to trust me. But I need to know the facts. Don't jerk me around."

Forbes composed himself. "This is difficult."

"Tell me what happened. Unvarnished truth."

Forbes took a deep breath and recalled the events of that fateful day. He explained as best he could what had happened. The photos of him and Feinstein, produced by the chief of staff, all the way to putting the opioid drops into the chief of staff's coffee. But he also spoke about shooting Francesca, the sex worker who had been paid to entrap Jack McNeal, at the behest of Karen Feinstein.

Iverson scribbled on his legal pad, brow furrowed as he got all that down. "Holy fuck, okay! This is seriously heavy stuff. But I appreciate you being honest. And that's everything there is to know?"

"Yes, it is."

Iverson was quiet for a few minutes. He stood up and walked over to the windows, staring down at the park, deep in thought. "We can deal with this. There are different ways we can approach this. Depends on a lot of factors. First, I'll reach out to the chief counsel for the Secret Service, Curtis Montgomery. Close friend from Harvard. We'll take it from there."

"What do I do? I mean, what do I do now?"

Iverson turned around. "You continue as per normal. You continue your work on your book. What I need to ensure is that there is no leak of this to the media. It won't come from our side. But it will be tricky to contain. *White House Body Man Accused of Murdering Chief of Staff.* It's got a certain ring to it."

"Things got out of control. I know that. But I was scared. I just wanted to protect the President. And then things got crazy. I panicked."

Iverson scribbled some notes.

"I spoke to my father when the President said he had a problem. He put me in touch with you."

"That was the right thing to do. Listen, I love the President too. We all want to protect him. That's why I got involved when your father initially reached out to me. No one could have known how crazy it was going to get, right?"

Forbes felt vulnerable after opening up so much. "The woman who died, the journalist. Caroline McNeal."

"What about her?"

"The plan started getting complicated when she got involved. And then she was taken care of, but Jack McNeal began to do some digging . . . and it spiraled from there."

Iverson took a few more notes. "I'm hearing Jack McNeal is a prime suspect in the disappearance of Henry Graff. Maybe another man too. So, things are going to get bad for him."

"I don't doubt that. But he knows the story."

"That is true. But we all know the story of what happened to Sophie Meyer. And that puts us all at risk. In different ways."

Forbes agreed.

"I would forget McNeal for now. He's not your concern. Karen Feinstein is more of a concern for you at this stage."

"Karen? Why would she be a concern?"

"She knows everything. She knows where the bodies are buried."

Forbes wondered what Iverson was getting at. "I don't know if I follow."

"She lured you into killing this honey trap girl, right? She knows you were the one who started this whole thing. She has you."

"So, what do we do?"

"Sit tight. I'll figure out your next move. In the meantime, not a word."

"What exactly are you going to do?"

"Let me worry about that. We'll talk again in a couple of days."

Sixteen

The storage facility in Brooklyn was thankfully empty again. The events in Miami had shocked McNeal to his core. He was convinced he was going to be killed. He knew O'Brien was just the start. It was a slow-burn operation, and he was still no closer to fighting back.

Who was Woodcutter? He needed a name. Even as a bargaining chip with the Feds further down the line.

McNeal sat in the private booth, the dossier once more in front of him. He marveled at the pile of papers. It must have taken Caroline months, maybe years, to accumulate all this information. State Department memos, numerous classified letters with redacted sentences, all leaked to his late wife or accessed via WikiLeaks. Pages of notes on Meyer and faded newspaper clippings.

He read the memos once more. Senior officials talking about the "national security risk" Sophie Meyer posed. She had been compromised. And her "numerous dalliances" with everyone from billionaire Chinese tech geniuses to Hollywood playboys on superyachts in the Mediterranean, along with powerful senators and, as McNeal had found out, even the President, made her "toxic." A national security adviser described her as a "real and present danger to national security."

The more he read, the more he wished he could turn back time. He felt sick thinking of his wife's solo investigation into such powerful players. But the fact that his late wife had pursued her investigation showed what a brilliant and uncompromising journalist she had been.

It had cost Caroline her life.

McNeal's mind returned to the day he had seen her body in the morgue. Her lips blue. Her twisted neck, her lifeless body. Her face like gray wax. Her dirty, mousy-brown hair with bits of leaves entwined with the strands. He prayed it was all a bad dream. He remembered his body going into shock. He wanted to tell her how much he loved her despite everything. He had never stopped loving her. He wanted to tell her that he read all her columns. He read the books. The wife he so admired. The pain of estrangement. It never went away. Not for him.

He felt tears well in his eyes as he waded through countless more official documents. He didn't let up. He read on. Hour after hour. He turned his attention to the newspaper clippings. Social functions. A glittering ball in Miami ahead of the Super Bowl. Meyer sashaying past the photographers.

He turned his attention to the dozens of other black-and-white photographs. He had scanned them already. But his natural curiosity compelled him to look again at the glamourous photographed at parties and social gatherings. A Hamptons fundraiser for the President. A world of privilege. Decadence. The tuxes. The Botox. The swollen lips. The glazed eyes. The vintage champagne. The exclusive guest list.

Eventually, he'd had his fill. He'd had enough for the day.

The sky was darkening as McNeal met up with his brother again on the deserted Westport beach. He didn't care if they were being watched. Just so long as they weren't overheard.

McNeal and his brother both wrapped up against the biting cold. Snow flurries blew in off the salty air of Long Island Sound.

"Is this really the best place to meet up?" Peter asked.

McNeal walked slowly as waves crashed hard onto the beach. Both men had scarves on, wrapped over their mouths. "It's the best place under the circumstances. We're probably being watched as we speak, but we should be fine as long as we don't have our cell phones."

Peter turned up his collar against the wind. "What a mess."

"I think it's just the beginning."

"What do you mean?"

"I don't think they're going to stop at killing O'Brien."

"You saying we're in their sights?"

"No question. I feel like the dossier is the most important thing. I was checking it over again before I drove up."

"Anything?"

McNeal shook his head. "I've been thinking about the people who sent this crew to spy on us. They're clearly the same people who took out O'Brien. They're why we need to identify who Woodcutter is. He's behind all of this."

"I think you're wasting your time."

"If we don't identify him, who the hell will? No one will know about him. The fucker will get away with it. We need to know who he is."

"I think we've got more pressing matters, Jack."

"He could hold the key to the whole thing. Who is he? We were told Woodcutter is a Secret Service code name. So, the chances are he either works at the White House or has some connection to the White House, right?"

"Correct."

"I don't believe this whole thing originates from Karen Feinstein. It's weird how it all started. Graff said so himself. They were contacted. By who? Nicoletti told us that Woodcutter was the initial contact, how it all began."

"I know all that. What's your point?"

"I have to find Woodcutter. It all comes back to him. We need to know what we're up against."

"I just want all this shit to stop."

"So do I. But it won't. See what I'm saying? We don't know how this is going to end. But we can at least know who the enemy is."

"What if you don't come up with anything, Jack? Look at what happened to O'Brien. I think it's just a matter of time before . . ."

"A matter of time before what, Peter?"

"Before one or both of us winds up dead."

Seventeen

The operative had listened to the entire conversation.

Ramirez had secured a military-grade parabolic long-range microphone, placed it beside the open attic window of the Airbnb, and pointed it at the beach. But despite the range of nearly two hundred yards, and the ambient noise of waves and wind, the microphone picked up the whole discussion.

The sound quality was impeccable.

The operative adjusted his headphones as he watched McNeal and his brother through high-powered binoculars.

Ramirez grinned and chewed gum. "We got those fuckers. They're nervous."

"Is this recording the conversation?"

"Absolutely. Feinstein will love this."

The operative sensed they needed to neutralize the brothers, once and for all. He had proof McNeal and his brother knew way too much. They had the code name for Andrew Forbes too. He couldn't understand why the green light to kill them was taking so long. Feinstein needed to be told in no uncertain terms. He looked across at Ramirez. "Is the audio feed live in New York?"

"Copy that. Real-time conversation. They've got it already. Monitoring every moment."

The operative watched as the McNeal brothers slowly walked off the beach, presumably back to Jack's home. His cell phone rang. He took off his headphones and answered the call.

The voice of Tom Steele. "Good work."

"Tom, do you mind if I speak frankly?"

A beat. "Sure."

"I'm not pulling the strings; I understand how it works. I know Karen is making the final decisions. I know she does a lot of painstaking work before she gives a green light. But I really, really, need to bring this up."

"I know what you're going to say."

"This is not my call to make, I know."

"That's right, it's the client's call. Don't ever forget that."

"I understand. But these guys, the McNeal brothers, know way, way too much."

"I know they do."

"Have you shared your views with Feinstein?"

"I'm about to."

"I think we need to take them out. Right now. We could've done it on the beach."

"I suggested that."

The operative wondered what was causing the delay. "And what did she say?"

"She's concerned one of our guys, such as yourself, could get caught in a police dragnet in or around Westport."

"Tom, we have options. We need to explore options."

"I know where you're going with this."

"Do you?"

Steele let out a long wheeze.

"Here's another option, Tom. A better option."

"What?"

"We could take them out from a boat on the Sound. Far out on the Sound. Long-range. Not a soul in sight."

"I already suggested that."

The operative's heart sank. "You did?"

"I gave her three clear options how we could do this today. Land, sea, or air."

"We had a chance today. We really did. I don't think it's smart to pass up chances when they're served on a plate. I don't understand it."

"Listen, Karen is in charge. She has been made aware of my concerns. But she is weighing numerous other aspects of this operation."

"Like what exactly?"

"It's complicated."

"Try me."

"She's worried about Woodcutter. That's taking up more of her time. And, from the discussion on the beach, not only are the McNeals aware of Woodcutter, they know it's a Secret Service code name."

"Which is surely all the more reason to neutralize them both."

"Karen is preoccupied with Woodcutter right now."

"She's right to be worried about him. He's a dark horse. But first she needs to shut down the McNeals, once and for all."

Eighteen

The covert audio captured on the beach between Jack McNeal and his brother should have preoccupied Feinstein to the exclusion of all other matters. But it hadn't.

Her mind was elsewhere.

She stood and stared out at the lights of the skyscrapers, as far as the eye could see.

Feinstein's cell phone rang.

"Karen, you got a sec?" The voice of Robert Bassett, principal director of Defense Pricing and Contracting at the Pentagon.

"Bobby, nice to hear from you."

"I just wanted you to be kept in the loop: we are in the final stages, and your proposal just needs the signature of the undersecretary of defense. In effect, we're recommending we go ahead. I imagine the contract could be signed within three days."

Feinstein closed her eyes. She wanted it to be signed and sealed right now, without delay. "That's great news. Thank you so much for the update."

"The contract is with our lawyers. Once they get the signature, you'll get an email."

"Delighted it's gone through."

"Long process, procurement. But we got there in the end. Anyway, take care, speak soon."

Feinstein ended the call and buzzed in Tom Steele. He sat down and stared long and hard at her. He handed over a SIM card. "Belonged to Finn O'Brien. Thought you might want it."

"Appreciate that. I'll get the data analyzed."

Feinstein relayed the news to Steele that the contract would be signed within a week. "So, we're in the home stretch. We need to be supercareful until then."

"Karen, you spoke to Garner. He told you in no uncertain terms that we need to deal with the McNeal brothers. The longer this goes on . . . I don't know."

"Tom, as long as we are involved in providing services for the government and government agencies, we need to appear whiter than white. Seventy-two hours and we can get them."

"We need to get back to basics. Let's clean house. O'Brien was a good start."

"He's small potatoes. He just knew too much. But Jack McNeal is a whole other matter."

"Karen, let's finish this once and for all."

"We'll get to him."

"When? Jack McNeal is a stubborn son of a bitch if nothing else. You heard the conversation on the beach?"

"I certainly did. Now I know what they're thinking. Which is good. But we can't make a move."

"I know it's your call, Karen, but I would feel a lot more comfortable if we could just neutralize them within the next few hours."

"I don't like being rushed. Slow, methodical research and electronic surveillance will indicate the optimum time. Besides, seventy-two hours. That's nothing."

"This is not an exact science, Karen. Algorithms can only take you so far. I say we take them out now. Literally, now. We have our

98

guys up there in Westport. They're both there. We have a separate team waiting to go. We could take out Jack McNeal in his house tonight. Make it look like an accident. And take the brother out on the highway."

Feinstein closed her eyes.

"I know it's not my call . . ."

"Exactly, this is not your call."

Steele raised his hands in a submissive gesture, surrendering the point.

"McNeal photographed our operative down in the Tribeca diner, right? And he sent it to O'Brien?"

Steele nodded. "For me, that was the final straw. We have to finish this. It's taking way too long."

"But we have to balance the strategic aims of the company. I'm having lunch tomorrow with an influential senator. Any whiff of death squads operating on American soil and the firm will be exposed. It won't be pretty."

Steele stayed silent.

"Can you imagine if we took McNeal out now? No one is going to buy it, least of all the Feds. We can stall and misdirect, but all it takes is some fucking rookie investigator who picks up the thread. It's all so fucking messy. I can't remember a job that got this fucked up. The timing with this procurement and audit of the firm, the employees and background checks. It's a fine balancing act."

"Let's boil it down," Steele said. "Who knows the real story who's not already dead?"

"Jack McNeal, his brother, Peter, their father, William Garner, and assorted Feds."

"The Feds have buried the information that was passed to them about the death of Caroline McNeal. Maybe they've sent it to the Secret Service. But they've washed their hands of that. Political hot potato, I don't know."

Feinstein was fixated on not making glaring errors. She was worrying about which way to turn.

"Jack and Peter McNeal should be our prime concern. Our only concern."

"If we make a move on all of them now, it will look way too suspicious. What if Ramirez or your guys are injured?"

"What's the alternative? Every minute that goes by is a minute that McNeal could blow us out of the water. Have you thought of that?"

"It's the way I want it. Don't worry, we'll get to them. But I want more than one option for the McNeals. Which leaves only Andrew Forbes. He's suddenly the wild card. And it worries me."

"What's the plan for Andrew?"

"We've got to assume he is under surveillance by the Secret Service or the Feds or both. I don't know."

Steele gave this some thought.

"Get electronic eavesdropping on Andrew Forbes," Feinstein said. "Don't you have a new guy, cyber-intelligence specialist? He's good, right?"

"He's the best. Joshua Pietsch, ex-NSA."

"How's he doing?"

"He thinks we're running military drills, military simulations of scenarios. He doesn't know what he's really doing for us. He believes this is just a Pentagon project to simulate real-life scenarios but using real people with real identities."

"Get him to start targeting Andrew Forbes. I need to know what Andrew is planning to do. I haven't forgotten about Jack McNeal. We'll get him. Don't worry."

Nineteen

The leaden clouds hung low over Staten Island, and the skirl of the pipes filled the freezing air as the coffin of Finn O'Brien was lowered into its grave.

Jack McNeal stood on the periphery of the mourners alongside Peter and their father, wrapped up against the icy January wind, cutting them to the bone. He thought back to his wife's funeral. The same emptiness and grief etched on the faces.

The priest offered some words of comfort to the assembled family and friends who had slowly filed into the cemetery, ruddy-faced old cops dabbing at their eyes as one of their own was laid to rest.

McNeal's mind again replayed the scene of the blood-splattered corpse in the bath.

O'Brien, like his own father, was old school. He had never earned much as a cop. But he had enjoyed a fruitful retirement down in Florida as a personal investigator. It was also the business that had gotten him killed. He had paid a terrible price for doing a favor.

McNeal wished *he* had been the one taken out. But, then again, this was these guys' shocking way of not only dealing with a problem, but also sending out a not-too-discreet message.

No one who knew Finn thought he killed himself.

Miami Beach Police had no suspects. It was reported that they were keeping an open mind. But it was all bullshit. They had nothing. But it was clearly a murder.

McNeal had read that the surveillance cameras in and around the Bal Harbour apartments weren't working. It was blamed on routine maintenance. McNeal knew it was a convenient excuse. It pointed to high-level planning.

It was homicide, pure and simple.

When the ceremony was over, the mourners headed to a packed Flanagan's Tavern.

McNeal squeezed past friends and family to offer his condolences to Finn's widow, Mary, who'd been visiting New York when Jack discovered her husband's body. She wore a long black skirt and jacket, and a small gold crucifix glinted around her neck. "I'm so sorry for your loss," he said.

Mary hugged him tight. "Thanks so much for coming, son. I think the last time I saw you was on St. Patrick's Day at your father's house."

"I think you're right, Mrs. O'Brien."

"We can't understand it, Jack. No one seems to know what happened. I don't believe he would leave me like that. I don't believe Finn killed himself. Do you?"

McNeal felt sick, standing before the grieving widow, unable to divulge what he knew. "Never in a million years."

"I can't believe you had to find him. What were you speaking to him about?"

"I was passing through Miami and was going to ask him if he wanted to go for a beer," he lied.

"I'm so sorry that you had to see him like that."

McNeal bowed his head, unable to look her in the eye.

"He always wanted to live in the sunshine. But he said, one day, he wanted to retire to Ireland. That was his dream."

McNeal felt his throat constrict and put his arms around her and gave her a hug. "He was a good man. He'll be sorely missed."

"Take care of yourself, son." She turned to face a couple of Finn's old pals paying their respects.

McNeal got to the bar and ordered a whiskey shot and Guinness chaser each for his father, brother, and himself. The bartender placed them on a tray, and Jack took them over to Peter and his dad. He tossed back the whiskey before slurping the head off the dark, thick beer. "I wish to God I could turn back the clock . . ."

His father wrapped an arm around him. "We all do, son. But life's not like that. It comes at you like you wouldn't believe."

McNeal drank some more.

"Finn wouldn't have wanted you or anyone else to go moping around. He would've said, *Have a good stiff drink,* wouldn't he?"

McNeal believed his father was right. O'Brien's tough upbringing wouldn't allow wallowing in self-pity. Liquor was a way to inoculate yourself against the cruelty of the world.

He bought another round of drinks and one for his boss, Bob Buckley, who sat in the corner. Buckley had known O'Brien when he was a young rookie cop. Finn had taken him under his wing. They patrolled Hell's Kitchen back in the 1970s, then home to many working-class Irish Americans. Finn was on a first-name basis with the Westies, the Irish mob who had aligned with the Gambino crime family. He knew the toughs that frequented the 596 Club at the corner of Forty-Third and Tenth. He also knew Micky Spillane and Jimmy Coonan. But it was a different city then. A time when Hell's Kitchen was far grittier and more dangerous, before creeping gentrification had taken hold of the West Side of Manhattan.

McNeal handed his father and brother their drinks. "Gimme a minute. Someone I want to talk to."

He walked over and shook hands with the head of the Internal Affairs Bureau, then handed him a drink.

"I'm glad you made it, Bob."

Buckley averted his eyes before he knocked back the whiskey. "Jack, I'm so sorry. I didn't have a choice. Christ, I don't know what to say."

"You don't have to say anything. I know how it works. It's procedure. It's the way it is. Seriously, don't sweat it, Bob."

"It wasn't the call I would have made. I just wanted you to know that."

McNeal patted him on the back. "Bob, it's nothing."

Buckley took in the rest of the drinkers at the wake. "Your father hasn't changed. I know your dad and Finn go way back."

"The bad old days, huh?"

Buckley smiled. "A whole different ball game."

"So my father says."

"We dealt with some real fucking roughnecks, let me tell you. Tough little ruddy-faced Irish."

McNeal chuckled. "Is there any other kind?"

Buckley moaned. "I feel so fucking awful about it all. You being suspended. But you know how it is."

"It's just a job. It's not the end of the world. The end of the world is when you lose the only person you loved. Mary O'Brien loved only Finn. That's the end of her world."

"She loved him, alright. And the church."

"How can I forget?"

Buckley sipped some Guinness. "I heard you were down in Miami. You found Finn, is that right?"

"How'd you hear about that?"

"A friend of my brother's is a cop down there. He contacted me." McNeal said nothing. "He said surveillance footage doesn't exist. Not a thing. He said it doesn't look like your garden-variety home invasion."

McNeal didn't want to get drawn into the discussion, although he was eager to know what exactly Buckley knew.

"He was asking about you."

"Who?"

"The friend of my brother in Miami."

"And what did you say?"

"I let him know that you were suspended. And that you had been interviewed about the disappearance of Henry Graff. I had to lay it out for them."

McNeal wanted to steer the conversation back to Finn. "What does he think went down?"

"He said it might have been a mob hit. They're speculating that with his connections to a few shady characters in and around South Florida and having been employed as an investigator for a Mafia captain in Jupiter, Florida, he was whacked. Finn was close to the Italian crew back in the day. He sailed close to the wind."

McNeal thought the theory had a semblance of truth. He knew all about the rumors and stories about O'Brien. His father said there were rumors that he took regular kickbacks from Spillane. His father never believed it.

McNeal had investigated various hits by New York Mafia families when he worked for the now-defunct Organized Crime Control Bureau, before he had joined Internal Affairs. It didn't tally with what happened to O'Brien. The method used in O'Brien's execution, the headshot while the guy was defenseless in the bath, had been used in numerous Mafia hits. But what didn't tie in with the mob was remotely cutting the surveillance. That alone pointed to a carefully planned, military-style operation. Besides, a lot of mob shootings simply involved a motorcyclist gunning down a rival on the street in broad daylight or a couple of goons stepping out of a car and into a bar before they killed their target. No one, invariably, saw a thing. Cutting surveillance footage didn't seem like their work. "It's a possibility."

Buckley spoke into his pint. "I don't know what's going on with you, Jack, but I hope you can sort it all out. I know you're a good cop."

McNeal offered a crooked smile in response.

"I don't know how things got to this stage, Jack. I had earmarked you as my successor. But none of what's happened has helped your prospects. I should have tried to see the pressure you were under. It's a lot to deal with. A lot of men would've gone under."

"What can I say? Since my wife died, the job doesn't hold the same allure."

Buckley gave him a grave look. "I hope you don't hold it against me for referring you to the shrink. That was just my way of trying to help you."

"I don't know what's worse, being psychoanalyzed or watching videos of degenerate New York cops in action."

"The job gets to you. You thinking about getting out while you still can?"

"Once this cloud has lifted, I'll be ready to move forward. As it is, Bob, my head isn't in the right place."

Buckley patted him on the back and checked his watch. "Listen, I'm running late for an appointment. Got to head back to the office. You know how it is."

McNeal shook his hand. "Nice of you to show up for Finn."

"Last of the old school. God bless him."

McNeal stayed for another twenty minutes. His family all paid their final respects to Finn's widow as she clutched her rosary beads in one hand, a glass of whiskey in the other.

When they were outside in the cold air, his father suggested a nearby hole-in-the-wall bar, McGuigan's. They walked to the bar, reminiscing about Finn.

Jack got the first round of drinks. The three of them sat at a small wooden booth. He toasted Finn O'Brien, drained half his beer, and stared at his father.

The old man's hands had a slight tremor, and his eyes were still bloodshot from crying at the graveside.

"I'm sorry, Dad. I know you'll miss him."

"He was one of a kind. A great man. What a character."

Peter leaned close to their father. "How are you holding up?"

"Me? Nothing fucking wrong with me."

Jack grinned and shook his head. It was his father's standard response if anyone thought he was getting emotional. "You're incorrigible, Dad."

"Yeah, whatever. I'm sorry we're all meeting under such circumstances, but I'm glad we're together. Your mother would have been very proud of you both."

Peter put his arm around his father. "I love you, Dad."

"I love you too. I love you both."

McNeal pushed thoughts about the death of Finn O'Brien to one side; he had to or else he would turn into a basket case. He needed to focus on himself, his brother, and his father. He needed to navigate a way out of the personal hell he was in.

His father put away a couple of beers in rapid succession, washed down by a couple of double whiskeys. It wasn't long before he was talking about their late, beloved mother. He always did that when he got to drinking. It was just the way he was. He grew maudlin.

McNeal didn't mind it at all. He liked seeing his father showing his true side. He was like Finn in that he had only ever loved one woman. Their mother.

Peter's eyes moistened.

His father talked about wishing their mother could see Peter's kids growing up. "She's always watching over us, Peter," their father said. "She'll always look down on us, making sure we're alright. Just like she always looked out for me from behind the curtains when I came home after work, sometimes late at night. She was always there. A little light on, no matter what time. And always soup. Beautiful soup she made."

McNeal felt his throat knot up as the memories flooded back.

Over the next couple of hours, they talked about New York. How much the city had changed even in the last twenty years. What it was like for a cop nowadays compared to ten years earlier.

His father took a final gulp of whiskey and sighed long and hard. Dark shadows under his heavy eyes. "You mind ordering me a cab? Your old man can't keep up anymore."

"You want me to get you home, Dad?" Jack asked.

"I can see myself home."

McNeal knew it was best to get a cab. He tried to flag down a taxi for the one-mile journey, but there weren't any. "I'll walk you home."

"Don't be an idiot."

McNeal reluctantly ordered a ride through Uber. A car pulled up in seconds. He made sure his dad was safely in the car, then watched it drive off into the night. Then he headed back into the bar.

Peter stared into his drink.

Jack and his brother had so much to talk about. He leaned in close. "You haven't got your cell phone, have you?"

"The new one? No, left it at home."

It meant they could talk. "What a mess. What a fucking mess."

"I can't believe you found Finn's body. Was it bad?"

"Awful."

"Where do we go with this? What do we do next?"

"Say nothing. Be discreet. And keep your nerve."

"It's one thing after another. It's easier said than done, Jack."

McNeal sensed his brother was starting to feel the pressure. "There's no other way. We need to stand firm."

"You sent the photo of the guy in the diner to Finn?"

McNeal said he had.

"That's what did it. What does the guy look like?"

"A regular guy. White. Thirtysomething."

"Could have been a hit man. Not too difficult to find in New York. But I suspect he was part of this Graff crew."

Jack nursed his beer.

"Or he was working for Feinstein."

"I feel like I'm losing my mind."

"Tell me about it. I'm not sleeping more than an hour or two a night. I'm having terrible nightmares."

Peter gave him a sour look. "Same. And flashbacks."

Jack drained the rest of the beer from his glass. "We stick together, come what may. It's the only way we're going to get through this. Remember what Dad used to say?"

Peter smirked, first wry, then stolid. "Blood is always thicker than water."

Twenty

The editorial director hogged the meeting as he droned on about the privilege of publishing the former body man's book on the president.

Forbes had endless hours of fun reading articles about Guy. The articles had the same message. Guy stressed how much his publishing company and the imprints were striving for greater diversity. He mentioned encouraging younger members of the staff to see themselves not just as editors, but as activists, trying to "raise the bar" as they worked toward better "inclusion." He spewed such shit as *We need to empower our communities to help themselves.* It could have been a slogan devised by Karl Marx himself. He talked about the need to "spread the power of the written word." And he talked more about diversity. But not about diversity of opinion. That wasn't allowed.

The publisher gave away a few thousand free books to minority communities in East New York. It was painfully patronizing stuff. But Guy and his company always ensured a photographer or reporter was on hand to capture the event. It was free PR for his company. And it generated a huge amount of newspaper column inches. If they had paid to advertise such events it would have cost them hundreds of thousands. It was cynical and it worked. Guy even talked about reaching out to "minority women, especially those who struggle with gender issues," as if such women were a monolithic entity.

White Savior Syndrome on a grand scale, that's what it was. It was neoclassical liberalism which stressed free markets but with a social conscience. And it made everyone feel better, at least for a little bit. If that.

Forbes wasn't buying the bleeding-heart bullshit. He looked at the facts. The publisher's multibillion-dollar parent company was part-owned by a Saudi prince. The thought of taking a lecture from such medieval nutcases truly appalled him. To compound matters, he had to listen to the fucker in front of him drone on about diversity, positivity, a can-do culture, and giving back. It was like Guy had read a book on being a social justice warrior and regurgitated the whole spiel. It was nonsense. Seven people around the table. Not a Black face in sight. Or brown. It was five young, highly educated, upper-middle-class white females almost certainly from liberal arts colleges. A white publishing director. No working-class Blacks. No working-class Hispanics. No working-class anything.

He listened patiently as some of the pretty young women around the table discussed the marketing potential for the book. How determined they were to get him on every primetime TV show to sell it.

A young woman named Amy asked, "How do you feel about that, Andrew?"

"How do I feel about it? I feel good. Who doesn't want to know what the President really thinks, what really interests him? What celebrities he likes. It's going to be salacious. Hard-hitting. And not for the faint-hearted."

The editorial director shook his head and grinned. "You're absolutely right. It's a powerful memoir. Last time I saw interest like this was with the Monica Lewinsky book. That was amazing, right?"

Forbes assented politely. It all felt surreal. Here he was, a cold-blooded murderer, the President's former body man, charming the pants off some editorial stiffs in exchange for the tidbits in the book. What it would be missing was the secret he would take to the grave.

His heart began to beat hard when he thought back to dropping the drugs into the coffee. He still got a kick out of thinking about it. He had surprised himself. And if that wasn't bad enough, he had also, at Karen Feinstein's insistence, killed the honey trap woman in cold blood. He hadn't thought he had it in him. But he had.

The more he thought about it, the more the taste of blood invigorated him. It was scary to start with. But once he realized it was possible to escape detection, he had become strangely calm. Sure, it had been unnerving for the Secret Service to interview him. But the chat with Iverson had allayed his fears.

He felt omnipotent.

The only cloud on the horizon which could darken his future was Karen Feinstein. She was a lingering concern. She knew about him. His involvement. The disappearance of Henry Graff, who had contracted her firm, could lead to a forensic trail all the way back to him.

Iverson was right. He needed to think about Feinstein and focus on ensuring she wasn't going to turn him in. The fact of the matter was he couldn't trust anyone.

"The thing about the Lewinsky memoir that I love," gushed the editorial director, as if unable to be quiet for five minutes, "was how she took us on a journey."

Forbes really had to concentrate not to piss himself laughing. *A journey? She had certainly taken the President on a journey,* he was tempted to say. But he didn't. He just sat there respectfully.

"And I see your memoir taking us on a similar journey, delving into the heart and soul of what makes you tick, what makes the

President tick, and frankly, what ticks the President off. We want to know that, don't we?"

"If I told you what ticks him off, we'd be here until doomsday," Forbes quipped.

A few forced smiles and awkward silences.

"But, yeah, sure, I want to show the readers what my day was like. Is that what you're talking about?"

"Precisely," the editorial director said. "But perhaps more than anything, I want you to convey how you felt. How did you feel when the President woke you on Air Force One on a flight to the Middle East to discuss a Cardinals signing? I mean, seriously, that's crazy!"

The young women laughed politely.

"I also love the anecdote where the President barges into the staff office in the West Wing and moans that his bedsheets aren't Egyptian cotton. Did he really say, 'Get Cairo on a secure line'?"

Forbes grinned. "Most certainly did. He was very off-the-cuff. He liked things just so, what can I say?"

A young female editor curled some hair behind her ear. "Andrew, I'm one of the team who will be working on your book, and the thing that resonates with me is the way you describe a young woman, a Secret Service agent, who winces when the President is close to her. There are a whole lot of little nuggets like that throughout the book, and my job is to try and tease out as many of those as possible, from a female reader's perspective."

Forbes smiled at the young woman. She was cute. "Appreciate that, thank you. I'll do what I can. And delighted I'll be able to work with all of you."

The editorial director beamed as he looked around the table. "Well, I think I can say on behalf of everyone around this table, we are thrilled and couldn't be happier and more excited to be publishing what I believe will be the sensation of the year. It's going to be huge."

"Have we got a working title yet?"

"We were thinking *Body Man: The Man Who Served the President*. But that's just a working title."

"Sounds good. Sounds great, actually!"

Forbes thanked them profusely. The gushing was rubbing off. He shook hands, had a few selfies taken by various members of the team. He rode the elevator down to the lobby. He stared at his reflection in the mirror. A monster in a bespoke suit smiled back at him.

Iverson leafed through a pile of papers on his desk. He motioned for Andrew to take a seat. He peered over his spectacles. "Mr. Forbes, did you enjoy getting schmoozed by the great and the good of the New York publishing world?"

Forbes sat down and shook his head. "Not so much. Smug, gutless, sycophantic wonders."

Iverson mused, "Privilege does that to people. No idea why. Anyway, can I get you a cup of coffee? Water?"

"Double scotch might be better."

"You really are old school, Andrew. A chip off the old block. Okay, glad you came in. How are you holding up?"

"I'm holding up fine. I'm looking for an update."

"Here's where we are. This is important stuff. I spoke to the Secret Service about an hour ago. They really have the hots for you. They find it compelling that you have opioids prescribed by your doctor, along with your being in a meeting with the chief of staff an hour before he collapsed on the plane."

"What did you say?"

"Purely circumstantial. A lot of indignation. And I threatened to file a lawsuit."

"How did they take that?"

"They took note of it. It's a game of poker, Andrew. You have to know how to play your hand. They're keeping their cards close to their chests."

"Have they got anything else?"

"Not a thing. No residue in coffee, nothing. Unless they do have something and they're holding it back. But I suspect they have nothing."

Forbes sighed. "Well, that's something, I guess."

"However, they have you in their sights. I believe they will try and work on this and hope you say or do something that would confirm their suspicions."

"You think they might bug my cell phone?"

"Guaranteed. So, be careful what you say and what you text. So, how are we going to deal with this? Well, I have assembled a first-class team of lawyers, handpicked, who will work solely on derailing whatever the Secret Service accumulates."

"What about my connections to Karen Feinstein? The photos?"

"That is an entirely different matter. I will be dealing with that aspect myself."

"Did they mention her?"

"They were more forthcoming than I had anticipated. They wanted to know how you knew about Karen Feinstein and Henry Graff. I told them to put any questions in writing. It gives us time and space to reach out to Feinstein, or her lawyer, to be more specific."

"You think that's wise?"

"Leave that to me. I'll reach out to her counsel. I know him."

"The fact that the Secret Service is sniffing around Karen is concerning. My photos, cell phone conversations, GPS tracking, piecing it all together."

"It takes time to amass all that circumstantial stuff. But none of that proves that you killed the chief of staff. And just because the messages came from your cell phone doesn't mean you sent them. Do you know how easy it is to hack a cell phone?"

"Are they going to believe that?"

"It doesn't matter. It's good to throw that into the mix so that if it comes to a court case, we have already planted those seeds of doubt."

"It's not going to go to trial, is it?"

"No guarantees. But you have me as your lawyer, so you're in good hands. I know what it takes to resolve issues way before we reach court."

Forbes shifted in his seat. "I'm concerned that the messages I sent on an old iPhone might point to my involvement in the deaths of Sophie Meyer and Caroline McNeal."

"My job, Andrew, is simple. To ensure you stay out of jail. Out of court. There is not one iota of forensic DNA evidence linking you to any murder, disappearance, or whatever. The messages and emails, they could have been hacked. Sent by Feinstein herself. Her firm has the technological know-how. That's another angle we will be using. My advice with regards to the photo? Karen Feinstein was a woman you met. Maybe a girlfriend."

"So, who took the photos of us together?"

"I don't think anyone really knows for sure."

"That wasn't my question, Iverson."

Iverson pinched the bridge of his nose and went silent, as if contemplating what had happened. "My thinking? My thinking is that this picture the chief of staff saw . . . Well, there may be other pictures of you two together."

Forbes felt a wave of nausea wash over him.

"They are also a great blackmail tool, which were passed to a newspaper, and on to the chief of staff."

"I still don't get it. Who benefits from the photo?"

"Karen Feinstein benefits. If you squeal to the Feds, Secret Service, or the cops, or reveal untoward details in your memoirs, this will keep you on a very tight leash, released only when she chooses."

"Are you kidding me? She must be crazy."

"Think about it. You told me she wanted you to kill the honey trap girl, right?"

Forbes noticed a knot of dread tightening in his gut.

"The photos would be a useful double lock on you. Karen Feinstein is a hugely intelligent woman. But she is also a trained CIA operative. What I mean is that she is a trained killer and knows tradecraft. If this reaches court, we will be exploiting that to full effect. I will get every company document and tax return subpoenaed. Every contract she has ever worked on pored over forensically. When I've finished with her, she'll wish she had never met you. Trust me."

"She played me, is that what you're saying?"

Forbes felt like the dumbest fool who had ever lived.

"I'm on this, 24-7. I have a team working for me who are animals. They will destroy anyone in their path. Is that the kind of legal representation you want?"

"That's exactly what I want."

"They'll turn up expecting a knife fight, in a legal sense. But they need to know that if this ends up in court, we will pick them off, we will destroy them, and we will stop at nothing to get our way."

Twenty-One

The corpses fell from the sky. Hundreds of them, pouring past his window. He watched. He opened his mouth and tried to scream. But try as he might, nothing came out. He felt numb, paralyzed with fear. The sound of soft flesh hitting hard concrete below. The sound of sirens off in the distance.

McNeal woke bolt upright as his cell phone rang. His heart pounded and his head hurt. He gathered his bearings. He lay sprawled on his sofa, still wearing his rumpled suit, a half-empty bottle of whiskey tipped over on the hardwood floor. He felt nauseous. It was a bad hangover.

He reached for his phone.

"Jack, you're late." The sound of Belinda Katz's voice was harsh to his head.

"What time is it?"

"You sound terrible. Eleven forty-four. You're fourteen minutes late."

"Shit, I'm sorry. I'd like to reschedule."

"I think it's important we talk. That you don't wall yourself off. I'm worried about you. I know there's something wrong, Jack. But we can fix it."

McNeal groaned, head pounding. "I need to shower and freshen up."

"I'll see you at twelve-thirty. I had a late cancellation. That okay?"

"See you then."

McNeal took a long, hot shower, shaved, and changed into a fresh set of clothes. He noticed a slight tremor as he fixed himself some strong coffee and washed down some Advil with orange juice. He caught a cab to her apartment.

Katz collected herself as he slumped in the seat opposite. "Rough night?"

"One of many recently."

"It's good to kick back now and again."

"It was a drinking session after a funeral."

Katz kept her face impassive. "Family friend?"

"Yes."

"You want to talk about that?"

"The guy I found dead down in Miami. Name's Finn O'Brien. He was laid to rest yesterday."

Katz pointed gently to his hands. "You're shaking."

"Way too much to drink. You going to give me a lecture on the dangers of drinking?"

"If you want. Talk to me, Jack."

"What about?"

"Let's talk about those recurring nightmares. Last night, too?"

"Yes. Every goddamn night."

"Falling corpses?"

McNeal nodded. "Just before I wake up. A feeling of dread. Panic. I see them falling from the sky. It's so real it's freaky."

"I want to delve into a subject area you have studiously avoided."

"What's that?"

"I want us to talk about Henry Graff."

McNeal wondered how long he could put up with listening to this.

"I know that might be difficult. In fact, I know it will be difficult. But I need to know more about how this person fits into your life."

McNeal shifted in his seat. "Why?"

"Why what?"

"Why do you want to talk about Henry Graff?"

"His disappearance is in some way playing a part in these nightmares. I would like to explore this aspect of your life."

McNeal closed his eyes.

"Do you have a problem with me asking such questions? Does that make you feel uncomfortable?"

McNeal stared at the floor.

"Do you know seventy percent of the people I treat with PTSD, and that includes cops, ex-cops, and veterans, have recurring nightmares? I would suggest the events from three years ago, disturbing events that you might or might not have been involved with, have triggered you. You are not sleeping as well. When we first met, when you were having a crisis, you didn't mention such dreams. A lot of your trauma then was dealing with the loss of your son and the death of your wife."

McNeal felt tears in his eyes. She knew him better than he knew himself. "I want to turn the clock back. Back to when my son was alive. My wife was there. We were a family."

Katz handed him a couple of tissues.

McNeal dabbed his eyes. "Goddamn it. Look at me!"

"Grief, anger, and rage are clearly at play, and I believe you are teetering on the edge again. The discovery of Henry Graff's body in the reservoir has triggered dark, deep, almost primitive psychological responses. It's the mind's way of coping. You're at risk of short-circuiting. You could be heading for a nervous breakdown if you keep suppressing all this deep anger."

"I feel . . . I feel I'm not here. I am, obviously, but I feel detached."

"I want to remind you what I said before, Jack. We are talking in strictest confidence. But there are two caveats. The first one is if you say you are having suicidal thoughts, I will have to call in doctors. The second one is if you talk about planning or telling me about a crime or potential crime you are *about* to commit. I'm going to ask you one more time so we're clear: You're not going to commit a crime nor considering committing a crime?"

McNeal felt his heart skip a beat. "I don't plan on harming anyone or committing any crime."

Katz scribbled on her legal pad. "I'll take that at face value."

McNeal didn't know if he could trust her. He didn't know if he could even trust himself in his current state of mind. He had put thoughts of tracking down Karen Feinstein and even the Woodcutter character in the back of his mind. He had already crossed the abyss. He knew what it looked like. He couldn't let it happen again.

Katz looked up from her notes. "I have a friend upstate whose sole specialty is PTSD cases. It's a pastoral setting; it will involve abstinence from alcohol or drugs of any kind. You will go cold turkey. Become clean. You will start again. A new beginning, so to speak. Talk therapies, cognitive behavior therapies, group therapies, lots of walking, swimming, usually a lot of tears as you confront your deepest fears and ghosts of the past. I know it sounds like a big ask. But I would like you to consider that. I would write a letter of recommendation."

"Where?"

"Finger Lakes area."

"It's nearly in goddamn Canada! One day. Not now."

"I would ask you to reconsider. Now is the time."

"Maybe it is. I feel I just need space to sort myself out before committing to that."

Twenty-Two

The freezing cold air roused McNeal. He felt famished and stopped off at a deli to pick up a turkey sandwich and a coffee. He ate the food at the counter in a matter of minutes, taking the occasional gulp of hot coffee.

McNeal walked a few blocks, his head clear and feeling better after some sustenance. He saw a passing taxi. Instead of heading back to his apartment, he took a twenty-minute ride to the storage facility in Brooklyn.

He walked into the facility and opened up the safe-deposit box.

McNeal sat alone in the room. He pulled out the files. He read a few pages of a classified Pentagon memo. He knew being in possession of this could mean serious jail time. But the memo did not contain clues to the identity of Woodcutter.

He weighed whether he needed his brother's help to scan the documents again. It would be quicker. But Peter had a family and a job to contend with.

His attention switched back to the photographs. Black-and-white images of Sophie Meyer. He looked through them just as he had the time before and the time before that.

Slowly it dawned on him. He realized that all the photographs his wife had amassed showed Sophie Meyer either by herself at functions or somewhere in the frame. There was only a single photograph *without* Meyer in it. One photograph. Why was that? What was the relevance of including a photo without Meyer?

McNeal looked at it closely. A guy in a tux dancing with a stunningly attractive young woman. The couple were the main people in the photograph. Everyone else in the frame was on the periphery. No sign of Meyer at all. He stared at the photograph. Definitely no Meyer.

He felt a frisson of excitement as he looked closely. The young man's well-bred features. The confident smile. The perfect set of teeth. Manicured fingernails. He looked to be in his midtwenties. Very young. The girl opposite him held a glass of champagne as she danced. But it was the guy in the photo that interested McNeal. He sensed this photo without Meyer was important. But why? More importantly, who was this guy?

McNeal's mind began to spiral. He looked at the young man's face again. It seemed vaguely familiar. But even though he racked his brains, the features didn't resonate with him.

He flicked through the rest of the photos. He realized the same young man was on the periphery of two of the pictures. And in one, the young man was standing within earshot of the President, eyes on Meyer.

Who was the kid? Was he a friend of Meyer? A lover of Meyer?

McNeal's interest was piqued. He knew from years as an experienced investigator that curiosity was essential in good detective work. He followed his nose. He didn't know where it would lead. Sometimes it led nowhere. But sometimes, just occasionally, it paid dividends to pursue an obscure line of inquiry. A hunch.

Who was this young man? Why was his photograph in his late wife's file on the Sophie Meyer assassination?

His heart began to thump just a little bit faster. McNeal took a few minutes to look through the dozen or so press clippings with photographs of Sophie Meyer attending parties. Then he saw it.

A photograph in the *New York Times* from four years earlier. The same young man. It was captioned, *Andrew Forbes, the President's personal assistant.*

McNeal sat and stared, holding the clipping in his hands. He took out his cell phone and photographed the newspaper clipping and the photo of Forbes dancing with the girl. He packed the dossier away into the metal box and locked it once again.

When he arrived back at his apartment, still buzzing from the lead he might have unearthed, he saw a couple of NYPD detectives waiting for him. He recognized them from the 122nd Precinct on Staten Island.

The bulkier cop stood up. "Hey, Jack. I'm Detective Al Kernohan. This is my colleague, Detective David Ortiz. We need to talk in private."

McNeal sensed something was wrong. "What's this about?"

"We'd rather talk in private."

McNeal's heart began to flutter as they rode the elevator up to his apartment. He showed them inside and shut the door behind them. He switched on some lights and led them into the living room. "Take a seat, guys."

Kernohan sat down on the sofa as Ortiz sat in an adjacent brown leather armchair. "Appreciate your time."

"So, what's this about?"

"Jack, this isn't easy."

"What is it? Spit it out."

"When was the last time you saw your father?"

McNeal felt his stomach harden with tension. "My father?" His mind spun memories from the previous afternoon and night with his brother and father. He grew wary as to whether they were fishing for information indirectly about O'Brien. He had to be on his guard. "Why do you want to know that?"

"Can you answer the question, Jack?"

"Yesterday, early evening, about seven, I put him in an Uber. It had been a tough day for him. Old friend's funeral. And a few drinks afterward. He probably needed to get some time to himself."

"Was he drunk?"

"What sort of question is that? What's going on?"

"Where did you last see him?"

"It would have been outside McGuigan's bar."

Ortiz scribbled in his notepad.

"Why are you asking that? Is he okay? Has there been an accident?"

"Your brother, Peter, called the precinct this morning."

McNeal got a feeling of dread in his gut. "Are we talking about the same person? My brother, Peter McNeal, right?"

"He's NYPD too, we know that. He called us, concerned."

"Peter called you?"

"You didn't answer your phone when he called."

McNeal believed he might have slept through the call. Peter was an early riser.

"He said your father wasn't answering his phone."

"So, why don't you go around and check."

"We already have. He wasn't there. We gained entry."

McNeal's mind conjured up worst-case scenarios. He closed his eyes for a split second. Corpses falling from the sky again.

"Are you okay?"

"My dad doesn't go anywhere."

"There was no sign of his cell phone. In fact, it appears his cell phone is turned off. So, we can't trace his whereabouts. Your brother is concerned."

McNeal's mind again pictured O'Brien's body. "My dad . . . He has his cell phone. It's an old Nokia, keeps it on 24-7. He likes to know what's going on. He likes to text us or call his pals."

"Your brother has already given us the names of a few friends. We've spoken to them. But no one knows a thing. How did he appear yesterday at the funeral?"

"My dad? Well, he was upset about it. But it was a funeral, what can I say?"

"The funeral for an old friend. Finn O'Brien. Ex-NYPD, I hear."

McNeal shrugged. "That's right. My dad and Finn go way back. But they hadn't seen much of each other in the last few years."

"Finn moved down to Florida, right?"

McNeal nodded.

"And you found O'Brien's body, is that right?"

McNeal shifted in his seat. "Sure, that's correct."

Kernohan exhaled. "Jack, you know how this works. We've got to ask. We need to know if your father has gotten mixed up in something. Something to do with Finn O'Brien. He represented some shady characters in his investigations."

"What do you mean?"

"Finn O'Brien is believed to be friendly with some mobsters down in Florida."

"My father knows nothing about that. Trust me. He is beyond reproach. Ask anyone."

"So, is this a coincidence? You discover O'Brien dead, and then your father goes missing?"

"I have no idea. I'm telling you what I know."

"What was O'Brien helping you with?"

"He wasn't helping me with anything. I was down there to get some sun. And I thought I'd look him up."

"And you found the body?"

McNeal nodded.

"Let's get back to your father."

"Of course."

"You sure he's never gone missing before? Maybe a sign of the beginnings of Alzheimer's? That kind of thing."

"I don't think so. He's sharp as a tack. Besides, the only place he goes is his local bar."

The detectives both gave a half smile. "Old school, right?"

"He liked routine. He liked Staten Island. He liked having a drink. He never ventured too far from home."

"Do you want to explain where you've been the past few hours?"

McNeal was reluctant to discuss what he viewed as private business. He didn't want everyone at the station house in Staten Island knowing he'd been seeing a shrink or about the storage facility. They definitely couldn't know about that. But he knew that refusing to say anything looked bad. "I was seeing a woman called Belinda Katz, East Tenth Street."

"Is that your girlfriend?"

"No. She's a psychologist."

"Are you in a relationship with her?"

"Purely professional, I can assure you. So, no, we are not in a relationship."

The detectives looked at each other. "Look, Jack, we know you are a person of interest for Henry Graff. And we know you're not working at Internal Affairs until that gets cleared up."

McNeal felt irked at the tone of their questioning. "I'm failing to see what your point is."

"Don't act dumb, Jack. We just want you to know that we've spoken to Bob Buckley, who was with you yesterday at the funeral and in the bar, so he has confirmed all that. But he said to go easy on you as you're under a lot of strain."

McNeal muttered his thanks.

"We're reaching out to various agencies, you know how it works, and I want you to know we're doing whatever it takes to find your father."

"I appreciate that. He's former NYPD, as you know."

"We will find him. Hopefully he's just wandered off for a few hours. Have you got a cell phone number in case we need to contact you?"

McNeal reluctantly gave the number of his new cell phone.

"We'll be in touch, hopefully with good news."

The detectives thanked him for his time and left his apartment.

McNeal called his brother.

"Where are you, Peter?"

"I'm at Dad's house. Sitting and waiting for news."

"Just had the cops here."

"I had to get them involved, Jack."

"I know."

"This is not like Dad. Not like him at all."

McNeal sensed something had happened to him. "Let's hope and pray that he just went to clear his head with a walk and he'll be back some time soon."

"You think it has anything to do with Finn?"

"I don't know."

"This is not good, Jack. I've got a bad feeling about this."

"Yeah, I got that too."

Twenty-Three

The operative scanned Hempstead Bay with powerful binoculars. Watching. Waiting.

He stood on a deserted beach on the outskirts of Sands Point, a village on the northernmost point of the Cow Neck Peninsula, on the north shore of Long Island. He had expected the boat, which had left Staten Island a couple of hours ago, to be in his sights. But still no sign.

His cell phone rang.

"We're on our way." The surprisingly soft voice of Ramirez.

The operative hissed. "Where the hell are you guys? I've got to check in soon. We're on the clock."

"We got stopped by a police river patrol."

"Are you kidding me?"

"Negative."

"Did they search the boat?"

"Thankfully no. Just asking us for our IDs and what tugboat maintenance contract we were working on."

"Have you got the package in place?"

"It's in place. And we're going to deposit the package very soon."

"ETA?"

"Within five minutes."

"Copy that."

The operative ended the call. He stood and waited, freezing-cold air fogging up his binoculars. He wiped them with a cloth. "Come on, where the fuck are you?"

Eventually, the lights of the tugboat came into view. The operative scanned the side of the boat as he waited. He saw two spectral figures. He assumed one was Ramirez. The package was dropped off the starboard side of the boat, disappearing from sight. It was done.

He waited until the tugboat turned around and headed back down toward the city.

A couple of minutes later, Ramirez called. "Package has been delivered. Do you copy?"

"Copy that," the operative said. "Good work."

"Speak to you in the morning."

The operative ended the conversation and called Tom Steele.

"We good?" Steele said.

"The package has been delivered. I can confirm the package has been delivered."

"Copy that. Get yourself out of there."

"Copy that."

The operative ended the call, put his binoculars in his backpack, and drove back into town. He headed to his room in a boutique hotel on the Lower East Side. He locked the door and afforded himself a smile.

Twenty-Four

Karen Feinstein studied the series of long-range telephotos of Andrew Forbes, taken from an adjacent skyscraper with a direct line of sight. The black-and-white pictures showed him deep in conversation with his lawyer, Jason Iverson. She took a few minutes to peruse the prints. She knew the name Iverson. He was one of New York's most formidable lawyers. Forbes had secured the services of a heavy hitter. A lawyer who could look after Forbes's interests. A lawyer who would stop at nothing to win a case. He didn't play by the rules. But then again, neither did she.

She questioned what exactly Forbes was talking to Iverson about. Was it connected to the publishing deal? Was Forbes's cell phone being bugged by the Feds or the Secret Service because he was a suspect in the suspicious death of the President's former chief of staff? She had to assume it was. But if the Feds were bugging Andrew's cell phone, it meant that Feinstein and her people couldn't deploy such tactics. Not without coming to the attention of the NSA. That wasn't an option.

Feinstein was behind the curve. She needed more intel. But the more intel she accumulated, the more concerned she got.

Forbes was paying for the best. His father had deep, deep pockets. Her intelligence suggested that the lawyer was a member of the same private club as the chief counsel for the Secret Service. She assessed the odds of Iverson cutting a deal for his client. She knew Forbes had been interviewed by the Secret Service. She knew how it worked. A deal would be dangled in front of Forbes in return for evidence or a confession of guilt. And that would compromise Feinstein and her whole operation. No deal would mean Forbes would remain a loose cannon. He had zero scruples.

The more she thought about it, the more she realized that just as there appeared to be no good options with Jack McNeal, she faced the same dilemma with Andrew Forbes. She had to get to them. The Pentagon contract would soon be in the bag. Once that was signed and sealed, she could clean house, so to speak. Her company would be off the leash. The oversight process at an end.

Feinstein stared at the photographs. The handsome, serious face of Andrew Forbes, the beautifully cut suit. Savile Row tailoring. Only the best. A young man born with a silver spoon in his mouth, if ever there was one. She needed to be very careful. William Garner was right.

How could she have been so dumb? Of course!

The publishing deal offered a chance for Forbes to spill the beans. He might be more forthcoming about his relationships in the memoir. Actually, that would be a given. He would be given free rein by his publisher to talk in depth about his relationships. His friendships. She had enough damning evidence to bury him. But conversely, he had the same about her. He knew everything.

Feinstein could see now that she had gotten too close to him. He was a client, after all. But she had fallen for him. She hadn't told her closest confidants. Not a soul. She thought he was funny. Clever. Well read. He made her laugh. Not the dark, morbid, sick humor of Henry Graff, who talked of posing for photos with dead members of the Taliban. Souvenirs of war, as he called them. Trophies of the victor. Forbes was a great storyteller. He talked about his father's vacuous mistresses and the British nanny who had looked after him as a child and who subsequently married a minor member of the royal family.

Forbes was seriously wealthy. Well, at least his father was. And that posed its own problems. The father was thought to be worth in excess of eight hundred million dollars. A conservative estimate, according to *Bloomberg*. It was believed that billions might be stashed away in offshore accounts in the Caymans, Switzerland, and the British Virgin Islands. No one knew the father's true wealth. Andrew Forbes was going to be no pushover.

Feinstein had pictured a future with Forbes, crazy though it seemed now. She had imagined herself giving up her business. The subterfuge. The foreign assignments. The shadowy world she and people like Henry Graff inhabited. She had imagined herself and Forbes developing a closer relationship. She yearned for intimacy. Her trysts with Henry over the years were strictly casual. Perfunctory. Graff didn't want commitment of any kind.

She and Andrew had grown closer, their relationship developing into something more meaningful. But she sensed after a few dates and sexual encounters that he wasn't as interested in pursuing the matter as she was.

It left her empty, once again, full of remorse. Full of what might have been.

She thought of her life in the shadows. Bugging, surveilling, and neutralizing threats, near and far. Year after year. She didn't have any qualms about it. She fit the psychological profile. She didn't do empathy. That was good in her trade.

Deep down, somewhere in her soul, Feinstein craved a normal life. She wanted to leave it all behind. She wanted to retire, despite only being in her early forties. She felt envious of other women. In her world she was surrounded by men. But they didn't want someone like her in their beds. Why would they when they could have a brighter, happier, twentysomething version of her? Her best years were behind her.

Her cell phone rang, snapping her out of her reverie.

"I just sent you a message." The voice of Tom Steele. "Click on the link. It's secure. I'll stay on the line."

"What is it?"

"Just do it."

Feinstein sat down at her desk, opened up her messages, and scrolled down. She saw the latest one from Steele. Then she clicked on the link.

The screen showed real-time pin-sharp color footage of Andrew Forbes naked with a hooker masquerading as a suburban college girl in the bathroom of an East Village bar. She watched him fuck her. And again.

Feinstein felt soiled and closed the window.

"You still there?"

"Yeah, I'm still here."

"Worked like a charm on Mr. Forbes."

Feinstein closed her eyes. She contemplated what type of existence she was living. Was this living? It was so reprehensible she had long ago forgotten how repulsive it was. The crushing reality when it was closer to home left her feeling empty in her core.

"I said it worked like a charm on Forbes."

"Yes, it did."

"Listen, I know you feel bad having to do this, but it needed to be done. Most clients, as you know, stay out of sight. This guy can't help himself. He's a wild card. And I don't trust him not to fold when the Secret Service or the Feds interview him again."

Feinstein quickly gathered her thoughts. "I think with a high-powered lawyer like Iverson, Andrew Forbes will be protected, come what may. Iverson's mandate will be to protect the father, the business, and the legacy. The father's largesse with both Republicans and Democrats is in the millions. He's not going to allow his son to go down, no matter what."

"You've got a call to make, Karen."

Feinstein closed her eyes. She wasn't ready to make that call right now. She had to keep her eyes on the prize. The multimillion-dollar Pentagon contract. She pivoted away from that discussion. "The business in Staten Island? That seemed to go well."

"It's a slow burn. But it's not playing out fast enough for my liking."

"This is the low-risk strategy, and I'm sticking with it."

"Can we get back to talking about Andrew Forbes?"

"If we must."

"What do we do? What's the call?"

"I'm not ready to make that call."

"If not now, when?"

"We'll talk in twenty-four hours. I need more time to think about this."

It was a ninety-minute flight from LaGuardia to Reagan Washington, and her mind was in turmoil the whole way. She stared out the window at the blue skies above the clouds. Eight miles high, sipping coffee, mindful of what was at stake.

She had a decision to make. A life-changing decision which could define her, save her, or ultimately destroy her. She needed to get it right, and for the first time in her life, she was having serious doubts about what she was doing.

Doubts about what the hell she was going to do. Doubts about killing the client. Doubts about killing a man she had feelings for. Despite everything, she cared about him. Maybe she loved him. Then again, she was probably fooling herself. He didn't love her. He didn't love anyone. He was fucking a hooker in the East Village, for

Christ's sake. He was writing a book about his time in the White House. And to cap it all off, he had been interviewed by the Secret Service. The guy was bad news.

Her flight landed, and she picked up the rental. She drove the familiar roads to the gated community outside McLean, Virginia. Manicured lawns. Order. Nothing out of place. At least on the surface.

William Garner's wife showed her in again and escorted her upstairs to her husband's study. "Good flight, my dear?"

"Surprisingly so, thank you."

"Good to hear."

The wife knocked on the study door and opened it up, then showed Feinstein inside.

William Garner stared out his study windows, over the fields and woods to the rear of the property, glass of his favorite single malt in his hand. He wore a shirt, no tie, thick wool V-neck sweater on top, navy chinos, burgundy leather slippers. "Come in, Karen. Have a seat."

The door shut quietly behind her.

Feinstein sat down in a leather armchair. "Thanks for seeing me again on such short notice."

"That's what I'm here for."

Garner turned to face her, face like stone. "What's the problem, Karen? I detect a reticence to go through with this."

"Who are you talking about?"

"Andrew Forbes, that's who I'm talking about."

"I don't know, I really haven't had to deal with such an issue before. It got personal; I think that's the problem."

"You're torn, aren't you?" he asked.

Feinstein mulled it over. "I'm more than torn. I'm genuinely unsure what the right call is on this. There are so many moving parts. And all the time we've got Jack McNeal, his brother, and the discovery of Henry's body."

"Don't forget the disappearance of Nico, Henry's trusted friend."

"How can I forget?"

Garner went across to a table in the corner of the room. A silver tray with half a bottle of Laphroaig and a cut-glass tumbler on it. He poured a generous measure into the tumbler and handed it to Feinstein.

"Thank you."

Garner sat down and took a large drink from his own glass of Laphroaig. "I find the eighteen-year-old hits the mark for an old man like me."

Feinstein sipped the scotch, savoring the tastes.

"Anyway, like most pleasures in life, it passes. Let's get down to business. I believe Andrew Forbes is consulting a lawyer? We got a name yet?"

"Jason Iverson. New York attorney. He's a pit bull."

"Forbes is an interesting character. Very sure of himself. And that makes him doubly dangerous."

"I'm worried I've underestimated him. I just thought he was some dumb rich kid. Don't get me wrong, he's a nice guy."

"Whether he's a nice guy is neither here nor there. It's not relevant."

Feinstein shifted in her seat. She detected the merest hint of malevolence in how Garner spoke to her. "Point taken."

"And yes, he might be rich, but he's clearly not dumb."

Feinstein conceded this point.

Garner fixed on her. "Do you really know what you're up against?"

"I believe so."

"You need to factor in Andrew Forbes's formidable father. He has tentacles in a lot of industries. You do know that, right?"

"I am aware of some of them."

"I'm aware of all of them. Karen, you need to know what exactly you are up against now. He has myriad connections. Media. High tech. He has decades-old links with powerful bankers in Hong Kong, mainland China, India, and Brazil, and he has political friends all over Europe. He has a publishing empire too. I'm just scratching the surface. Mining, biotechnology, government IT contracts—he has his fingers in a lot of pies."

Feinstein took a large gulp of the single malt. It warmed her belly. "You're saying we need to be very careful."

"Indeed."

Feinstein shook her head.

"Let's take stock again," Garner said. "Andrew Forbes has been interviewed by the Secret Service, has a tell-all book deal—what it contains only the editors will truly know—and we have a honey trap, which shows him to be hopelessly compromised. He is reckless. He is a worry. But he also has a great lawyer and a powerful father. That is a potent mix."

"What do you think his next move will be?"

"It's not so much what his next move will be, it's what *yours* will be. You need to define how you are going to approach this. Don't try and second-guess him."

"That's why I'm here. I'm conflicted. I like him."

Garner arched his eyebrows. "We should never let emotion get in the way of what needs to be done. You know that as well as I do. You need to take emotion out of the equation. Let's not make it personal."

"I know."

"So, why are you letting emotion get in the way of making the decision?"

"I'm thinking of the ramifications of any decision. The President's former body man. Think about it. Where will that lead?"

"You're absolutely right to be concerned and wary about this decision. But you need to be very focused. My thoughts, for what they're worth? There is no easy decision. Both ways have risks to a greater or lesser degree."

"Knowing what you know, what would you do if you were in my shoes?"

Garner leaned closer. "I'm reminded of a journalist, a woman, who was increasingly indiscreet. She was an American, based in Managua, and she was playing all sides. I liked her."

"You had a thing?"

Garner whispered, "She was my mistress at one time. You know how it is."

Feinstein averted her gaze. She knew only too well from her long affair with Henry Graff.

"I received photos showing the young journalist drinking with various leftists. She was also the girlfriend of a leading Sandinista."

"Not good."

"The following night, she was chatting with a CIA political officer from the Managua station. A nice kid, tough, from Nebraska, but head over heels for her."

Feinstein closed her eyes.

"We did some digging. He was so dumbstruck that she was paying attention to him, he didn't realize she had stolen his notebook."

"Notebook?"

"Yeah, it had important numbers. So, he let his guard down. And she passed it on to her boyfriend, a Communist."

"What did you do?"

"I'll tell you what I did. The Sandinista—a very bright fellow who had been educated at Brown—we had his truck bugged. She was riding with this Brown-educated Commie in the back of the truck with some fellow guerrillas. We listened to the whole conversation in real time. And I gave the go-ahead for one of our operatives to remotely detonate the truck, killing everyone, including the American journalist."

Feinstein felt her blood run cold. "Tough call."

"Not really. It was a dirty war. You do what you have to do, right?"

"I'm not sure Andrew Forbes has compromised us so overtly."

"That's where you're wrong. He's unpredictable, like that journalist. He thinks he got away with killing the chief of staff. What sort of person would even consider doing that? You'd have to be seriously unhinged. It can't be allowed to stand. The way I see it? He has brought the heat on himself. And he has brought it on us."

Feinstein took another gulp of single malt. Her instincts told her that Garner was right. But a small part of her, a little piece of her heart, was going to die if she gave the go-ahead for Forbes to be neutralized.

"Have you got what it takes to handle it?"

Feinstein snapped, "I know what needs to be done. Let me deal with McNeal first. Then I can green-light it."

"Good. Then do it. The only questions you face now are how and when Andrew Forbes must die."

Twenty-Five

It was nearly midnight as McNeal paced his apartment, unable to sleep or think straight. There was still no word about his dad. He prayed with all his might that his father had just wanted some space and time to himself. But deep in his heart, McNeal feared the worst. He knew something bad had happened.

McNeal fixed himself a strong cup of coffee. He took a few gulps, hoping the caffeine hit would revive him. He called his brother, who was back at their childhood home on Staten Island, waiting for any news.

"Any word, Peter?"

A long sigh. "Not a goddamn thing."

"What about the police?"

"They stopped by again an hour ago asking me more questions. But nothing. No sign of the old man."

"It's not like him, Peter. Not like him at all."

"I know. He's always sound asleep at this time, seven days a week."

"You ask any of the cops at the 122nd if they had any inkling, off the record, what's going on?"

Silence.

"Peter, I asked you a question."

"I know you did. You remember Johnny Edgar? He's now at the 122nd."

"He's on the force? Edgar? He was a roughneck."

"He's okay. Sorted himself out after the army, a bit like me. So, I reached out to him. And Johnny, well you know what he's like. He tells it like it is. He says, off the record, they spoke to an Uber driver. And he says Dad might've been followed from the bar."

McNeal felt as if his insides had been ripped out. "Might've been followed?"

"That's what he said."

"Let me get this straight: Police think a car followed the Uber I helped Dad into?"

"So Johnny says. Some Hispanic woman in the following car, according to the driver."

"So, we got an ID on this woman apart from Hispanic? License plate?"

"Nothing."

McNeal got a sick feeling in his stomach. "That's very unusual."

"I know it is."

"No one on God's earth would want to do him harm." McNeal felt as if he was coming apart at the seams. "Peter, I'm going to come over. That okay?"

"What for? There's nothing you can do. Besides, I've got this here in case anyone calls or Dad turns up."

"I know you do. But I need to be back home."

It was a half-hour drive out of Manhattan back to the family home on a quiet street in New Dorp, Staten Island.

McNeal saw the light inside, his brother staring out of the front window, as if keeping watch. He went inside and hugged Peter tight.

"This doesn't look good," Peter said. "Not good at all. Christ, I can't take it."

"I know."

McNeal made them both strong black coffee. They sat at the kitchen table, their mother's silver crucifix still on the wall. The same scuffed table they had eaten at as kids. The same table their mother had fussed around, trying to keep her two argumentative sons from constantly bickering and fighting. The same table their father would lay his hands on before saying grace. Where they had listened in hushed silence as their father talked about the bad guys he had encountered that day.

McNeal and his brother would listen, rapt. The stories about the hoodlums and thugs—whether in Harlem or on the Lower East Side or in Midtown Manhattan—they couldn't get enough. They loved hearing about the knife fights. The killings. The murder. The mayhem. The sketchy bars. The alley where a panhandler was found dead. Not because it turned them on. But because they wanted to be like their dad and fight the bad guys on the street, day in, day out. Their mother often told Dad to just "hush now." But when she had gone into the living room to watch a TV show, they listened to their father. They heard about the nightclubs. The all-night bars. The corrupt politicians with drug habits. The rock musicians who had overdosed in fancy Manhattan hotel suites.

The more Jack heard about the NYPD, the more he wanted to join. And he did, almost as soon as he could.

His father had been proud. His mother had tears in her eyes.

"I feel like I'm going out of my mind," Peter said, snapping Jack out of his reverie. "I know what this is about. And so do you."

McNeal felt the weight of the world bearing down on him. The feelings of guilt were turning him inside out. It seemed as though he was drowning in quicksand, unable to extract himself or those he knew from the nightmare currently unfolding. He had inadvertently embroiled not only O'Brien, but also their father, in his personal battle to find out who had killed his wife. He feared the worst.

He prayed his father would turn up after having met up for some drinks with old pals. But somehow, somewhere in his soul, he knew that was a lie. His father was missing. He dreaded to think what had happened to him.

It was like a descent into hell, a hell of his own making.

His mind conjured images of O'Brien's corpse. Was this how it was going to end for his father? Killed at the hands of Feinstein or her crew?

Retribution had led him to a cycle of recrimination and violence. He had perpetuated it by wanting to find the people who had organized the murder of his wife. But he couldn't see where it would end.

"I don't understand," said Peter. "Why Dad? He has nothing to do with this."

McNeal stared at the table. "Let's not get ahead of ourselves."

Peter flushed. "What the fuck do you mean? You know this isn't like him!"

"I know."

"I swear to God, this better not be what I think it is. I don't get it! Why Dad?"

"You know perfectly well why."

Peter scrunched up his eyes as if unable or unwilling to face the harsh reality.

"It's a way of getting at us without getting to us directly. The same with O'Brien, although he had direct involvement with us, helping us. They're sending a message."

"How did it come to this?"

McNeal sat in silence, unable to give an answer.

Twenty-Six

The night dragged. The waiting continued.

McNeal could see Peter was growing more agitated. He tried to keep his brother's mind distracted. He made strong cups of coffee and ham-and-cheese sandwiches for sustenance. He made small talk. But Peter seemed to get more and more morose.

He needed to change his brother's mood. The same dark mood Peter had been locked into when he returned from Iraq. Interminable silences. Monosyllabic responses.

"It's strange to be back on Staten Island," Jack said.

"It's home."

"Hey, do you remember the time we went into town before you got deployed?"

Peter raised an eyebrow. "We drank for nine hours, didn't we?"

"Helluva day."

"I enjoyed it, bro. We don't seem to sit down, just me and you. Like the old days."

"I know. I miss it."

Jack and his brother reminisced about growing up on Staten Island twenty years earlier. The thrill of going into Manhattan on a Saturday night. The dive bars they hung out in. The views of the Manhattan skyline from the Staten Island Ferry. The frenzied excitement the city offered. The possibilities. The incessant noise. The summer heat. And the temptations. The barhopping. Riding the subway. The thrill of being in the epicenter of New York City. So near to their home, but it could have been a lifetime away.

"I remember the day I saw you after the ferry crash, you remember that?"

McNeal's mind flashed back to 2003. He had been thrown across the deck of the Staten Island Ferry, knocked unconscious, and sustained a compound fracture of his wrist. He came to in the hospital after the operation, his father by his side with tears in his eyes. A metal external fixator on his arm, keeping the fractured bones aligned and stabilized. He remembered his father kissed the back of his hand. It wasn't like his dad. His father wasn't normally one to show his emotions. Unless it was anger. He was not one who opened up and bared his soul.

All of a sudden, the happy memories flooded back.

McNeal remembered playing baseball as a kid. He looked around and saw his father watching him, enthralled, big grin on his face. That was as close as he ever came to glimpsing that side of his father. What he usually got was the ferociously hardworking, no-nonsense, gritty, blue-collar cop, who kept his emotions in check. His dad was a diehard Mets fan. McNeal had always rooted for the Yankees, after he and his friend Frankie Callaghan had skipped school to watch them play the Red Sox one afternoon. The sun shone. The Yankee fans screamed abuse. They drank. It was a great day out in the city.

The brothers talked long into the night, trying to keep each other's spirits up. McNeal didn't mention the name *Andrew Forbes*. It wasn't the right time. He needed more concrete information.

When the first rays of the new day flickered through the kitchen blinds, McNeal sat and stared at his reflection in the TV screen. He wondered for the millionth time what had happened to their father. Where the hell was he?

It was then that the headlights of a car washed over the dark living room.

McNeal heard it pull up outside. Footsteps. Then a heavy knock at the front door.

The sound snapped McNeal and his brother back to the present. He looked at his brother. Peter closed his eyes, knowing what it meant.

McNeal got up and opened the front door.

Detectives Kernohan and Ortiz from the 122nd Precinct were stone faced. He knew what they were going to say. He showed them into the living room. He switched on a lamp.

Kernohan asked them both to take a seat.

McNeal sat down beside his brother as he felt his stomach drop. He wrapped his arm around his brother's shoulder, dread etched in Ortiz's eyes.

"I'm so sorry to have to tell you this," Kernohan conveyed. "We just recovered a body washed onto a beach on Long Island."

Peter began to sob. Like he never had before. Childlike sobs from a tough cop like his brother. A guy who had served on the front line in the hell of Iraq.

Jack had never seen his brother like that. He hugged him tight. His brother was the tough one. The stoic. He tried to speak, but no words came out. Jack wrapped his arms tighter around Peter. He felt his brother shake as he sobbed.

"We believe it's your father. His wallet was on him. But you'll have to formally identify him."

"When was he found?" Jack asked.

"Just over an hour ago in Brooklyn."

It was a short drive to the morgue.

Peter rubbed the tears from his eyes as he stared at their father through the glass. The blueish-gray body was bloated from being in the water.

McNeal felt numb. Shocked to the core. He couldn't believe this had gotten so crazy. He hadn't foreseen any of this. He felt as if he was being eaten alive. Remorse. Guilt. He knew in his heart, in his bones, this was *them* sending a message.

He wanted to die. More than anything, he wanted to die. He felt ashamed. This was all his fault.

He felt like falling to his knees and wailing. But he didn't. He just went numb. It felt as though part of him had already died. Inside, he felt empty. A chasm. He tried not to think about what had happened to his father. He said a silent prayer in the hopes his death had been quick and painless.

Ortiz drove Jack and his brother back to the house. He escorted them inside and handed Jack his card. "You need anything, let us know. I'm so sorry for your loss, Jack."

McNeal shook his head. A few minutes later, Ortiz drove away, leaving the brothers alone to grieve. Jack hugged Peter tight. His brother began to weep again. "I'm so sorry, bro."

Peter began to shake. He cried and wailed. "I want to get them. I want them to pay for what they did."

Jack held his brother's contorted face in his hands. His own anger and rage had been extinguished by a deadening and suffo- cating grief. "Now is not the time, Peter."

"Dad's gone! We need to get them!"

"We need to pay our respects to Dad and his memory." Jack handed his brother a handkerchief. "This is not the time to go crazy."

Peter wiped his eyes. "I say it is. Don't you want to get who did this?"

"I just want it to end."

Twenty-Seven

A bone-chilling northerly wind cut through Andrew Forbes's layers of clothing as he finished his stretching exercises. He watched his breath turn to vapor before he set off around the frozen Central Park Reservoir. He began his run, the path icier than he would have liked, struggling to stop himself from slipping on a few occasions. It wasn't long before he felt the endorphins kick in. Despite the arctic conditions, running was one of his favorite releases. The rush of chemicals through the blood. His mood elevated. He eventually warmed up. His blood flowed. His mind focused. His thoughts turned to yesterday's intense conversation with Iverson.

Forbes had been thinking over what his lawyer had said. Not only with regard to the Secret Service having him in their sights. That was a problem in itself. But the possibility, the very real possibility, that he might have been played by Feinstein.

The more he thought about it, the clearer it got. Feinstein had already asked him to commit a murder, locking him into the conspiracy. But the compromising photos would be another piece of leverage in case it all went south for Karen Feinstein and her company. He knew it would mean she would trade whatever she had for a minimal sentence, even no sentence. No charges. He hadn't seen that coming.

He ran on, pounding the track, heart pumping harder and harder. Red-faced joggers in over-sized fleeces, discussing business as they wheezed by.

Forbes was fortunate to have the best lawyer in the city in his corner. He needed a fighter. Iverson impressed him. He wanted to win at all costs. He needed that counsel at this time. But he must be smart while under investigation.

He knew the Secret Service didn't have much, if anything, to go on. But he would have to trust Iverson to deal with that side of things.

Which only left the business with Feinstein. She was outside of his control. She was also outside of the control of Iverson.

Forbes could see in stunning clarity the very real threat she posed to him. He was at her mercy. He knew if she talked to the Feds or the Secret Service, assuming they would check Forbes's text messages and calls, he could be in deep trouble. The messages, albeit coded, showed interactions on a weekly, sometimes daily, basis. If she was in the picture, Feinstein could turn witnesses against him. She would look after her own interests. He had to seriously consider where that would leave him.

Forbes ran harder as the icy wind buffeted him. His cell phone vibrated in his pocket. He slowed down. He caught his breath and checked the caller ID. His heart jolted hard. A number known only to a few.

"Andrew Forbes speaking."

A silence. "Andrew, this is the White House switchboard. I have the President on a secure line."

Forbes wondered what the hell he wanted. "Put him through, please."

"Andrew . . ." The familiar booming voice, loud enough to scatter birds from trees. "How the hell are you, son?"

"Mr. President, what a delight. I hadn't expected a call from you, or I would've taken this in my apartment."

"Forget that. I just wanted to say I heard about your new book deal. Out the end of next year, I'm hearing. Very, very exciting. Congratulations."

"Thank you, sir. I'm rather humbled that you've taken the time to contact me."

"Why the hell wouldn't I contact you? The best body man I ever had. You wouldn't reconsider, would you?"

"I would in a heartbeat, Mr. President, but I couldn't keep up with your pace. How do you do it?"

The President gave an uproarious guffaw. "Great fitness tests, they say. Terrific genes in my family. Tough people."

"I believe it, sir."

"Well, anyway, I just wanted to take a couple minutes to express my admiration on this book. I have to say one thing, though, Andrew, and I hope you don't take this the wrong way."

"Not at all, sir."

"I hope it's all going to be nice stories about yours truly, huh?"

"Mr. President, it goes without saying that you, without a shadow of doubt, come out of this smelling of roses."

"Fantastic. I've got a lot to thank you for, Andrew. You were a great sounding board. And lots of fun to be around. Made me feel twenty years younger, if you know what I mean."

Forbes grinned. "I do, Mr. President."

"And listen, that tailor you put me in touch with, he's sent me over ten bespoke Savile Row suits, scores of fantastic silk ties. I've got you to thank."

"Every man needs a great suit."

"And every President needs a great body man. One last thing, Andrew, I'm in New York in just over a week."

Forbes had a pang of anxiety trying to remember what he was in town for, before remembering that wasn't his job anymore. "New York? Business or pleasure, Mr. President?"

The President pronounced, "It's a little fundraiser for my library, organized by my supporters in Manhattan. Pressing the flesh. Want to meet up?"

Forbes weighed what he was hearing. What was the catch?

"That is if you don't have anything else happening on a Saturday night."

"Mr. President, I'd be honored to meet up with you and support the fundraiser."

"Great. I'll get my secretary to send the details over to you later tonight. Take care of yourself."

The line went dead.

Twenty-Eight

It was a long, agonizing, and painful wait until the funeral. The medical examiner had seen no sign indicating violence. The cops speculated that Daniel McNeal might have wandered off into the night and fallen into the water. But McNeal knew one thing for sure—his father wouldn't have taken his own life. Never. Just like O'Brien, it was not in his nature.

When the day came, a deepening cold front was moving in over the tri-state area, snow falling on the mourners as they gathered around the open grave.

McNeal stood beside Peter and his wife, Muriel. Heads bowed as they laid their father to rest. He felt numb, from not only the chilling wind but also the thought that their father's death was unexplained.

He watched his father's beautiful coffin being lowered slowly into a hole in the ground. The sound of the bagpipes of two NYPD pipers in the distance playing a stirring lament carried on the icy breeze. He felt his throat constrict. But McNeal didn't shed a tear.

He felt spent. Drained of emotion. He almost felt detached from the proceedings.

The priest shook his hand. "Your father was a good man. I hope you know that the Lord above will be greeting your father as we speak. God rest his soul."

McNeal nodded. "Thank you, Father."

His brother shook the priest's hand and began to cry. Peter was a hard case. Seeing him like this cut Jack to the bone. He felt as if his heart was being ripped out. He had never counted on this happening. He couldn't prove it was related to his investigation. Or to O'Brien's death. But he knew it was. Deep down he and Peter both knew it. What they had done, killing Henry Graff and Nicoletti, had returned to haunt them.

The mourners shook his hand. Ex-cops, old friends of his father, ex-army buddies of Peter's wearing their Sunday best, they all either hugged him or patted him on the back. Inside he felt like an empty shell. He didn't feel like he could handle it. He didn't feel like he deserved sympathy or condolences. He wished he was dead.

McNeal hung around the graveside for a few minutes as the mourners drifted out of the cemetery. He saw the grave diggers approaching. When he looked up at them, they decided to move elsewhere for a while. They could see he needed time.

He stared down into the grave at the coffin. Soft white snow fell slowly, covering the polished mahogany and nameplate.

McNeal wanted to say so much. He wanted to tell his father how much he loved him. He wanted to tell him how much he meant to him. But it was all too late. Way too late. He looked up at the sky, feeling the cold flakes cool his skin. Covering his eyes. Shrouding his grief.

The reception after the funeral was held at a neighborhood bar, a couple of blocks from the McNeal house. Hushed conversations as the tea, coffee, sandwiches, soft drinks, and small glasses of Irish whiskey were served.

McNeal had pushed aside his sadness and talked to the former detectives he had worked with, friends of Peter's, neighborhood faces. He nursed a drink as he listened to them talk about his father. A man without reproach. Nobody's fool. Old-school New York cop and all the rest. It was all true. Said with sincerity by good people. But he didn't want to hear it. He didn't want to be consoled. He was paying a price. This was his penance.

McNeal swallowed the whiskey. It burned his insides. He felt better. A waiter handed him another. He talked some more. He tried to appear interested and engage in conversation. But his thoughts were elsewhere. He doubted he would ever get over what had happened.

Muriel stepped forward and hugged him tight. "I'm so, so sorry, Jack."

"Thank you. How are the kids?"

"The usual. Leaving me ready to tear my hair out. But I love them."

McNeal grimaced. The loss of his own son still lingered. It always would. He dreamed of how his son would have turned out. Would he have joined the NYPD too? Maybe he would have become a journalist like his mother.

"I've got to get back."

"Not staying for a drink with me and Peter?"

"I have to get back to the kids. I'm so sorry."

"Thank you."

Muriel pecked him on the cheek. "Make sure to look after my husband tonight. You know how maudlin he gets."

"He can stay at my place. It's not a problem."

After she left, Jack and his brother stood alone in the private back room of the bar.

"You okay if I stay over?" Peter asked. "I don't want to be too presumptuous."

"You're my brother. Shut up and let's go somewhere else. We can talk. And get a few drinks. It's what Dad would've wanted."

It was a weirdly silent taxi ride into Manhattan. Neither brother said a word, as if the events of the day had made them mute.

McNeal picked a basement dive bar where he occasionally hung out, three blocks from his Manhattan apartment. It felt as if there was nothing else for them to do but wallow in their sadness and anger.

The brothers sat in a booth opposite each other.

Jack ordered a Jameson each to throw back and a couple of bottles of beer. The whiskey was knocked back gratefully, the burning in McNeal sending warmth into his belly.

Peter leaned forward, his voice a whisper. "I can't deal with this. I feel like I'm going out of my mind."

Jack took a long gulp of the beer. "Slow down."

Peter stewed as he nursed his drink. He breathed hard, as if getting himself worked up. He scrunched up his face, clearly unable to block out the bad thoughts in his head.

"I know how you feel."

"It's just . . . It's too fucking painful. I can't turn the other cheek."

McNeal felt the same. He worried that Peter was in *kill first and ask questions later* mode. He wanted to douse the rage. At least for now. "Tonight I want to think about Dad. We remember Dad. What a great man he was. What a great father he was. And what a great husband."

Peter was quiet. "He's gone. And it's because of us!"

McNeal bowed his head. It was all true.

"We know who's behind this."

McNeal leaned in close and whispered. "This is not the time to lose our minds."

"Isn't it? I'm telling you, Karen Feinstein and that fucker Woodcutter—whatever he calls himself—they are behind this in some way."

Jack gulped some of his beer. "You want to keep it down? I think there's a couple of guys at the bar who didn't hear you."

Peter closed his eyes tight, trying to block out the pain. "A line has been crossed for me."

"So, what are you planning to do, huh? Just get a ride over to her office and beat her brains in?"

"Not a bad idea." Peter shook his head. "But no, I'm not."

"So, what is the plan?"

"I don't have a plan."

Jack gripped his brother's wrist tight. "Listen to me. I understand you're hurting. We don't know for sure what happened. As far as we know it was a drowning. Nothing suspicious. How did he end up way out there at Sands Point? We just don't know. He was a confused old man, that's what they're saying."

"I'm not buying it. None of the cops are buying it."

"Neither am I."

"Sometimes you need to take action, Jack. The time for talking is over. It's time to take some action."

"I agree with you."

Peter swigged some beer. "This is my dad. I want to know what happened to him. I want someone to be held accountable."

"We will take action. But we can't let the blood rush to our heads and cloud our judgment."

"What, and your judgment wasn't clouded when Caroline was murdered?"

McNeal was stung by the remark. He knew his brother had a point.

"I'm going to do something, with or without you. First O'Brien and now Dad. Fuck that. I'm going to deal with this."

"I will too. I promise you."

"I'm prepared for whatever they throw at me."

"So am I."

Jack could see that their father's death had pushed Peter worryingly close to the edge.

"I want to kill. I want revenge. This is my father."

"I thought I had put all of this in the past. But I can see that's not the case. We'll do this. I promise."

"I want to kill the fuckers who did this. Who organized this. I feel like I'm dying. I'm telling you, I think they're going to come after us. And sooner than we think."

Jack got very close. "There's a way out for you. I've got money. You can take your family and move away. It's not a problem. I'll deal with this my way."

"I'm not going anywhere. They came after my dad. So, I have to go after them."

"We go after them together."

Peter swigged some more beer. He studied the near-empty bar.

"Why don't we talk tomorrow? I might have stumbled onto something that's going to help us finish this."

Peter shrugged.

"I don't want to get your hopes up. But there was a photo of this guy in the dossier. Didn't mean anything to me until I noticed it was the only photo without Sophie Meyer in the picture."

"Who was it?"

"Andrew Forbes. The President's former body man."

"What does that mean?"

"The guy who carries the President's bag. Hangs around with him. Accompanies him on trips. Sits in on meetings. That kind of thing."

Peter stared at Jack, deep in thought. "You think he might be Woodcutter?"

"I think he is. But I'm going to find out for sure. You want to help me?"

"I'm in."

"Tomorrow, without any liquor involved? Clear heads, do you understand?"

Peter closed his eyes tight. "What if we find out that this Forbes is Woodcutter?"

"Then we'll deal with it in the cold light of day. We'll have a few drinks tonight. You stay over with me. We'll talk in the morning. What do you say?"

Twenty-Nine

The operative sat in the back of a white surveillance van parked near the dive bar. He checked the monitor which showed real-time video of the front of the pub. Still no sign of life. The brothers had been in the bar for a couple of hours. Just when he thought they were going to make a night of it, the McNeal brothers emerged from the bar.

"Game on," he said to Ramirez.

Ramirez was glued to her monitor as Peter pointed at his brother. "Jack looks stone-cold sober."

"Peter looks unsteady on his feet. He's had a few."

Ramirez quipped, "Lucky him."

The operative watched the brothers turn and head along the street, directly past the van. He waited until they were at the end of the street before he spoke. "Where to now?"

Ramirez tapped in a few keys on her laptop, and a mobile surveillance guy's real-time feed went live. "We're in. You got the new feed?"

"Got it."

The footage, taken from a concealed pinhole camera in the mobile surveillance guy's woolen hat, played on. It showed the brothers meandering slowly back to Jack's fancy apartment in Hudson Square. Then the brothers went inside.

The operative's earpiece buzzed to life.

"Okay, what do you suggest?" The voice of Tom Steele.

"I say we get the mobile operative off the streets, and we can head over to Jack's apartment."

"Right now?"

"That's where they are. I think they're in for the night."

"They might not emerge until tomorrow morning. Could be a long wait for you guys."

"Probably. But that's fine."

"I mentioned to Karen what you told me."

"What did she say?"

Steele sighed. "She's getting there. But she's still trying to pick the right moment."

"It's taking too long. The longer this goes on, the greater uncertainty it brings. We could take them both out tonight."

Steele went quiet. "For what it's worth, I agree. And I've shared my views."

"Tom, for Christ's sake, we'll have the pair of them holed up in the same apartment. This is a perfect opportunity."

"That would mean virtually no planning. There's a twenty-four-hour doorman in the building. I haven't got a plan for that."

"I'll give you a plan: remotely disengage the surveillance alarms, walk in, spray fentanyl in the face of the doorman, dump the doorman's body down the garbage chute, then head up to the apartment. He opens the door, we get them cold. Then get a clean-up team to dispose of the three bodies. No one would even know."

Steele paused a long while. Then: "She's incommunicado for the next couple hours. She has an important meeting."

"It's nearly midnight, seriously?"

"Seriously."

162

"So, we just sit?"

"You watch and wait."

The operative felt as if the window of opportunity would close if they didn't take them out tonight.

"I will need you to stand by. I'm meeting Karen after her meeting. Then it could be a go."

"Does she ever sleep?"

"Not much. So, be alert, it could all be a green light very soon."

"Let's hope so. It's dragging now."

"Not for long. Have a cup of coffee."

The operative shook his head. "I just want to get this job finished."

"Be patient. We will neutralize these fucks sooner than you think. We're in the home stretch."

Thirty

It was after midnight when William Garner arrived at Karen Feinstein's office. He wore an impeccable navy suit, a starched white shirt with a black tie, and black shoes. He meandered past the views.

"Nice place you've got here," he said.

Feinstein indicated for him to sit down in a leather chair opposite her. She looked at her personal assistant, Nadine. "That'll be all for tonight. Get yourself home."

Nadine quietly shut the door behind her.

"So nice to see you again, William," she said.

Garner sat down in the easy chair. "Likewise. Congratulations on getting the contract finalized."

"Signed and sealed!"

"I think a drink is in order to celebrate."

"The usual?"

"Please."

Feinstein fixed them both a single malt scotch on the rocks and sat down in the chair beside him. "Glad you could make it."

Garner looked deep into his glass before taking a small sip. "Wonderful news for the firm. I thought it would never happen. I made a couple of calls. The signing was brought forward."

"Very much appreciated. Clears the decks for me."

"Indeed it does. Sorry for the unannounced visit. I'm in town, arrived a day early. So, made sense. But I just want to see if the McNeal operation has finally been green-lit."

"As of five minutes ago."

"So, we're underway."

"The last I heard it is proceeding nicely. Slowly and surely."

Garner mused, deep in thought. "It would be nice to have it all sorted out within the next couple of days."

"That is the aim. It's a fluid situation. But it's vital that the deaths not look suspicious. I'm very mindful of that."

"That all sounds good. So, hopefully by Sunday night, this business could be wrapped up?"

"That's the plan. I have my schedule of appointments, so it has to fit in with that."

Garner took a small sip of his drink. "That is very, very good, my dear. The liquor, I mean."

"I broke out a thirty-year-old bottle of Laphroaig. Henry's favorite tipple."

"He was a man of impeccable tastes."

"I wanted to thank you for your guidance on this issue."

Garner took a few moments to respond. He was always careful how he calibrated his words. They were always very calculated. "That's what I'm here for."

"Is there anything that you want to bring to my attention?"

"The only outstanding concern I have now is our young friend, Andrew Forbes."

"I heard what you said."

"Did you understand the depth of my concern? My real concern?"

"I think I did."

"What are your thoughts?"

"We're tracking Andrew's movements very closely. Electronically, mostly. But we are combining that with close physical surveillance when we can."

"I like the sound of that. That's a good first step."

Feinstein reached over to her desk and picked up an envelope. She handed it to Garner.

Garner put down his drink and opened up the envelope. He pulled out the black-and-white photos. He studied them closely. "Andrew Forbes in a park? Where exactly were these taken?"

"Central Park. He's become a fitness nut since he moved back to New York."

Garner studied more of the photos. "I see he's taking or making a call in this one. Do we know more about that particular call?"

Feinstein winced. "No, we don't."

"That's unfortunate."

"All his other conversations we've captured perfectly. This one? Nothing."

"Some electronic jamming by chance?"

"Correct."

"That's a strange one."

"Within a minute of the call ending, we picked up another call of his to his publisher. So, yeah, weird one. Still trying to figure it out."

"Never mind. We've got him in our sights?"

"Trust me, we're waiting for the right moment. I have three teams assigned. They are working independently of each other, but each reporting back to Tom Steele. He's in charge of the operation. Once McNeal is out of the way, Forbes will be next."

"I like it. I like Tom. Listen to what he says. He's a smart operator."

Feinstein gulped the rest of the scotch. "We will take Forbes down. He just doesn't know it yet."

Thirty-One

McNeal floated on a river of darkness as corpses drifted past. The sky was black, only the billions of twinkling stars giving glimmers of light. He turned his head away. The waxy, bloated faces of the dead slipped past, eyes open as if frozen in time.

He woke bolt upright, heart rate high. He struggled to catch his breath, images of the nightmare etched into his brain. He got his bearings. A sudden pain in his head, and he remembered the liquor he had consumed the day before. He felt sick. And he felt down, not only with a low-level hangover, but knowing his father was no longer around. He felt an emptiness in his soul. A yearning to turn back the clock.

He had always pictured his father falling asleep one night, thinking of his long and full life, his beloved late wife, his family that loved him. A long, long sleep. Peaceful. Nothing more to give.

McNeal's mind was already in overdrive. He tried to organize his fragmented memories of the events. Kernohan and the NYPD said there were no suspicious circumstances. No signs of foul play. He didn't believe it for a minute. The autopsy had brought up nothing untoward. No signs of torture.

He should accept that at face value.

The problem was that McNeal didn't accept the official version. He knew in his heart it was a professional hit. No sign of injuries on the body. They might have just dropped him into the water. His father was old, could barely swim. Was that it?

McNeal couldn't reach out to any old NYPD contacts and friends. He wasn't even allowed to go into Internal Affairs HQ. His sketchy memories from the night before flooded back.

McNeal got up and clapped his hands, remembering his brother had passed out first. "Hey, Peter, you up yet?" He headed to wake his brother, who had fallen asleep in his spare bedroom. He knocked on the door hard. "Time to wake up, man," he said. He rapped on the door again. No reply. He opened the door.

The bed was empty, unmade. Peter wasn't there.

McNeal had no idea where the hell he had gone. He might have gone out to grab some coffees and breakfast for them. His brother had always been an early riser. Up and about. He called Peter's cell phone. But it rang and rang.

He scrolled through the apps on his phone. He checked the FindMyPhone app to check his brother's location, but it wasn't showing up. He might have turned it off, or maybe Peter had gone back to Jersey, missing his wife and kids. So, why didn't he say so before he left?

McNeal thought about calling Peter's wife. But he was aware that his fiery brother might not have gone straight home. He didn't want to unduly concern his wife, who would be asking where he was if he wasn't with Jack.

Had Peter caught a cab back to his dad's house on Staten Island?

A place to mourn in peace. A place to grieve. Was he back at their old house? Where was better than that?

McNeal could see that their father's sudden death had been a hammer blow to Peter. It had hit him hard, shaken him to the core.

Even worse than Jack. But surely he wouldn't have just walked out on his brother without letting him know where he was. It would be out of character.

He picked up his phone and called the lobby to see if they knew anything.

"Hey, it's Jack McNeal, apartment 322. My brother, Peter, stayed over. Can you tell me when he left the building?"

"Morning, sir. Yes, I wrote it down. He left just after three this morning."

"Three? Are you kidding me?"

"No, sir."

"Was he picked up by cab?"

"No cab. He just headed out onto the street. I asked if he was coming back. He said no. Said he was going for a drink."

"A drink? At that time?"

"I didn't question him, sir. I told him it was late and a good night's sleep might be a good idea."

"What did he say?"

"Nothing. He went out. And then he was gone."

A few minutes later, Jack's landline rang.

"Jack, sorry to bother you so early." The voice of Muriel. "I was just hoping Peter was there. He's not answering his cell phone."

McNeal's heart sank. It was the last thing he needed. "I was just about to call you. Listen, he stayed at my place, but when I woke up this morning, he was gone."

"Gone? Gone where?"

"I don't know."

"Jack, I'm starting to get worried."

"I know you are. I checked with the doorman. He said Peter left at three in the morning. No cab. He must've headed out when I was asleep. We were back in here by eight or nine last night. Peter told the doorman he was going out for a drink."

169

"Oh my God. I don't like the sound of that. You know what Peter is like when he gets too drunk."

McNeal closed his eyes. He had thought the very same thing. "Listen to me. I'm going to make a few calls. He's probably just grieving, missing our father."

"So, where do you think he went?"

"That's what I'm going to find out. I'll let you know as soon as I find him. I imagine he went for a nightcap or two if he couldn't sleep . . . or checked into a hotel to be by himself."

"That doesn't sound like Peter. Not at all."

"I'll get back to you as soon as I have news."

Thirty-Two

A sense of dread and fear gnawed at McNeal. He sensed something was wrong. Really wrong. He was frightened that his brother had snapped. The scenarios in his head were all bad. He began to imagine discovering his body in the woods near the family home.

McNeal needed to get a grip. He needed to do something. He needed to speak to people. He called the 122nd Precinct on Staten Island. It was located only seven blocks from his father's house. He asked to be put through to Detective Kernohan.

"Kernohan speaking."

McNeal quickly explained the situation.

"And this is out of character, I'd imagine?"

"First my father goes missing and winds up dead, now my brother is missing. What do you think?"

"I didn't mean to sound so callous."

"Something is wrong. This is completely out of character. He stayed over after my dad's funeral. Now he's gone. What are you going to do about it?"

"I'm going to put a couple of officers on this. He might turn up later today at his home. I'll liaise with officers in Manhattan to keep them up to speed. I'll check with the hospital too. But you know how it is. If he's been drinking, he might've passed out somewhere."

McNeal closed his eyes, knowing that could be true.

"So, let's not get ahead of ourselves. Leave it to me."

McNeal thanked Kernohan and disconnected before he called his sister-in-law and explained that he had reported Peter missing. "They're on this."

"So unlike him." Her voice was quiet. "He hasn't done anything stupid, has he, Jack?"

"Like what?"

"I don't know. He's devastated, losing his dad. You know how much he loved him."

"Listen to me. Peter wouldn't even consider that, I can assure you."

"I think you're right. I'm just scared that he might do something in the heat of the moment."

"We'll find him."

"Promise?"

"I promise."

McNeal ended the call. His mind was struggling to take it all in so soon after his father's shocking death. His head was pounding. His mouth felt dry. He called Peter's cell phone again. Still no answer.

He paced his apartment as he tried to clear his thoughts.

Where the hell was his brother? What was on his mind? He hadn't seen Peter so emotional since he got back from Iraq. He remembered those days when he first returned. His brother was in pieces. Mentally broken. Blackouts from drinking. Disappearing for days at a time. Had their father's death provoked the same sort of response? Drinking until he blacked out? He had lost count of the number of times Muriel had called him saying Peter had been found passed out on a sidewalk in New Dorp, sometimes yards from the nearest bar.

He looked out over the street, the dark waters of the Hudson in the distance. He hoped and prayed Peter hadn't done anything stupid.

McNeal stared at the Hudson River. His apartment was only a couple of blocks from the water. He used to like jogging in the summer on the waterfront walkway all the way up to Fifty-Ninth Street. Then jogging all the way back.

He conjured up a scenario in which Peter had wandered out in the middle of the night, trying to clear his head, needing space to come to terms with everything.

The more he thought of Peter walking around near the water, and what had happened to his father, the more he felt a sense of foreboding.

It wasn't long before Jack's thoughts became darker. What if Peter hadn't just gone for a drink? Maybe he had snapped. He had a gun. Maybe Peter had taken his own life.

McNeal began to consider his own situation. He thought of the mental strain and the nightmares he had endured since he'd killed Graff and Nicoletti. Were all these dark memories plaguing Jack's dreams and turning them into nightmares doing the same to Peter? Would it be too much of a stretch to imagine their father's death triggering Peter's darkest fears?

Jack's cell phone pinged. He held his breath. He peeked at his phone. A text message from Peter. It said simply:

Sorry for walking out on you. I caught a cab over to the cemetery. I've been sitting beside Dad's grave all night. Hope you're not mad. If you can pick me up, that would be much appreciated. Love, Peter.

Jack closed his eyes. "Thank God!" Waves of joy washed through his body. "Thank God." He said a silent prayer before he sent a text straight back to his brother.

Glad you're okay. I'll be right over.

It was a forty-minute drive in snarled-up traffic.

McNeal crossed over the Verrazano-Narrows Bridge to Staten Island. He had blankets and some hot chicken soup for his brother. He figured Peter would be freezing cold if he had been out in glacial conditions half the night.

He arrived at the cemetery looking forward to getting his brother back to his family. He drove slowly down the winding road, past hundreds and hundreds of graves. Predominantly Italian, Irish, and American flags dotted the headstones. He negotiated the road until it came to the section where his father had been buried at the far end of the cemetery.

He pulled up close to the plot.

McNeal got out of his car and walked over to his father's grave. He walked between the beautiful, ornate headstones. The memories of yesterday flooded back. The mourners. The faces. The dark skies.

McNeal's peripheral vision saw birds fly out of nearby trees. His senses were switched on. He approached the grave. Sticking out beside the rear of his father's grave, a pair of shoes. That had to be his brother. No doubt passed out.

"Hey, Peter, you okay?"

Peter didn't reply.

"Your ride's here!"

Jack took another couple of steps and stopped dead in his tracks. Lying prostrate over his father's grave, brain matter splattered over the granite headstone, his dead brother.

A bloody bullet wound in the back of his head, gun still in his mouth.

"Oh for Christ's sake, Peter!"

Jack fell to his knees and cradled his brother's bloody head. He felt congealed blood on his skin as he pulled him close. "Peter! Peter! No!"

He felt himself shake. Then he began to cry as he held his brother close to his chest.

Thirty-Three

It was as if his world had exploded in slow motion.

Blue lights swirled around his head. The sounds of cops, paramedics, and sirens echoed in his shattered mind. Shouting. He stared at the blood congealing on the frozen ground.

McNeal blankly watched the blizzard of activity all around, while still holding his brother. He sensed he was going into shock. He felt numb.

"Sir, can you hear me?"

McNeal couldn't move, unable to respond to questions. He was in a waking nightmare. A suffocating hell of his own making. More muffled voices in his head.

"Did you discover this man?"

Blurred faces. Blue lights.

He felt himself being helped to his feet. He noticed his bloody hands were shaking.

He was in acute shock. Then a terrible emptiness began to consume him.

He tried to piece it together. Like a jigsaw from his shattered mind. Was his brother really dead?

His beloved, tough veteran brother dead? The brother who he had fought alongside as a kid against the neighborhood bullies on the streets of Staten Island? The brother who had served his country? The brother who had returned a broken man, but who had rebuilt his life in the NYPD?

The brother who had killed Graff and Nicoletti with him? The brother who had now been taken from him?

McNeal threw up. He was checked over by a paramedic for a few minutes. They cleaned him up.

Detectives Kernohan and Ortiz stood above him. "You need to come with us."

McNeal stared at them.

"Do you understand what I just said?" Ortiz said.

McNeal snapped back to reality. He sat in the back of an SUV as Kernohan and Ortiz took him to the nearby 122nd Precinct. Inside, the harsh fluorescent lights hurt his head. He followed Kernohan into a windowless room.

McNeal shivered as he pulled up a seat opposite Kernohan.

Kernohan called in Ortiz, who instructed a uniformed cop to get a hot coffee and a blanket.

"Jack, just so you know, this is obviously being recorded. You know how it works."

McNeal gave one sharp nod. The cop returned with a blanket. He wrapped it around McNeal.

"That better?"

McNeal bowed his head.

"Sorry, I meant are you warmer?"

"Yes."

"Let's get down to business. Did you kill your brother? Did you guys have a falling out?"

"Are you fucking serious?"

"Answer the question."

"No, I didn't kill my brother. What the hell are you talking about? I spoke to you. I was the one who called the precinct and reported Peter was missing."

"Who do you think did kill your brother?"

"How the hell do I know?"

"Jack, we already took a statement from your doorman. Your brother was staying with you last night. Why did he leave in the middle of the night?"

McNeal lifted up the coffee. His hands were still shaking. He took a couple of large gulps of the lukewarm coffee. "I have no idea."

"How did you know your brother would be at the cemetery?"

"How did I know he'd be there . . ." It felt as if his brain had begun to seize up.

McNeal closed his eyes for a split second. His mind spat out images of his dead brother sprawled on the grave. He needed to get a grip. He couldn't let the NYPD know about the text telling him where his brother was. He figured it would implicate him in his brother's death. Then the cops would want to get his cell phone. And if they got his new cell phone, it might lead to questions about his old cell phone and what happened to it. The old cell phone he had gotten rid of after Graff was killed. Besides, the wrong answer could incriminate him. He knew how it worked. His one saving grace was that his cell phone records were only retained by his provider for two years.

The questions raged in his head.

"Do you hear me?"

McNeal sat and sipped his coffee as he gathered his thoughts. "Give me a second. I'm trying to focus."

He thought back. It had all begun with *his* thirst for vengeance. He had wanted to find the people who had killed his wife. He had wanted justice. But in the end, there was no justice. It was a blood reprisal. He had killed Henry Graff and Nicoletti, his brother, Peter, at his side. And now, here he was, alone. His wife dead, his father dead, O'Brien dead, his brother dead.

A trail of blood. The vengeance and bloodlust had come back to haunt him. His family had been torn to shreds because of his wish to avenge his wife. It had consumed him. They had taken everyone close to him. He was the only one who remained.

"Jack, are you refusing to answer questions?"

McNeal's mind began to focus. "No. I'm still in shock, I think."

"We know Peter suffered from PTSD in the past. Are you saying he might have killed himself?"

"I don't know. I know Peter was heartbroken, utterly bereft at our father's death a few days ago. The funeral yesterday was a tipping point."

"Did he kill himself?"

"I don't know. It wouldn't be in his character at all."

Ortiz scribbled some notes. "And yet," he said, "your brother was a veteran. He was pretty strung out when he came back from Iraq, or so I hear."

"That was a while ago."

"You never get over stuff like that. I should know. I was out there too."

"I don't know. I just know my brother didn't appear suicidal. He was heartbroken."

Ortiz gave a sideways glance at Kernohan, whose gaze was boring into McNeal.

McNeal sipped some more coffee.

"Your brother stayed with you last night?" Ortiz said.

"That's right. I need to talk to his wife. Can I make a call?"

"We'll deal with that. When did you realize he wasn't there?"

McNeal recollected the events of the day, starting with his hangover. "Let me think. I woke up this morning, about eight, and he was gone. I checked with the guy at my front desk, and he said Peter had left around three by himself, no cab."

"Does your brother usually stay over?"

"No. Well, once in a blue moon, if we're going out for a drink in town, he might spend the night at my place."

"Nice place you've got. How do you afford that on an NYPD salary?"

"My late wife left me an inheritance."

The detectives exchanged glances.

Ortiz leaned back in his seat. "So, you've got money. And you also found a body down in Miami a few days back. Your father died after falling into the water in or around New York, we don't know where, then washed ashore on a Brooklyn beach. And now your brother, who stayed with you last night, is found with a gunshot wound to the head, lying over your father's grave? How can you account for all that? Are you saying you had nothing to do with their deaths?"

McNeal shook his head. "This is crazy."

"Were you involved in his death? Did you get someone to kill your brother?"

"Who the hell do you think I am? I loved my brother."

"And you weren't involved in the death in Miami?"

"No, I wasn't involved."

"And your father?"

McNeal leaned forward. "Don't ever suggest I would harm my father. I loved my father. I loved my brother. I'm a cop. I investigate cops."

"So, what the hell happened to them? Three people, three deaths. Gimme a fucking break, Jack."

"I wish to God I knew."

Ortiz shrugged. "You know more than you're telling us, Jack. I can look into your eyes and see the whole story there. I can see

179

you're frightened. But you need to tell us what's going on. You need to tell the truth."

McNeal grew anxious about what had happened to Peter's cell phone. The cell phone he had given him. Then he thought back to the text message. The message from Peter. But was that it? Had it been sent by them after they had killed Peter, making it look like a suicide? To lure him out there? His wife's death had been made to look like an accident or suicide. Same with Sophie Meyer's.

Slowly he began to piece together a scenario. He didn't buy it that Peter had killed himself. It was then, with sudden clarity, he realized what they had done. It was pure evil.

Could they have been watching his apartment, then followed Peter to their father's grave in the middle of the night? Would he have caught a cab? Had they tracked him? He might've been drunk. Not aware of his surroundings. Then they had interrogated him. They would have taken his cell phone. And killed him.

It was entirely possible that *they* had sent a text message to Jack from Peter's cell phone as a sick joke to lure him out to the graveside and discover his brother's body. They had made it look like a suicide. But, with Jack turning up, he would have been the main suspect. The perp. It was cute. Sophisticated. Grimly effective.

McNeal's investigative knowledge kicked in. A lot of cops would assume it was a suicide. Grief. But he saw a pattern. And so would detectives like Kernohan and Ortiz.

A pattern of killings, made to look like suicide. O'Brien's was the same modus operandi. Gunshot in the mouth. His father's death? A confused old man who had taken a drink or two too many and fallen into the water. But how did he get washed all the way from the city to a beach in Brooklyn? The old man had thrown himself in, killed himself after his friend O'Brien died, they would deduce.

His mind flashed back to the chain of events in the middle of the night. They had been watching Peter when he left Jack's apartment. His apartment had been under surveillance the whole time. Then they had followed Peter to the cemetery.

He wondered if they were watching as Jack arrived.

So, why didn't they kill him there and then?

They must be waiting. One death could be viewed as a suicide. But two bodies? Not so much.

Ortiz said, "Jack, did you hear what I said?"

"Sorry, I was miles away."

Ortiz scribbled some more notes. "I asked you a question."

"Can you repeat it?"

"You had no idea Peter was going out there to your father's grave?"

"No idea at all. No indication. We had a few drinks after my father's funeral yesterday. His wife went back to Jersey to be with her family, knowing Peter wanted time alone with me to talk, brother to brother."

Kernohan intoned, "I understand." He was playing the good cop. "This is tough, Jack, I understand. Terrible. But I'm sure you understand we've got to ask questions. You see, you found the body of Finn O'Brien in Miami, right?"

McNeal nodded.

"That's problematic. Help me out here. I'm still trying to wrap my head around the fact that there have been three deaths in the space of the last ten days. You found two of the three bodies. You've got to admit, it is straining credulity to believe you had nothing to do with any of this."

"What are you saying?"

"You used to be in my shoes. A detective. This is a pattern, isn't it? And you're incriminated in all three deaths. It's either that or a vendetta against your family or people associated with your family."

McNeal sat in silence.

"I could see you being involved. I could also see you being innocent of everything. But you need to help us help you."

McNeal said nothing.

"Let's imagine you didn't kill your brother and O'Brien. Let's imagine that your brother didn't commit suicide, since you say you don't think he would do that. That means someone is taking people out. Killing those close to you and your immediate family."

"You wanna ease up a little? I'm still trying to take it all in."

Kernohan leafed through more papers. "It says here your wife died in tragic circumstances too. Drowned in the Potomac River. Do you see what I'm getting at?"

"What?"

"That there's a pattern."

"We seem to be going around in circles! Do you seriously think I'm involved in this?"

"You're our number-one suspect."

"I was not involved in their deaths in any way. That's a shocking accusation."

"It is. But I have to ask. You understand that, don't you? You investigate bad cops, don't you?"

McNeal detected a slightly sarcastic tone in the detective's voice. "I'm suspended."

"All these facts paint a picture. Perhaps your family and acquaintances are being targeted. The question is, why? And by who? The Mafia? Associates of O'Brien?"

McNeal felt himself flush. He knew they were trying to rile him up. Get him to say something dumb. Make a slipup. His brain felt foggy again.

"A couple members of my team are speculating this is all connected to the disappearance and death of Henry Graff, down in

Maryland. The Feds have already spoken to you, haven't they? He was a shadowy figure, wasn't he?"

McNeal sighed.

"Graff's own wife was the victim of an apparent suicide. You see how this pattern is starting to look? It goes on and on and on, all the way back and forth. And you are the common link."

McNeal wasn't going to be drawn into talking about Graff. That was off limits. And it might dig him into a hole even deeper than the one he was already in.

"Jack, talk to me. We want to help. You just need to be more forthcoming. Why are you being targeted? Did you have something to do with the disappearance of Henry Graff? Do you know anything about that?"

McNeal sat in silence.

"We believe you're involved in some way."

McNeal stared at Ortiz, who was scribbling notes.

"If it was me, and my family was being targeted," Ortiz said, "I would cooperate fully with the police. Absolutely."

"Listen, I know you guys are just doing your job," Jack said. "I'm horrified by all of this. I don't know anything about my family or acquaintances being targeted. I think my brother has been grief stricken and appears to have taken his own life."

Ortiz consulted his notes. "But you told me, Jack, that you brother wouldn't, in your estimation, have taken his life."

"I don't know, I'm not an expert."

"What about O'Brien?"

"What about him?"

"Did he shoot himself in his bath a few hours before you turned up at his apartment?"

"That's what the Miami Beach Police said, according to the *Miami Herald*."

"Jack, listen to me. Do I look like a stupid man?"

"Certainly not."

"So, don't try to make a fool out of me."

McNeal couldn't decide if the killing of his brother was the work of the guy from the diner. The man whose picture he had taken. Was the man part of a team taking orders from Karen Feinstein? Just like the orders that had killed his wife? That had killed Sophie Meyer?

The questions raced through his head like a freight train.

How did the Woodcutter character fit into this? Was Andrew Forbes definitely Woodcutter? Was he still working at the White House? He must have been at one time if he had a Secret Service code name. Was he still pulling the strings now?

McNeal felt himself disassociating from the questioning. Was this his way of coping? Was he going out of his mind?

He considered that the nightmares were a signal of his descent into madness. Corpses falling past windows. Nightmares shrouding reality.

"You don't look too good, Jack. Do you need medical attention? Are you in shock?"

McNeal cleared his throat and finished the dregs of the coffee. "I'm shaken up."

"Do you need medical attention?"

"I just need some time and space to get my head around this. I just want to go home."

Kernohan leaned in close. "I'm sure you do. But we've got a lot more to ask you."

The hours dragged throughout the morning and into the afternoon.

McNeal was interrogated by a succession of detectives. He tried his best to keep calm. He tried to keep his story consistent. But they kept picking away at the "statistically impossible" sequence of events. They were correct, of course. But McNeal played it straight. He just reiterated that it was a terrible sequence of events. Bad luck. Coincidence. It was clear that they weren't buying it.

"Just a heads-up, Jack, the FBI are now involved. I believe the Secret Service is also carrying out an investigation in a parallel inquiry. Two federal agencies along with the NYPD."

McNeal knew it was time to just sit quiet. Eventually, exasperated by him not giving them what he knew, he was released. It was nearly four p.m.

A young cop drove him back from the precinct to pick up his car at the graveyard. He thanked the kid. Then he headed back to his apartment in Lower Manhattan. He said a muted hello to the new guy on the desk in the lobby.

As McNeal rode the elevator, he caught his reflection in the glass-paneled interior. Dark shadows. Pale face, drawn. Unshaven. He looked fucked. The events had aged him.

When he got back inside his apartment, door locked, he lay back on the sofa in silence. He stared at the walls, wishing he was dead.

Thirty-Four

The New York sky was ablaze. Shards of bloodred winter sun peeked through the trees, casting long shadows over Central Park.

Andrew Forbes squinted as he sat on the penthouse terrace of the ultraexclusive Knickerbocker Club on East Sixty-Second Street, warmed by the patio heaters. He sat alongside his lawyer, Jason Iverson. He brushed a speck of dandruff off the shoulder of his bespoke tuxedo. It wasn't long until the private fundraiser for the President at a nearby townhouse. He nursed his single malt as Iverson sat quietly with his martini.

"Nice place," Iverson said.

"What can I say? My father got me in when I was twenty-one."

Iverson whistled. "Lucky guy."

"Said it was a great place to network."

"And is it?"

"It can be, I guess."

Iverson clinked his glass with Forbes's. "To networking."

Forbes took a gulp of the malt, the liquor warming his insides. "What do you think of the tux?"

"It's a killer look. Very James Bond."

Forbes purred, "Behave."

"How do you feel about meeting with the President again? And in such close quarters?"

Forbes mulled over what it would feel like to see the big guy again. He missed him. But he hadn't missed the crazy pace he set. "Looking forward to it. But overall, glad to be out of there. I like taking things at a more leisurely pace. It was exhausting just being in his presence."

"Word of advice, for what it's worth. Make sure you don't have anything on you that shouldn't be there."

Forbes rolled his eyes.

"I'm talking drugs, recreational or otherwise. Secret Service will be all over the townhouse, and they'll have sealed off the first block of East Seventy-Second Street."

Forbes gave a wicked smile. "Rest assured, I won't be carrying any pain medication."

"For Christ's sake, definitely not!"

Forbes stared at Iverson. "So, what did you want to talk to me about?"

"I just wanted to stress to you, in person, that you have to be very careful. Don't do anything that could be used against you if the case makes it to court. Even a fleeting remark. You need to be on your very best behavior. And don't get trashed on free champagne. I know how these events are. It starts off nice and civilized. Half a dozen drinks later, the party is in full swing."

"Are you speaking from experience?"

"Listen to me. I remember I got invited, when I joined my first firm in New York as an associate, to a Christmas party at the Plaza."

"Wild?"

"The partners were good people. A few drinks in, and then more drinks, and they were acting like demented animals. One threw up on the wife of a client I had invited. Not a good look."

"Sounds like quite the party."

"It was. But not in a good way. Remember, it's business."

"I got this, relax."

"Consider this—a lot of powerful people will be there. And the Secret Service will be mingling, and you won't know they're there. Walls have ears. Microphones. Cell phones. Don't let your guard down."

"Is the lecture over?"

"Not quite. There's one more aspect I want to talk to you about."

Forbes sipped his scotch. "Shoot."

Iverson leaned in closer, his voice low. "Got a call a few hours ago. Secret Service legal counsel, Curtis Montgomery. He mentioned that they were going to be speaking to Karen Feinstein next week."

"Really?"

"Yes. So, that concerns me."

"It concerns me too."

"She knows where the bodies are buried. She knows how this whole thing started. Do you see what I'm getting at?"

Forbes thought about that. Feinstein might be able to cut a deal with the Secret Service. He couldn't cut a deal as he was a suspect in the death of the chief of staff. She was still a hypothetical risk to Forbes. "What do you propose?"

"You visit my office tomorrow, one p.m., and we will discuss how we can deal with this. My firm is already hard at work finalizing our strategy. But I want to outline that to you tomorrow."

Forbes pulled out his cell phone and put the appointment in his schedule. "Done. You think Karen is someone I should worry about?"

"Be under no illusions. She is no one's fool. Karen Feinstein is someone you should absolutely worry about."

Thirty-Five

Unable to sleep, tormented with grief, McNeal turned to prayer for solace.

He sat alone at the dimly lit Our Lady of Pompeii Church on Carmine Street in the West Village. He needed sanctuary. A place to feel protected. A place to hide. One day he would stand before his maker. He would be judged. He knew he would have to atone for his sins. But first, he had to confess.

He got up from his pew and headed inside the confessional box.

"Bless me, Father, for I have sinned. It has been ten years since my last confession. I have killed men."

The priest whispered prayers. "What else, son? What else do you have to confess?"

"I don't know if I want to go on. I don't know if I want to live. My father and brother have died. I believe they've been killed. A reprisal for my actions."

"My son, think long and hard about what you are saying."

"What do I do? God help me, what do I do?"

The priest listened intently and suggested he seek help, counseling for his grief. He talked about going back to church. "God will never turn his back on you. Know, my son, you are not alone."

"Father, I'm hanging by a fucking thread, so help me God."

He listened as the priest implored him to seek help. To confess all his sins.

McNeal did. He let him know everything. A man he had never met. A church he had rarely given a second thought to. But now, at this time of torment and hell, he sat in church. Just like he had as a boy. Just like his brother had. Just like his beloved mother had. He returned to his faith. It was all he had left.

Their father never went to church. He said he was either too busy or grimaced at the idea of spending an hour listening to a priest. His dad viewed priests as lost souls themselves who couldn't function in the real world. And his father became even more antichurch after the cases of pedophilia among the priesthood became a national scandal.

McNeal felt the same. He thought he had no faith. Not since he was a boy. It had deserted him years ago. He felt, as a teenager, that church was for people who were old. Men and women clinging to superstition the closer to death they got. But here he was, a man in his late thirties, back in church.

A place of peace amidst the bars, bodegas, restaurants, and 24-7 hubbub of the West Village. He knew in his heart only God would judge him. He would have to stand before his maker one day and confess. Make peace. Was he going to hell? Was he going to burn in eternal damnation? The killings. The vendetta. The violence he had meted out to avenge his wife? Maybe he would. Maybe it was all God's work.

He felt tears cloud his eyes. His looked through the glorious ornate interior of the building. Paintings on the wall celebrating the Rosary. The ancient Christian faith. A cross on the wall. He felt he was dying a thousand deaths. *They* had nailed his family to their cross. It was just a matter of time before they came for him. For all he knew, they were watching him now.

"Find your faith again, my son. The same faith that brought you here tonight. You will find a way to go on. Trust in the Lord. May almighty God have mercy on you, and having forgiven your sins, lead you to eternal life. May the almighty and merciful Lord grant you indulgence, absolution, and remission of your sins. Amen."

McNeal felt tears on his face.

The priest asked him to say three Hail Marys.

McNeal left the confession booth and headed back to his seat. He just sat in silence. He prayed as if he could ever atone for his sins. He would burn in hell and would deserve to. Penance. He would need to show repentance. Was this his way of acknowledging his sins and kneeling before God?

He asked himself, not for the first time, what he had become. *Thou shalt not kill*. He had killed. But he hadn't killed innocents. He had killed men who had organized or participated in the killing of his wife. Was there a moral argument that his killing of such people under such circumstances could be justified? *Never*, most would say. And they would be right.

The more he ruminated on the chain of events that had resulted in the deaths of those closest to him, the less spiritual he felt. He might have walked into the church hoping to find solace. Crumbs of comfort. But it was fleeting. The truth was he felt empty. Sickeningly empty.

What the hell should he do? His mind plunged forward again. He thought seriously about flying abroad and saying to hell with it all, but the dark memories would always be there, following him to his grave.

He knew *they* had the means and wherewithal to find him, wherever he went. Perhaps he should speak to his lawyer, cut a deal with the Feds. But even if they did agree to that, there was no guarantee he wouldn't be locked up for the rest of his natural life. There was no guarantee that *they* wouldn't get to him.

The church doors at the back of the chapel creaked, snapping him back to reality. The sound of heavy footsteps. He wondered if this would be it. Were they going to kill him here and now?

The church doors slammed shut.

McNeal sat and prayed, head bowed. A man's footsteps. Heavy breathing. A whiff of cologne.

The wooden pew behind him creaked.

McNeal held his breath.

"Don't turn around." The whispered voice of Mafia captain Luigi Bonafessi. "I hope you don't mind me joining you."

McNeal sat frozen in silence. He dreaded whatever the hell it was Luigi wanted. He hadn't reached out to him or any of his crew.

"I'm so sorry for your loss. Peter was a man I knew all my life. It's a lot to take in, I know."

McNeal realized that, if he hadn't already, he was headed for the abyss. Eternal damnation.

"When I lost my brother a few years back, I got a card from Peter. He wrote a personal message on it. I didn't expect that. I've never forgotten that."

McNeal rubbed his face.

"I'm heartbroken that you've lost your brother like this. You're both neighborhood guys. Lot of water under the bridge and all. But you know what it's like. We all go our separate paths in life. Anyway, I wanted to pass something on to you."

McNeal whispered, "I don't know if this is the time or place, Luigi."

A small envelope appeared at his feet.

"Pick it up."

"What is it?"

"Just pick it up."

McNeal bent down and picked up the envelope.

"Put it in your pocket."

McNeal tucked the envelope into his jacket pocket.

Luigi's smoky breath was warm on Jack's neck. "Late last night I got a call. Peter reached out to me."

"What?"

"He said he wanted to talk. Nothing more, nothing less."

"What did he want to talk about?"

"He wanted to know where two people lived and their cell phone numbers."

McNeal's heart rate hiked up a notch. He couldn't believe what he was hearing. He didn't want to know any more.

"It's in the envelope. Feinstein and a guy you know as Woodcutter."

The mention of the names set McNeal's teeth on edge. "I don't know what you're talking about."

"You had the correct name, Jack. You're a smart guy. We're going to help you with this. We know people, Jack. People who can give you answers. I know what you're thinking: Why would you want to be associated with someone like me? I get it. It's not a problem. But there's a young guy, a kid, he helps us. He can help you too."

McNeal wondered if Luigi was under surveillance. "You got any cell phone or device on you?"

"No. Better safe than sorry."

"This is not the right time."

Luigi pressed on. "I told Peter about this kid. And Peter said he was going to speak to you about him."

"I want to be left alone. Is that too much to ask?"

"I don't mean any disrespect. I'm here to show you that I can help. I ain't going anywhere. I want to help."

"Just leave me alone."

"The kid works for my people. He's smart. I'd appreciate it if you would listen to me. Peter definitely indicated he was going to speak to you."

McNeal wanted to grieve in peace in the sanctuary of the church. But even that was being denied.

"He's superbright. His father, tough little Italian man who knew my parents, owed my father a lot of money."

McNeal closed his eyes and shook his head. He knew the Mafia moved in when people were at their weakest and most vulnerable. Like he was now.

"And when I say a lot of money, I mean six figures. He was a successful man, a pillar of the community, had a few restaurants, but he was a degenerate gambler. He had debts all over town. He couldn't pay it back. It was tough for him as it was one of our gambling dens in Chinatown where he racked up forty big ones in a poker game. We had his address, his work address, phone number, cell phone, his bank details, and so we knew everything we needed to know."

"Luigi, you want to get to the fucking point?"

"Relax. We came to an agreement with him. He brought his son to me. And he began to work for us, and in turn, this will pay off his debts in probably a couple years. The kid is a hacker. And this kid gets details for us, as and when we require. Hard-to-get numbers. Addresses of people. Businesses of people. Acquaintances of people."

"I'm not interested, Luigi! Besides, you can't access information like that."

"Is that right? Well, the kid did. Cool as a cucumber."

"How?"

Luigi cleared his throat, leaning close.

"I'll tell you how. He accessed Feinstein's SIM card just by having her cell phone number. Would you like to have that? I bet you would."

McNeal had heard of that hacking technique.

"And from that, he accessed messages and all sorts of interesting stuff. Feinstein was messaging a person called WC. It turns out Woodcutter is a Secret Service code name. Feinstein occasionally used the anagram Ted Outcrow, otherwise known as . . . a preppy kid who worked for the President."

"Are you trying to get us killed?"

"You want to know who this is? We do. We know everything. We're calling in some favors. And I've been asked by other people in my organization to give you any help we can."

"This is bullshit!"

"You were right. The guy's name is Andrew Forbes. I've got his address here in New York. Feinstein's address here in New York. We have it all for you."

McNeal sat stunned, not knowing what to say or how to respond.

"My cell phone number is in the envelope. You call me if you need any help in any way. I want to help you."

"Help me do what?"

"Get revenge for your family."

Thirty-Six

The operative sat in a hip coffee shop, perfect line of sight to the church. He nursed his black coffee as he watched the portly man, smoking a cigar, get back into his Lincoln. A few minutes later, McNeal slipped out a side entrance of the church.

His cell phone rang within seconds.

"We got a real beauty here," Tom Steele said.

"Who's the big guy?"

"You're not going to believe this."

"Try me."

"One hundred percent match for Luigi Bonafessi, a former street thug, now Mafia boss. Made man. He has a small army of enforcers and killers in his ranks. And he's as bad as his men."

The operative gulped the rest of the coffee. "Are you serious?"

"Deadly."

"I'm guessing Jack's pals at Internal Affairs don't know about this relationship."

"Exactly. We've got team two in the van, and they've got photos of them leaving the church within a few minutes of one another."

"What about electronic surveillance on Bonafessi?"

"Negative. He has cell phones, but the ones that are registered aren't able to be activated."

"Cute."

The operative mulled over what exactly Bonafessi wanted with McNeal. What was the plan? "So . . . only Jack remains. Last man standing."

"And Woodcutter. Let's not forget about him."

"Where is he?"

"We have eyes on him. He's uptown. And we have him in our sights."

Thirty-Seven

The townhouse on East Seventy-Fourth Street was an eight-bedroom, neo–Italian Renaissance masterpiece, located on a leafy street, only yards from Fifth Avenue.

Andrew Forbes was frisked and asked to produce his ID as he approached the cordon.

"Thank you, sir," a Secret Service agent said.

Forbes approached the swanky townhouse, its limestone facade looking fabulous in the media lights. Inside, it was all marble, gold, and dazzling lighting. He walked through airport-style screening in the lobby, a biometric retina scan done and his photograph taken.

A Secret Service agent frisked him again and politely ushered him up the grand staircase. It led to a drawing room with impossibly high ceilings. The impeccably white walls were adorned with modern art and some European masters. Sitting on a chaise longue, a couple appeared immersed in deep conversation, with glasses of champagne in their hands. It was decadent and it was beautiful. The woman, all of twentysomething, wore pearls and heavy makeup, as if determined to look more mature. A debutante on show for the movers and shakers, the rich and powerful.

Forbes smiled at the girl, who smiled back. She looked like the well-bred daughter of an Upper East Side multimillionaire, back in her natural environment after being away at college. The guy had high cheekbones, possibly a model.

A man wearing a tux, Secret Service lanyard around his neck, pointed into the room next door. "This way, sir."

Forbes walked into the grand ballroom, chandeliers hanging from the ceiling. Black-tie waiters with silver trays of canapés and champagne mingled with the guests. All the while, other Secret Service agents watched like hawks, talking into their lapel microphones.

"Sir, champagne?" a waiter asked.

"Don't mind if I do, thank you." Forbes picked up a glass of pink champagne and sipped the perfectly chilled bubbly. He scanned the walls. He recognized a Van Gogh and a Rubens.

He inserted himself into a cheery group talking real estate prices in the Hamptons, their children's private schools, cryptocurrency, and every other issue under the sun. He listened politely. He didn't have kids. He didn't have any intention of having kids. And the more he heard people bemoan or badmouth their children, the more he was determined never to entertain the thought.

The children of these people were, if you believed the parents, lazy, drunk, drug-addled, promiscuous, selfish social-media obsessives.

Forbes himself was on the promiscuous side, and, admittedly, he was selfish too. But the thought of having a son or daughter who even remotely resembled this crowd's offspring put him off kids completely. Unlikely that would change. The toll it took on their parents he found quite exhausting to even listen to.

He zoned out.

Out of the corner of his eye he saw a phalanx of Secret Service men approach.

Forbes spotted the President coming right for him. He stepped forward. "Mr. President, how are you this evening?"

"Couldn't be better, Andrew. Nice to be among like-minded people. Good people like yourself."

"We only want a better America, Mr. President."

The President grinned and shook his head like a proud dad. "This is what I'm talking about. Positivity. A can-do attitude. So, how's life in New York treating you?"

"What can I say? It's great. I'm enjoying it, sir. I live ten minutes from here. Nice part of town."

The President turned around. "Let me introduce you to the host," he offered.

"That would be great."

Forbes's placid veneer turned to an astonished gaze. Were his eyes deceiving him? Standing in front of him was Karen Feinstein. The host?

She wore a taffeta gown and beamed, radiant, basking in the vibes of the President attending a party in her house.

The President didn't miss a beat. "Andrew, this is Karen Feinstein, tremendous business lady. Karen, my former body man, Andrew Forbes."

Feinstein blushed as she extended her hand.

Forbes shook her hand and didn't let on that he knew her. "Fantastic place you have here."

"Thank you so much. If you're ever looking for opportunities to work overseas, my firm has some fantastic challenges for the right people in the Middle East."

"Great, thanks."

Feinstein handed him her business card. "Email address and cell phone."

"I really appreciate that."

"Not at all. Make yourself at home."

"Beautiful party."

Feinstein gave a professional smile. "Enjoy yourself. If you will excuse me, I need to meet a few guests who have flown in from London."

"Of course."

Feinstein turned away to greet her other guests.

Forbes grinned at the President. "What an impressive woman. You mind me asking what line of work the host is involved in?"

"Global consulting. Let me tell you, Karen's company is killing it. Growing in markets across the world. Advising governments. Very influential person. Give her a call. Tremendous entrepreneur and great American."

"Might do that, thanks."

The President looked at his watch as the Secret Service man beside him whispered in his ear. "Listen, great talking to you, Andrew, glad to meet up again. But I'm on the clock."

"Pleasure's all mine, Mr. President."

And with that, the President turned and faced another group of guests. A group of Manhattan hedge fund guys, talking way too loud, eyes glazed, best tuxes, and close shaves. Each one looked like he had sniffed ten lines of coke. Red faced, excitable, guzzling the bubbly, glass after glass.

Forbes finished his drink and nibbled on a wild salmon canapé. He felt slightly frazzled that the party was being hosted by Feinstein. In the flesh. It was way out of left field. Perhaps he should have reacted differently. But upon reflection, it was probably best not to draw attention to their relationship.

In a way, it all started to make a bit more sense. The President had never reached out directly to Feinstein or Henry Graff. He had reached out to Andrew, who had reached out to his father, who had put him in touch with Iverson. And Iverson put him in touch with Feinstein and Graff. A network of friends and influencers and powerful people.

He felt, more than ever, as if he was being played. Like a cog in a wheel. His job as the body man was to do whatever it was the President needed doing. Small stuff, annoying stuff, trivial stuff. Carrying bags, picking up a pizza delivery, having a beer or two, watching a ball game, being with him in downtime or when he was bored. On planes, in limousines, and on state visits. The body man was always there.

So, when the President confided in Forbes that he was concerned about the revelations of Sophie Meyer's affair with him, he took it upon himself to do what he could to protect him. The fateful decision was still being played out. The death of Meyer had cast a pall over them all. The subsequent death of her husband, Henry Graff, who had been in on the plot. And the disappearance of a shadowy acquaintance, Nicoletti, the hit man. The man who had killed Jack McNeal's wife when she started her investigation. It seemed like it would never end.

Forbes thought it was all under control at one point. He wasn't so sure now.

The more he thought about it, the more he began to question if Feinstein was playing a game with him. He wondered if he was being used. But by whom?

He finally began to wonder if Feinstein herself was having an affair with the President. Was this a quid pro quo? It would certainly improve her business for lucrative government contracts and Pentagon connections. He remembered what Iverson had said about Feinstein meeting the Secret Service. The lingering doubts were there.

The more he learned, the more he began to distrust Feinstein. What should have been the quietly effective death of Meyer had snowballed. It was partly due to Jack McNeal going rogue. But the revelation from Iverson about the upcoming meeting was gnawing at him. He feared Feinstein's meeting with the Secret Service could spell his demise. He was being lined up to be the fall guy. The compromising photos of them. Had that been Feinstein? A third party? If so, who? The questions kept piling up. None of it made any sense. It was likely paranoia on his part. But, then again, maybe he was being set up to be the patsy.

His senses were switched on like never before.

Forbes mingled some more. He listened politely as people talked about themselves. He watched them become animated. How much their last deal made, their children, their ex-wives, their lawyers, their dogs, their alimony, their *this*, their *that*, on and on and on.

He was on his third glass of Krug.

A woman raved about how she had found Buddhism after her husband ran off to Mexico with a "younger soulmate." He almost burst out laughing. He wanted to tell them to move the fuck on with their lives. But he didn't. He feigned interest, sipped the phenomenal champagne, and nibbled some more canapés.

He caught Feinstein's eye as she mingled at the opposite end of the huge reception room. A familiar look appeared in her eyes.

He watched as she left the room, attentively speaking to those she brushed past. She was a brilliant networker. How many people would have attended the fundraiser if the President wasn't in attendance? His presence guaranteed a full house. She was seriously connected.

Karen was also the perfect hostess. She had come far. Not the ruthless ex-CIA analyst whose company employed trained killers from the Agency. But a gracious, wealthy American business success story. It was very beguiling. She was beguiling. He had been beguiled by her. So had others. But she was as cold as they came. Her work dictated that. He needed to bear that in mind.

The guests were ushered upstairs to another beautiful room. Crystal glasses were filled with the finest champagne. An auction to raise funds for the future presidential library had numerous six-figure bids for outlandish items. World cruises, a Swiss Alps chalet for the month of January, a Beverly Hills mansion for Oscar Week, and a Hamptons beach house for the summer.

The auctioneer invited the President to say a few words.

The big guy was beaming, looking slightly bemused, like a village idiot who had stumbled on a magic formula quite by chance. He proceeded to give a rousing off-the-cuff speech about the importance of defending democracy and our way of life. He quoted Benjamin Franklin and talked about the Founding Fathers.

"This is a great country, people," he said.

The guests cheered.

"You better believe it. You think people head to China for better opportunities? Believe me, they don't. They don't head to Cuba. Quite the opposite. They head to places like New York. The number-one stop. America is a beacon of light in this world. Don't ever forget that."

Forbes felt his heart swell with pride. He listened as the President rambled on about friendship, freedom, and the joys of capitalism. He felt quite giddy. The guy was something else. A force of nature. Cheers, whooping, and clapping.

The President gave a final little wave, and then he was off, swept away by his Secret Service entourage, well-wishers clapping and cheering him out of the room.

Forbes thought the fun had finished. He was wrong. It was only beginning. Fifteen minutes later, a Beach Boys cover band took the stage, knocking out "Barbara Ann," then "Surfin' USA," as the donors got more and more trashed. It was insane.

He danced with a few young women who had helped Karen organize the evening.

"So, you're the body man?"

"You got it."

"I've heard a lot about you."

"It's all true!"

Blue bloods, old money, some new money. But mostly old money. European heritage. Like himself.

He spotted Feinstein. He danced with her for a few songs.

"I never knew you could dance, Andrew."

"There's a lot about me you don't know."

"Like what?"

"What I'm really like."

"I think I know a bit about what you're like. You remember that night?"

"It was fun."

Feinstein rolled her eyes. "What is it with guys?"

"We're wired differently."

"Hey, really glad you got invited. Why don't you stay over?"

Forbes's mind charged with possibilities. He was tempted. He thought she was incredibly attractive. But he also couldn't get what Iverson had said to him out of his head. "I'd love to, but I've got a friend coming over later." It was a barefaced lie.

"A friend? What kind of friend?"

"Friend from college."

"Uh, the worst. Who wants to revisit memories from their college years? You need to move on."

"He's a nice guy, and he's in town for the night. So, I'm letting him crash."

Forbes noticed a Secret Service guy watching from a corner of the room, talking into his lapel.

"Well, let me know when you're free for lunch. What do you say?"

"Sounds great. By the way, awesome place."

"Isn't it? I got a great deal on it. But I've done a lot of work to bring it back to life. You want a tour?"

Forbes shrugged. "Now?"

"Why not?"

"Let's do it."

Forbes followed Feinstein off the dance floor and up the grand staircase. He saw that Karen was in her element. It was a side of her he hadn't seen before. The social butterfly. The hostess. She had come a long way since she'd been a lowly CIA analyst. She had made a fortune in the global consulting and security business.

She sashayed out of the room, glass of vintage champagne in hand, Forbes by her side. He followed her up another flight of stairs.

"I think I'm getting vertigo, Karen."

"You like it?"

"Like it? I fucking love it."

A breathtakingly beautiful drawing room, Italian frescoes on the ceiling, and a wood-paneled library adjacent.

"Impeccable."

"Right? A client in London has a sister who's a top interior designer. It's her work."

"But you made this happen. You brought this to life. Amazing. It's a masterpiece."

Feinstein pecked him on the cheek. "You're sweet."

She took him up two more flights of stairs to her personal quarters on the top floor of the townhouse. She went up a spiral staircase and reached up to a hatch in the low ceiling which led out onto the roof.

The freezing cold air rushed in.

Feinstein led Andrew onto the roof, her breath turning to vapor. Views over the Upper East Side all around. He saw Central Park. The buzz of the traffic and police sirens wafting up from a great distance.

"Are you serious, Karen? This is a knockout."

Feinstein stood and stared at him, eyes heavy. "You like it up here?"

"I like it a lot. It's a statement home. It tells the world you've arrived."

"We could do it here if you wanted."

"Now? On the roof?"

"The President has left the building," she said with a giggle.

"What about your guests?"

"They're not going anywhere. Besides, the band is playing. There's booze. Who doesn't like free booze?"

Her hair was blowing in her eyes. She seemed to teeter on her heels and lose her footing. But she regained her composure and balance.

"I think we need to get back to the party," he said.

Feinstein stared at him. He sensed her mood change. He didn't know why. But he just knew. "You're right."

Forbes helped her down the spiral staircase and followed her into her private apartment. Forbes noticed a door ajar to an adjacent bathroom. He needed to piss. Badly. "Any chance I could use your bathroom?" he asked. "It's a bit crowded downstairs."

"Sure. Go right ahead." Feinstein turned on her heel. "I'll see you downstairs. And remember to flush the goddamn toilet and put the seat back down. I know what you guys are like."

Thirty-Eight

Forbes locked the bathroom door, glad to have a moment to himself. He enjoyed a long piss. He flushed the toilet and washed his hands. His mood was oscillating after the rush of champagne and the coke he had done earlier. But he wanted more. Someone always had coke at these parties, no matter how tight the security. Andrew had a knack for finding that person. He stood and stared at his reflection in the bathroom mirror. Pupils like pinpricks. Instead of leaving the bathroom and returning to Karen's party, he let curiosity get the better of him.

He opened the cabinet. Inside, there was an astonishing array of female beauty products. Blush, foundation powder, mascara, Touche Éclat for lightening shadows under the eyes. He noticed hair dye and disposable plastic gloves on the glass cabinet shelf. He gave a small chuckle. He sneered, noting that she hadn't gone to one of the top salons dotting the Upper East Side. Maybe she had just wanted to touch up her roots at the last minute.

Forbes felt a little crazy with the high-quality champagne and coke racing through his blood. He looked at himself again in the mirror. He straightened his tie. He looked sharp in the tux. He recollected the conversation with Iverson at the Knickerbocker a few hours earlier. How problematic was it really that Feinstein would soon be talking to the Secret Service?

The Secret Service could get a court order to access Feinstein's cell phone. Or they might already have accessed it from Graff's cell phone. That could have set things in motion. And in turn, the NSA would have accessed Graff's messages to and from her. It was the unknowable. He didn't know what Feinstein was thinking. He hoped, in a sense, that he was way off base, as well as Iverson. Seeing plots when none were there. Or that the coke was making him paranoid. But, then again, Karen wouldn't go down easily. She'd cut a deal before taking heat herself. And that's where the real problems could start for him.

Forbes stared long and hard at his reflection. He needed to understand the threat she posed. The more he thought about Karen Feinstein, the more he realized Iverson was correct. She had come too far to throw it all away. She was a pragmatist. A realist. She had her reputation and an empire to maintain. A multimillion-dollar Lenox Hill townhouse, a global business with lucrative security contracts from around the world. She wasn't going to give that up. She had worked her way to the top over many years. She could also afford the best lawyers money could buy, just like him.

Forbes figured she wasn't going back to being a lowly CIA analyst, hanging out in shitty bars in Beirut and Kabul, living off a modest salary. She couldn't face incarceration. Could *he*? That thought had never really concerned him before. But it did now. Not only surviving the rigors of life in captivity, but also the humiliation of his family. The disgrace.

Forbes checked his watch. He had been in the bathroom six long minutes. He opened the bathroom cabinet again. He didn't know why. Maybe just curiosity. But a little voice was whispering in his ear.

This could be your last chance. The last opportunity.

He stared at the pair of plastic gloves. Then an idea began to form. Slowly at first.

Forbes pulled on the gloves. A bottle of contact lens solution, packets of contact lenses, nasal spray, dissolving Xanax tablets. It was the same antianxiety medication he bought anonymously every month for the President. Hairbrushes and a large tube of lube. He thought about what other mischief she got up to. He scanned the shelves. The eye drops, mouthwash, nail scissors, lipstick, cotton balls, nail clippers, nail polish, face masks, tubs of beauty creams, on and on.

He pulled out the Visine eye drops and studied the list of contents. He saw the ingredient tetrahydrozoline.

Forbes stared at the bottle. He knew what that ingredient meant. What it could do. It felt as if a switch had been turned on in his head. His alcohol- and coke-fueled mind was gripped with possibilities. Dark possibilities.

He wondered if what he planned was too outlandish or just plain insane. Perhaps a mixture of both.

Forbes looked at the ingredients of the eye drops again. He had read an article which had intrigued him at the time. It was in *Time* magazine, about a paramedic who hated his wife. The chemical, if slipped into an unsuspecting person's drink or food, constricted the blood vessels. Suddenly, he could see as clear as day. It was a chance. Holy shit, he was in Karen's private bathroom on the top floor of her beautiful New York townhouse, and he had a fucking plan.

He was in full-blown *I don't give a fuck* mode.

Forbes knew he was about to make a momentous decision. There was no going back. He had to do it. And it had to work, come what may.

He took a long, deep breath and began.

He unscrewed the plastic eye dropper from the bottle, then the lid of the mouthwash bottle. Finally, he picked up the eye drops

210

and squeezed a dozen droplets of Visine into the turquoise-colored mouthwash. But that was only the beginning.

He took out four soluble Xanax tablets from their tinfoil wrapper and dropped them into the mouthwash. He watched them dissolve in a matter of seconds. But he still wasn't finished.

The pièce de résistance!

He took out his wallet, pulled a small zipper, and removed four pills in foil wrappers. Fentanyl, dissolvable. He had imagined dropping the drugs into Karen's coffee if they ever met up. But this was better. Way better. Out of sight, out of mind.

He pushed the four pills through the foil wrappers into the bottle of mouthwash.

Forbes watched the chemicals dissolve in under a minute. He put the foil back in his wallet.

Then he carefully screwed the lid back on the mouthwash, shook up the contents, and placed it carefully back on the shelf. He screwed the eye drop lid on, making doubly sure to place it back on the shelf exactly where it had been. He stared at the line of products. It appeared to him that nothing was out of place.

He shut the cabinet.

Forbes caught his reflection one final time. He was grinning like a jackal. Full-on wolf mode.

He carefully took off the disposable plastic gloves and put one in each of his trouser pockets. He took a few deep breaths. His fingerprints were in the bathroom. But not on the bottles of mouthwash, the eye drops, or the packet of Xanax.

Forbes had a reason to have been in there. He was taking a piss. He took a deep breath. He was ready. He unlocked the bathroom door, switched off the light, and walked down the grand staircase to rejoin the party like a conquering king.

Thirty-Nine

The encounter with Luigi at the church had chilled McNeal to the bone.

He returned to his Hudson Square apartment and poured himself a large glass of scotch. His hand was shaking as he took a gulp. The booze warmed up his insides. He sat down on the sofa, glass on the table. He opened the envelope Luigi had passed to him. Inside were the addresses and cell phone numbers for Karen Feinstein and Andrew Forbes.

He scanned the addresses. The two addresses were in prime territory on the Upper East Side, close to Fifth Avenue and Central Park. Lenox Hill.

McNeal had no way of knowing for sure if those two people were responsible for organizing the murder of his brother. But he did have sufficient proof that they had links to those who were involved in the murder of his wife.

The fact was Peter's death might have just been suicide, after all.

His brother's experiences in Iraq had traumatized him. Jack asked himself if helping him kill Graff and Nicoletti in such violent ways had sparked dark memories of the past for Peter. It was feasible.

McNeal realized he had three clear choices. He could do nothing and proceed as if nothing had happened. He could flee abroad and hope to live out his days without being hunted down. Or he could kill the people on the list. Feinstein and Forbes.

No good choices.

McNeal didn't know if they were even responsible for his brother or father's death. It was only supposition that they were linked to Peter's murder. Perhaps Feinstein had taken the reins of the operation and had directed the killing.

He longed for it all to disappear. To be forgotten.

The encounter with Luigi had rekindled the same dark feelings he had felt three years earlier. The opportunity for vengeance. The thirst for blood. But it also stirred up feelings of dread and anxiety. The same feelings he had nursed since his son had been so cruelly taken from this world.

McNeal finished his drink. He stood up and walked across to the window. In the distance, across the Hudson, the lights of downtown Jersey City. Peter had worked the streets of Jersey City when he started as a rookie cop straight out of the army. He had taken to the life like a duck to water. It was what he needed. He needed the uniform. The structure. The brotherhood he had enjoyed as a soldier. He enjoyed the cop bars. He enjoyed socializing with cops. He was a great street cop. He also enjoyed getting out there. He didn't mind breaking up fights and dealing with knife-wielding panhandlers. After Iraq, Jersey City had seemed like a breeze.

Jack's cell phone rang, snapping him out of his reverie.

McNeal composed himself. He worried it was his sister-in-law again. She had called him throughout the day, crying and wailing. He didn't know what to say. He tried to reassure her that it wasn't her fault. That Peter had been devastated by their father's death. But she wasn't buying it. She knew her husband. She knew his moods. She knew when he wanted quiet from the kids. She knew him well because she loved Peter McNeal. She knew, as Jack did, that Peter wouldn't have killed himself. Ever.

He checked the caller ID. It was his lawyer, Leonard Schwartz. McNeal moaned, then answered.

"Jack, thank God I've finally gotten you," he said. "I just wanted to say how heartsick I am for your loss."

"Appreciate that, thank you."

"Jack, I'm sorry to call at this hour."

"What is it?"

"The FBI has just been in touch again."

"What did they want?"

"They're going to be speaking to you again very soon. I suspect it's to do with Henry Graff."

"Have they got anything?"

"Who the hell knows? They didn't indicate anything. But I got the sense that they have the hots for you."

"This is not a good time."

"I understand. Anyway, the Feds said they'll wait until after Peter's funeral before they interview you."

McNeal took this in.

"It was the best I could do. From what I could gather, they might have more footage of you guys on the road that night, even a witness. Not enough to charge you with. But enough to ask more questions."

McNeal contemplated what this meant. "I appreciate the update."

"The day after Peter's funeral, they will come knocking. Just so you know."

It was impossible to ascertain what new information the FBI or Secret Service had on him. That was frustrating. He wondered if they had given a scrap of information to his attorney to set him on edge. But it also could have been designed to nudge McNeal into making a false move.

He thought a few moves ahead. If they were lulling him into thinking they didn't have much on him, it could have been a ploy so McNeal would let down his guard.

It wouldn't matter to him. His default position was to take the Fifth. They would have to prove that he and Peter had killed Graff. It would be virtually impossible, in his opinion, to link them to the body. And he thought it would be the same for Nicoletti, dropped down an abandoned mine shaft in New Jersey. They also first had to find the body.

He was truly alone. He had no one to turn to, apart from his lawyer. His father was dead. His brother, dead. His mother, long dead. His wife was dead. And his son, a child, dead, living on only in McNeal's shattered memory. The boy he had been teaching the rules of baseball. How to pitch. How to read the game. He was just a kid when he died. The son Jack would never see grow up.

McNeal was paying for his sins. He had confessed all to a priest. He thought he might feel better afterward. But that wasn't the case.

He had also told his psychologist of his involvement in the death of Graff and Nicoletti. With hindsight, he was shocked that he had done that. She could very well go to the cops or the FBI. Though she had said what he told her would be kept in confidence.

A black mood was enveloping him. Reaching deep into the furthest recesses of his mind. Alone with his thoughts in the middle of the night.

McNeal thought back to the church, Luigi slipping the envelope to him.

He paced his living room. His head burning with fevered thoughts. He felt the emptiness replaced by a wild rage. It began to gnaw at him. Again.

The more he thought of his options, the more his mood began to harden. It was true, he could flee, never to be seen again. He could wait for them to hunt him down. He could afford to get a new identity and set up a new life. He could do nothing and wait until after Peter's funeral for the FBI to take him in for an interview. He could be arrested. And charged. But none of those sounded like great options.

It left one option. Kill Karen Feinstein and Andrew Forbes. In cold blood. It might not end the cycle. It might result in his own death. But he figured he had run out of viable options. Nothing made sense apart from revenge. Blood vengeance.

Fuck it.

McNeal looked again at the names on the list. He wanted to talk again with Luigi. He wanted to know more. He didn't believe that Luigi was doing this out of the goodness of his heart. A part of him was. But that wasn't the motivating factor.

Jack knew there was more. He knew there was always an angle. They were never just doing you a favor. It was always a quid pro quo.

What was the real reason he had passed on the addresses and numbers?

McNeal needed to be careful in his approach to Luigi. He needed to be smart. He remembered the new nano SIM card he had bought a month earlier in case of emergencies. This was an emergency.

He opened up his cell phone using a paper clip. He inserted the new nano SIM. It took a few minutes to reboot, switching on the virtual private network, concealing his tracks.

McNeal pulled on a thick overcoat, hat, and scarf and headed out onto the street. He called Luigi's cell phone number.

"Yeah?" The distinctive New York accent.

"We talked in the church."

A beat. "Glad you called back."

"I hope I didn't wake you."

Luigi laughed. "I do a lot of my business at night, you know what I mean?"

"Got it. Is this number secure?"

"Who the fuck knows? I change my cell phone number every other day, so I'm assuming it's pretty secure."

"I want to talk one more time."

"What about?"

"I need help."

"What kind of help?"

"I'd prefer to talk face-to-face. Again."

"Where are you?"

"Hudson Square."

"Do you know a steak house, not far from you? Corner of Greenwich and Harrison in the middle of Tribeca?"

"Been there many times."

"When do you want to meet up?"

"As soon as possible."

"I'm in a car crossing Midtown. I could be there in fifteen minutes."

"I'll see you then."

McNeal ended the call. He took the nano SIM out of the phone. Then he set off.

Forty

The lighting in the steak house was kept low, candles on the tables doing most of the work.

Luigi was there, a bottle of expensive red wine already opened, at a table by himself.

McNeal pulled up a seat opposite. What was Luigi going to think? The mobster had already given him the addresses of Feinstein and Forbes. What else did McNeal want from him? He wanted answers.

McNeal was still shocked that Peter had reached out to Luigi. He wondered if meeting up with Luigi had sealed his brother's fate. Had Feinstein's people, through their FBI sources, known Peter had met up secretly with Luigi after their father died? Had Feinstein worried that Luigi was going to help him and Peter out? Was that it? Was this a warning? Then again, he wasn't sure if Luigi was nothing but a double-crossing Mafia psychopath who would murder his own crew if required. That was a distinct possibility.

Two general rules of thumb: Luigi knew more than he let on, and Luigi was using McNeal for his own ends. He wasn't buying the line that Luigi was simply helping out an old neighborhood guy. There was more to this than met the eye.

McNeal needed to find out what.

"Appreciate you seeing me on short notice."

Luigi shrugged. "I've told you before. I help people. People can get the wrong impression. But I like to do what I can if people are in trouble. People from the old neighborhood."

McNeal absorbed the restaurant. He saw a table with five menacing guys in a corner booth. "Those your guys?"

"They're fine, don't worry." Luigi poured him a large glass of red wine. "Go on, drink."

McNeal took a sip. "Thanks."

They made small talk for a few minutes before a waiter took their order. They both ordered medium rare Angus steaks with large fries, onion rings, the works. When the waiter was out of earshot, Luigi patted the back of McNeal's right hand. "Look at me."

McNeal did as he was told. He stared at Luigi's unfathomable dark brown eyes.

"When people are in trouble, I mean real trouble, they realize they are alone. I want you to know, and I say this with utmost sincerity, you're not alone. We can help you. We have friends. We have colleagues. We're a family, right?"

McNeal gasped, unable to believe that he—a suspended Internal Affairs detective—was reaching out to a crazy like Luigi. He knew his rap sheet. Killings. Torture. Kidnappings. Disappearances. Witness intimidation. Now here he was, sitting meekly in Luigi's presence.

"I know everything there is to know about you, Jack. I can look into your eyes and know what you're thinking. You know what I see?"

McNeal said nothing.

"I see a man on the brink. I see a man who is hanging by his fucking fingernails. A man who knows he could lose it all. Might lose it all."

"I've already lost it all. I've lost my brother. My father. I lost my wife."

"You've suffered a lot. Are we not put on this earth to suffer?"

McNeal averted his gaze.

"I want to help you end this cycle. But in order to do that, you must trust me. You must trust that I am a man of my word. And you need to trust me with your life."

McNeal sipped his drink.

"I don't do favors for everyone. But I'm doing this for you. And also for the memory of your brother, God rest his soul and your father's soul. Your family . . . We grew up together. Same neighborhood. Same streets. Same fucking streets, right? Did you know a guy, back in the day, Ray O'Halloran? Nasty fuck."

"Yeah, he was a year older than me."

"Did you know he said he was going to attack you for going out with a girl he had a crush on? Brianna O'Connor."

"I have no idea what you're talking about."

"Ray—we were in the same class—he confides in me that he is going to give you a beating."

"I don't remember getting a beating from him."

Luigi grinned. "That's right. You didn't. You know why?"

McNeal shrugged. Luigi went on, "Peter was my closest friend at school. I told Peter. And we decided to teach Ray a lesson he would never forget. We beat the living shit out of him and warned him never to go near you. Do you know that?"

McNeal shook his head.

"Long time ago. But it's true. Peter was looking out for you all the time. He wouldn't have allowed anything to happen to you. He was the tough one. But you were the smart one. He knew it."

"I don't know what to say."

"You don't have to say anything. My point is our families go way back. Me and Peter were tight. Not as tight as you brothers, of course. Then we left school and went our separate ways. But here we are again."

McNeal sipped the wine. "I need to ask you something. Something that's bothering me."

"What's on your mind?"

"You said you're doing this because of Peter, his memory, my father. And the neighborhood, all that stuff."

"Sure."

"There's more to it, isn't there? You didn't just approach me at the church out of the blue?"

"What can I say? Peter called and confided in me, man to man."

"He didn't tell me."

Luigi shrugged. "He didn't want to speak to you about it. He respected you too much. He knew what you thought of guys like me. And that's fine."

"I don't care about that anymore. I want the truth. Don't lie to me. I can't abide liars."

"Peter spoke to me. The death of his father was a blow. And he explained things to me. Things you guys did. He told me all of it."

McNeal sat in silence.

"That time you and Peter brought that car to me?"

McNeal nodded.

"I helped you, right?"

"Why?"

"I had my reasons."

The food arrived, and they both ate in silence. When they were finished, and on their second glass of wine, Luigi smiled. It was a strangely warm smile. Like a jocular uncle at Christmas. But McNeal knew behind the lamb's exterior lurked a rabid wolf.

"What do you want to know, Jack? I have secrets. You have secrets. And that's fine."

"You helped us out once. But now you're helping me out for a second time. I need to know why."

"Why do you think I'm helping you out again?"

"I believe Finn O'Brien is the reason you're helping me out."

A silence opened up between them. "You're a perceptive man. I like that."

"I know what you want from me. And I'm prepared to give it to you. But I need to know more about O'Brien. He was connected, wasn't he?"

Luigi stared at McNeal for a beat too long.

"Was he connected?"

Luigi leaned closer and whispered. "Mr. O'Brien looked after some of our interests in South Florida. He had connections in the police down there. Real estate investments. Golf courses. Condos. Some bars and restaurants. Cops can make life difficult if you're running a business. He made problems go away."

McNeal reflected on this information. He'd had no inkling that O'Brien had any links with the mob. He knew from his time in the NYPD working the gang unit what names were known. He knew the corrupt cops. "I need more details."

"He was set up in business when he retired to Florida. He also did a few private investigations into politicians and citizens who had caused problems for our business with regard to planning, zoning. He gave us the dirt. And the problems went away. Business as usual."

"He wasn't a *made man*, obviously."

"That's right. But he was someone we trusted, implicitly, with business affairs. He was a trusted associate."

"So, he wasn't whacked?"

Luigi stared at him, eyes suddenly black as coal. "Don't ever say that. You know who did it. And you have the names."

"Can I ask you a question?"

"What?"

"If he was the family's go-to guy down there, and he's crucial to your operations, why don't you take out the people responsible?"

"We considered it. But after making a few inquiries, it was clear that it was not a home invasion murder and it wasn't no suicide. It was planned with military precision. Surveillance cameras being deactivated. No trace of evidence. We know who did this. As do you."

"You're not doing this because it would bring the heat on your crew, right?"

"Some might say that, I don't know. Listen, I've answered your questions. What else do you want?"

"I just want to forget everything," McNeal said.

"Just like that. You want to turn your back on the world and walk away, as if nothing has happened?"

McNeal realized how absurd it sounded. "It might sound crazy, but I feel very conflicted. I don't want to go down the road me and Peter went down before. The consequences were appalling. Terrible."

"Sometimes we need to do things we don't want to. Sometimes walking away is not an option."

"And when is that?"

"I wouldn't tell you what to do. That's your business. Me? If it was my family? I would take down who was responsible. I'd kill the sons of bitches. And every fucker they knew."

"I'm not you."

Luigi presented a beatific smile, like a benevolent priest. "No, you're not. But Peter let me know that you have what it takes. You can do what needs to be done."

"So could you."

"O'Brien was only business for us. He wasn't blood. Peter was your blood."

"I don't know."

"You do know they will come for you. Sooner rather than later."

McNeal had grown acutely aware of that point. "I know they will. The Feds want to speak to me after Peter's funeral."

"Which gives you time."

McNeal gulped the rest of his wine.

"Sometimes, you need to take the fight to them. Sometimes, you've got to spill blood. It's just the way it is. If you don't have the stomach for it, I have some friends in Miami, a Colombian crew, who can do this for you. A favor. But it will cost you."

"Colombians, huh?"

"They are also our associates down there."

McNeal sat in silence, staring at the starched white tablecloth. A drop of red wine had fallen on it. It looked like a speck of blood. He saw once more Peter's bloody head wound. Brain splattered on their father's headstone. The images seared into his mind.

"We can do this for you. We can avenge these people, once and for all."

Forty-One

When McNeal arrived back at his apartment, he saw an SUV waiting outside. His senses switched on. He braced himself to be taken out. He considered turning back. But he didn't.

He walked up to his front door, key in hand. Four well-dressed men stepped out of the vehicle.

"Jack McNeal?" one of them said, flashing a wallet with an FBI ID card inside.

"That's right."

"We have a search warrant for your apartment."

"Can I see it, please?"

The Fed handed him the warrant.

McNeal scanned the details. He wondered if they had jumped the gun. His attorney had told him they would be visiting after Peter's funeral. But here they were, unannounced. He should have foreseen that.

They took the elevator to his floor and followed him inside his apartment.

"We are formally executing this federal search warrant for these premises. Do you understand?"

"Yes, I do."

The other Feds brushed past him as they began to bag up his MacBook, iPad, and all the rest.

"We'd also like to interview you again, Jack, in connection with the death of Henry Graff."

McNeal already knew how he was going to play it. "I'd like to talk to my attorney first."

"Plenty of time for that."

Four Feds accompanied him down the elevator to the lobby and into the waiting SUV. He was taken to their nearby office in Federal Plaza.

The offices were on the twenty-sixth floor, and he was shown into a large interview room. Two Feds were waiting for him.

"Take a seat, Jack," the lead Fed said.

McNeal felt exhausted and drained. "Am I under arrest?"

"No, you are not. You are helping us with ongoing inquiries into the disappearance and death of Henry Graff."

"I'd like to have my attorney here."

"We can arrange that later."

"What the hell is this? I'd like to make that call right now if that's okay."

"It's not okay. We have questions to ask."

"This is the second time I've asked, but you have not allowed me to make a call. I want that noted."

The lead Fed shifted in his seat. "We just want to update you on what we've found. We can talk about legal representation after we have talked about that."

"And then can I see my attorney?"

"Yes, of course, if you insist."

"I insist."

The lead Fed scrutinized him closely. "You seem a bit rough. Been out drinking? I can smell alcohol on your breath."

"My brother and father just died. I've got a reason to appear *rough*, as you say, don't you think?"

"Where were you drinking?"

McNeal knew he would be walking into a bear trap if he told them. "Listen, are we here to discuss what liquor I have consumed?"

"You don't need to be flippant."

"So, are we going to talk about if I drank a glass or two of wine to drown my sorrows, or are we going to get down to business? What is this all about?"

"I think you know what this is about."

McNeal leaned back in his seat, arms folded.

"We've been looking over some very interesting data. GPS data from your car. The car which seems to have vanished. Do you know what happened to your car?"

McNeal knew, alright. The vehicle had been pulped by Luigi. It was the same vehicle they had used to carry Graff's body in the trunk before they dumped the trussed-up corpse in the Liberty Reservoir.

"Do you understand the question? It's very easy. What happened to your car?"

McNeal stared at the lead Fed, who scribbled something in the legal pad in front of him.

"Jack, everyone knows where their car is. Unless it's stolen. It might be in the driveway. Parked on the street. A parking garage. I know where my car is. My wife knows where her car is. Why don't you? Can you account for it?"

McNeal sat in silence.

"Are you refusing to say what happened?"

McNeal still said nothing.

"Was it stolen? If it was, that's fine, we need to know. Was it sold? If so, who did you sell it to?"

McNeal still sat in silence. He knew they wanted to box him into a corner with answers that wouldn't match up with the facts they had in their possession.

"We contacted the manufacturer, and, as it's a virtually new car, it's pretty high tech."

McNeal had already anticipated this. It was still unwelcome and made him feel uncomfortable.

"Modern cars, as you probably know, upload location data and various other interesting things to the manufacturer. When you bought the car, it's all there in the contract, giving explicit consent to share this data with the manufacturer. Who, in turn, shared it with us."

McNeal sat quietly.

The lead Fed flicked through his notebook and picked up a road map with red markings showing a route. He showed it to McNeal, using his pen to identify the various points on his route. "This is the road you traveled. You stopped in what is a field, according to the data. And then after forty-two minutes, the vehicle is driven from this location near Frederick to cross the bridge at the Liberty Reservoir in Maryland. It stops for less than two minutes. Then it travels on to a salvage yard owned by a well-known New York mobster. The data stopped being uploaded a short while later. Can you tell us what that might mean? Did you sell the car privately to the company who owned the salvage yard?"

McNeal stared blankly.

"Do you know, or have you ever met, a gentleman by the name of Luigi Bonafessi?"

McNeal stared at the Fed.

"We don't have to explain who he is, do we? You know this name. You, having been employed by the NYPD gang unit several years back . . . you know all about Bonafessi. You working with the Mafia, Jack?"

McNeal closed his eyes.

"Closing your eyes won't block out the facts. You need to explain to us why your car can't be traced. We know the route it took. And it seems to have gone to a salvage yard. Did you ask Luigi or did your brother, Peter, ask Luigi to deal with the vehicle? Did you ask him to make it disappear? He specializes in making things disappear."

McNeal said nothing.

"I want to know where you went that night. The night Henry Graff disappeared off the planet. Would you like to explain this journey? Who was with you? Did you meet up with Henry?"

McNeal cleared his throat.

"Are you taking the Fifth?"

"Until I see my attorney, yes."

"The reservoir is where we pulled out the body of Henry Graff." He produced a photo of McNeal in the foyer of Graff's offices. "And this is you, not long before Mr. Graff disappeared. Turning up unannounced at his office."

McNeal stayed quiet. The FBI only had the journey his car had taken. They had no proof he had been inside the car or that it had contained the body of Graff. He wondered if they were holding anything else back.

"Now, your journey, in the dead of night, might be entirely coincidental to the disappearance of Mr. Graff. But we checked the GPS data from his Porsche, which we recovered from near the scene where you stopped for nearly two minutes. It was behind an abandoned gas station. This is quite an incredible coincidence. And then, in the dead of night, not long after your paths crossed, Graff vanishes into thin air. Until we found his body."

McNeal knew they were fishing for information. Wanting to get him to deny he was there or agree he was. Then work forward or backward from there, tying him in knots of his own making.

"Doesn't that concern you? We believe you know far more about the disappearance and death of Mr. Graff than you are letting on. We know you are seeing a psychologist. And we know you are experiencing extreme stress and anxiety, we get that. And that's before the sudden death of your father and the violent death of your brother. You need to talk to us. We can help you. If you are in trouble or got yourself mixed up in something, if you are in too deep, now is the time to let us know. I can help you. But only if you are forthcoming."

McNeal averted his gaze.

"That's how you're playing it? Well, we're not going away. We will get answers. We will get to the bottom of this. We have your computer and other tech to pick over."

McNeal wheezed out a full breath.

"You have suffered quite incredible personal losses. Your ex-wife's death."

"My wife."

"Sorry?"

"She was my wife when she died."

"I'm sorry, your wife's death. And there's the issue of the considerable sum of money she left entirely to you. Can you see what we're getting at?"

McNeal fixed his stare on the lead Fed until the guy blinked first.

"A lot of questions to answer. The thing is, Jack, maybe it wasn't you driving the vehicle. But if it wasn't you, you need to let us know. Did you let your brother borrow it? Was that it? Are you protecting your brother?"

McNeal knew they were trying to rile him up. He was being given an opportunity to put his dead brother in the car, alone. That wouldn't happen. No chance.

"So, one final time, Jack, can I clarify if you're taking the Fifth?"

"I'm taking the Fifth until I can see my attorney."

"Then, we have no choice but to end this interview."

Forty-Two

The harsh glare from the morning sun peeked through the trees as Forbes headed out on his morning run. His head was still pounding as he commenced the circuit around the Central Park Reservoir. The booze and coke still in his system, earbuds blasting Van Halen.

He was wrapped up in multiple layers against the arctic blast. Sunglasses shielding him from the dazzling early-morning light. He had taken a couple of Advil with a couple of cans of Coke. Eventually, he felt his hangover slowly lift.

He ran hard, passing walkers, strollers, amblers, light joggers, and some serious athletes. They were all there. Keeping fit, keeping focused, and looking after their minds, bodies, and souls.

He had enjoyed the champagne too much the previous night. He was glad to sweat the liquor out of his system and get the endorphins kicking in. Raising his mood. Elevating his happiness.

Forbes kicked it up and passed a jogger with a prosthetic leg. The man grunted every step as if in agony. Forbes was in awe of his determination. Who was he? Was he a veteran who had lost his leg in combat? An IED in Iraq? What a waste. But what an inspiration too.

His mind dredged up the events of the previous evening. He couldn't believe what he'd done. Had Karen woken up? Was she dead? Had she gone to bed last night without using the mouthwash? Perfectly possible. It was the not-knowing which allowed the frisson of excitement to build up in him.

He figured she was so wasted she had probably just flopped onto her bed. She would be more likely to use the mouthwash when she woke up, trying to freshen her breath.

Yeah, that sounded plausible.

He felt wild. He *was* wild. Truth be told, he hadn't slept much the night before. He'd tossed and turned, thinking of Karen Feinstein, the eye drops, and the mouthwash.

Forbes knew the effects of the Xanax on the President. He would take one before bed, and then it would be lights out until three hours later, four hours maximum. But it worked like a charm on him.

The President liked to take half a tablet in the middle of the day too. But there was strictly no alcohol if he was popping Xanax in daylight hours.

Diet Coke was his thing.

Gallons of the stuff.

The fentanyl was Forbes's nuclear option. It was up to one hundred times more potent than morphine. He knew it could work, undetected, even with the insane amounts of drugs in her system. It would blow everything else out of the water.

Forbes only warmed up when he finished his run. He strode down Fifth Avenue and back to his apartment on East Sixty-Fourth Street. Leafy townhouses. He only had a one-bedroom apartment. But that was all he needed. At least for now. No doubt his father could have bought him a townhouse or three. But he had time on his side. Besides, he got a generous allowance. He didn't want to abuse that trust. After all, he was going to inherit his father's enormous wealth. One day.

He showered and put on a polo shirt, fleece sweatshirt, jeans, and sneakers. He wrapped himself in a thick Canada Goose coat before he headed out to a nearby diner for brunch.

Forbes was sorely tempted to stop by Karen Feinstein's townhouse to see how she was. He almost couldn't help himself. But he somehow resisted the temptation.

Besides, he was famished.

He ate his omelet, washed down with a couple of cups of coffee. He wanted an update. He was desperate to find out how she was. But he didn't want to arouse suspicion.

Think, Andrew, think!

He could walk over. Press the buzzer. But why? It would place him at the scene if she had died. *Don't be a dummy.*

Forbes remembered his meeting with Iverson. He pushed the thought of heading over to Feinstein's place to one side. He ate his meal. He felt revitalized and took a cab down to Iverson, Walker & Faulkner.

A personal assistant ushered Forbes into Iverson's office. His lawyer, wearing a gray, single-breasted Savile Row suit, pale blue shirt, and red silk tie, was on the phone. He signaled Andrew to sit down.

Forbes pulled up a leather office chair and quietly checked his messages. None. He had expected something from his publisher about a marketing plan. But that was still to be released to him.

Iverson put down the phone and leaned back in his seat. "How you doing?"

Forbes put his cell phone back in his jacket pocket. "I'm good."

"How was your night? You look like you're going to the Arctic."

"Trust me, it is seriously cold. Nearly got frostbite on my run this morning."

"You ran?"

Forbes grinned. "I need to ease up on the booze."

Iverson laughed. "Oh, to be young, right?"

Forbes shrugged. "What can I say?"

"Have I got news for you!" Iverson lifted up the *New York Times* from his desk and showed him the front page. A photo of the President laughing as he chatted with Forbes, Feinstein in the background. "You believe this? This will be great for preorder book sales, right?"

Forbes took it in. "Wow! I hadn't seen that."

"Front page, baby! You can't buy publicity like that. That's knocking it out of the ballpark. Great stuff."

Forbes felt even crazier than he had felt in a while.

"So, tell me, you know I like some juicy gossip. What mood was the President in?"

"Elevated mood."

Iverson grinned. "Oh yeah. If the public only knew the chemicals rushing around that guy's bloodstream, they wouldn't believe it."

"He was in fine form."

"Delighted to hear it. Well, I had expected a call this morning from Curtis Montgomery, but I'm still waiting. I had hoped to give you an update on exactly where we were."

"Don't sweat it."

"That's what I get paid to do. I worry about stuff."

Forbes was tempted to confess to his lawyer how he had laced Feinstein's mouthwash with a killer cocktail of drugs. He meditated on if that was a part of his personality, to crave attention. "You think Feinstein is going to be forthcoming?"

"I've put in a few calls to contacts in the Justice Department and to the FBI, but no one seems to know a thing. So, that's problematic in and of itself."

"She might cut a deal."

"She might. She might also say nothing."

"I guess it's the uncertainty. I don't like uncertainty."

"Who does?" Iverson's cell phone rang. He picked up, holding his finger in the air. "Jason Iverson speaking." He went bug eyed at

Forbes. "Are you kidding me? Seriously? Curtis, I'm shocked. Are you absolutely sure? But sure, of course I understand. We'll talk next week." He ended the call.

"What is it?"

"Holy fucking Christ, Andrew!"

Forbes felt his stomach roil with anticipation.

"You're not going to believe this."

"Believe what?" Forbes feigned disinterest.

Iverson picked up the remote control and switched on the TV. A CNN reporter was standing outside Feinstein's townhouse. Police tape, cops, and media everywhere.

". . . the woman hosting the party, a longtime supporter of the President, reclusive Manhattan businesswoman Karen Feinstein, is in a coma, fighting for her life, after being found unconscious by her staff this morning in New York."

Forbes stared at the TV, trying to stop himself from smiling. "Good God. Now that is very shocking."

Iverson slowly turned on Forbes. The look lingered too long. "Andrew . . . what do you know about this?"

"Me? I swear to God. Jason, this is the first I've heard about it."

"Did you have something to do with this? I need to know."

Forbes shook his head. "Jason, I'm in shock."

"Now listen to me, Andrew, I need to know if you were involved."

"Absolutely not. I swear on my father's life."

Iverson watched the TV attentively. "I'm going to need to know exactly what you did at the townhouse. I need you to account for the time you spent there."

"Why?"

"The Secret Service will want to ask you some questions, be assured of that."

Forty-Three

It was a fifteen-minute cab ride from the FBI's field office to Madison Square Park. McNeal picked up a coffee at the Snack Shack and sat on a freezing park bench. He needed time to clear his head. He need time to think. He guessed how long it would be before the Feds charged him with the murder of Henry Graff. If the Feds didn't get him, he figured he would be next on the hit list after his brother and father.

He scanned yet again to determine if he was under surveillance. Maybe they were looking for the right time. But as his father had been found on an empty Brooklyn beach and his brother in a deserted cemetery, he believed that being in a crowd, surrounded by people, wasn't the perfect place to kill him. The safety of crowds. That said, it would be the easiest thing in the world for an assassin to jab him with a syringe of Sux. He would be paralyzed within seconds. Then he could die within minutes. No one would know. It would look like a heart attack.

He looked up at the beautiful prewar buildings surrounding the park. He feared his demise. He could see how easy it would be for a sniper to set up position and take him out. His mental state was fragmented.

His cell phone vibrated in his coat pocket. The caller ID showed it was Belinda Katz. He didn't really want to speak to her. "Belinda," he murmured wearily, "how are you?"

"You didn't get back to me two days ago, Jack."

McNeal closed his eyes. "My brother died. And my father. I've been dealing with that."

"What the hell? Are you serious?"

"Sadly, yes."

"I am so sorry. That was insensitive of me, under the circumstances. Your brother and father both died?"

"You couldn't have known."

"Do you mind if I ask how they died?"

"I'd rather not talk about that."

"This might sound like a dumb question, but how are you coping after such shattering news?"

"It's not easy."

"I understand."

"I'm struggling to take it all in. I'm having a very, very bad year."

"I'm so sorry. Do you want to talk about it now? That would be therapeutic."

"It's nice to hear your voice."

"It's nice to hear your voice too. But . . . But I can hear the sadness." McNeal closed his eyes. "You've had so much hurt and misery."

"It's been a rough time."

"I'm curious . . . I'm sorry for asking again—how did your brother die?"

"I found Peter, gunshot to his head, slumped over my father's grave."

"That's so terrible, Jack. I mentioned before about a friend of mine upstate, a clinical psychologist, and I would like to refer you to him. I think you need help. There is only so much you can endure."

"My brother endured worse."

"I'm not so sure."

"He did. He made it through Iraq. And he was a cop. He made it through that. Then he got shot, point blank, just hours after our father was buried."

"Was it a vendetta? A guy he had put away in the past?"

"It was a vendetta. But not from a guy he had put away as a cop."

"You're opening up. That's good. Is the vendetta linked to the disappearance of Henry Graff and the discovery of his body?"

"I don't want to say any more. One day."

"How are you going to get over this without regular therapy to help you come to terms with these traumas?"

McNeal shielded his eyes from the glare of the winter sun reflecting off the windows of a building opposite. "I need time to myself. Some space."

"I think that's wise. A long vacation. You need to get away from New York. Get some sun. Even go abroad for a while if that's an option."

"I hear what you're saying. I appreciate your time and guidance since we met. It's much appreciated."

"I wish I could do more. Jack, there's one final thing I'm going to ask you. And please don't take this the wrong way."

"What?"

"Are you having suicidal thoughts?"

"Surprisingly, no, I'm not."

"That's good. Jack, I hope you can find your way out of the dark place you're in. And I want you to know that I'll be there for you. Every step of the way. No matter how long it takes. Deal?"

"You got a deal."

"Look after yourself."

"You too."

McNeal finished his coffee and ambled around the park, thoughts scattered. He wasn't going to kill himself. He had considered that when his son died. But despite the bleakness, he had endured the pain.

The problem was that he realized that he was going to do something. His mood was oscillating wildly. It threatened to overwhelm him. He wondered if he should head to a nearby bar. Have a drink or two to take his mind off things.

He remembered a place where he was always welcome. A place where he could let off steam. A dingy, low-key place full of regular guys. Law enforcement, truckers, security guards, you name it. Blue-collar people.

The gun club was three blocks away.

McNeal needed a release. He was ready to explode. He needed to find an escape hatch for his boiling emotions.

The owner was wearing fatigues, ear protectors on. He gave the thumbs-up to Jack.

McNeal took up his usual position. He fired off round after round from his Glock. The sound echoed around the old brick and wood that had been there since the place was built, in the 1960s. He took another fifteen minutes at the shooting range. Round after round. He felt his anger spike as each shot hit the target. On and on, he fired. He thought of the information Luigi had given him. He thought of what his psychologist had said. Maybe he did need to move away, at least for now.

When he finished, he was handed a strong cup of black coffee by the owner.

"Haven't seen you around for a little while, Jack," he said.

"Lot of things going on."

"Nice firing by the way. We're a dying breed in New York. They say we don't want guns on the streets. But that doesn't stop those thugs and punks shooting up innocent people. It's fucking crazy."

McNeal let the man rant.

"A friend of mine, Andy Cortez, he's a member of the club, Puerto Rican security guard up in the Bronx, took down two gangbangers last weekend who tried to shoot up the nightclub he was protecting."

"The city is getting rougher."

"My wife wants to move out to fucking Montauk. She says I should just sell, and to hell with it all. But, for a lot of people, this club is a second home. I don't know what I'd do if I wasn't opening up the club, making sure the people that needed a facility to practice shooting had that opportunity. Imagine if this wasn't here?"

"I hear you. I like it."

"Thank you, appreciate that. Thing is, I don't know if I could live in Montauk. Don't get me wrong, it's a beautiful place, nice people. But you know, it's not the city, right?"

McNeal realized he wasn't really part of the conversation, just someone for the owner to talk at.

"I'd miss the fucking craziness of it all. The energy."

"I could do with less of the craziness."

The owner laughed.

McNeal sipped his insanely strong coffee and grimaced. He turned to the wall-mounted TV showing news footage, volume off. Then he saw it: *President's Manhattan Supporter in Coma* on Fox News. "You want to turn that up for a second?"

The owner pointed the remote at the TV. "What the hell happened?"

McNeal watched the Fox News reporter give some background as he stood outside Lenox Hill Hospital.

The reporter said, "Ms. Feinstein had lived in the beautiful townhouse, which was owned by her company, FeinSolutions, a global security consulting firm, for five years."

McNeal felt his heart begin to beat faster.

"She was a major fundraiser for the President in New York, especially among Manhattan's elite, and contributed nearly a million dollars to his future library in the last six months alone. But this morning, Feinstein was found unconscious by her housekeeper. She was rushed to this hospital, only a couple of minutes away. Sources say she is in a coma."

The gun club owner shook his head. "You fucking believe that?"

McNeal stared at the screen, transfixed. He wondered what the hell had happened. He didn't believe in coincidences. He wondered if she had been killed by Graff's people.

The more he thought about it, the more he realized one thing. Now there was only one name on Luigi's list. Andrew Forbes. Secret Service code name: Woodcutter.

Forty-Four

The sound of gunshots from the range almost drowned out the TV coverage. McNeal was trying to block it out when his cell phone rang.

"Jack?" It was Luigi. "Is that . . . is that someone shooting?"

McNeal thanked the owner of the gun club and headed outside to take the call. "Yeah. Visiting a gun club."

"You keep some weird fucking company. You saw the news?"

"Just saw it."

"What do you think?"

"I don't know what to think."

"You think someone might have tried to whack her in her own home?"

"I really don't know."

"She's out of the game now. Which leaves one name left, am I right?"

McNeal was running out of time to figure out what he would do. He weighed whether this was a medical condition or a serious attempt to neutralize Feinstein. It could have been a suicide attempt. But in the shadowy world she inhabited, she already knew too much.

"Have you decided what you're going to do? This kind of changes things, I'm guessing."

A police cruiser drove past. "I want one more meet, face-to-face again. Out of sight. I've got a few questions."

"You don't ask much."

"I need to go over some things. Yes or no?"

"When?"

McNeal felt his heart rate quicken as he began to conjure up scenarios. There and then, he made up his mind as to what he was going to do. "When are you available?"

"Tonight, eleven o'clock."

"Name a place where we can talk without interruption, if you know what I mean."

"You know Joe's, Italian restaurant on West Fifty-Seventh Street?"

"Been in there a few times."

"I know the owner very well. It has a little private dining room at the back. We can have a private chat. What do you say?"

The hours dragged.

McNeal showered and changed again. He ordered an Uber and headed uptown. He walked into the restaurant. A couple of Luigi's crew wearing smart suits escorted him through the main restaurant, past a handful of late diners, to the private area near the back.

A dead-eyed Mafia henchman frisked him for weapons and electronic devices of any sort. "He's clean."

McNeal followed the man down a dimly lit corridor. The walls had black-and-white photos of old stars and entertainers. Judy Garland. Frank, of course. Dean Martin. Jerry Lewis. Sammy Davis smoking a cigarette.

The hood stopped and slowly opened red velvet drapes. Behind them was a snug dining room.

Luigi sat alone, eating a bowl of pasta, a bottle of red wine on the table next to two glasses. He cocked his head for McNeal to enter. "Pull up a seat and take a load off."

The goon pulled the drapes shut behind him.

"Best pasta in Manhattan, seriously," Luigi said. "Friend of my father. His son, brilliant cook. From Palermo. Your classic Italian cooking."

"Sounds good."

"Tastes fucking good too." Luigi poured McNeal a glass of wine. "Don't worry, it's swept regularly for bugs. Wouldn't trust those Feds for a second."

McNeal took a gulp of the wine. "Appreciate you seeing me so soon."

"You need to eat. You're looking a bit thin."

McNeal began to eat.

"You like it?"

"It's delicious."

"What a shocker, the news about Feinstein, huh?"

"You can say that again."

"It's pretty fucked up, the shit you got involved with. But there's always a way to deal with it."

McNeal sipped his wine. "Very nice vino."

"You like that? I'll get a case sent down to your apartment."

"That won't be necessary. But thank you anyway."

Luigi shrugged as if slightly put out. "So . . . we meet again. What are you thinking? You want my help?"

"I think I know what I want to do. I hope you can help me."

Luigi wiped his mouth with his napkin. "See, I respect that. You come here, not making any demands, just a man who is humble. And reaches out for help. I like that. I want you to know something. I know your background. I know all that. But I sit down with you. It's business, right?"

McNeal nodded. It was hard to believe he was sitting opposite one of the most feared Mafia hoods in the city. A man who would take a chain saw to another man. A man who ordered killings left, right, and center. A man certainly not to be trifled with.

"When I came to you at the church, it was an act of good faith. I need to know that this is in good faith too. Are you acting in good faith?"

"What do you mean by that?"

"I mean, don't ever jerk me around. Don't waste my time. I'm not a fucking man to cross. You understand?"

McNeal cut his eyes. "I'm not here to waste your time. I want to talk business."

"Good. Business, I understand. I am a very good friend to have. If a person comes to me, and I know them, I know their family, and they are straight-up guys, you won't have a problem with me. The only time you have a problem with me is if you cross me."

"I don't intend to, trust me."

"What do you want to talk about?"

"I want to talk about Karen Feinstein."

Luigi began eating. "I heard a few rumors already."

"Like what?"

"That she overdosed."

"Is that right?"

"I put in a couple of calls. The doctors did some tests. They think she had taken some drugs. A cocktail of drugs."

"Seriously?"

"That's what they're saying."

"I don't know. Why would she kill herself like that?"

Luigi shrugged. "This whole thing is way out of fucking control. I don't know what the hell you've gotten yourself messed up with."

"Here's the thing. I've got a plan. I want to talk about my plan."

"Go ahead."

McNeal took a large gulp of the wine. "I'm going to lay my cards on the table."

Luigi nodded, mouth full of pasta, as he topped off McNeal's glass.

"You have helped me out before. Well, you helped me and Peter out before. You know what I'm talking about?"

"Sure. So, how can I help you again?"

"I want to give you some money. Think of it as a retainer."

"You want to give me money? For what?"

"For your services. This is a one-off. And I'm prepared to compensate you."

"I don't want compensation. This is a favor."

"I don't want a favor. I want a service. Consider me a client."

Luigi laughed. "You want to give me money? What can I say, knock yourself out."

McNeal cleared his throat and leaned closer. "When my wife died, she left me a lot of money. I didn't grow up with money, you know that."

Luigi remembered unprompted. "We're working guys," he said like a mantra.

"I want to give you money for a bit of help and ongoing assistance, further down the line, as and when required."

"I don't want any payment."

"I know you don't. But what I have in mind is complex. It will take money."

"How much we talking?"

"Five million."

"Holy fuck. Are you crazy?"

McNeal shook his head.

"Five million? You've got that kind of money?"

"I do now."

"Holy mother of God." Luigi dabbed his perspiring forehead with his napkin. "Let's say I'm interested, just for argument's sake. What kind of help you looking for?"

"For starters, the information your whiz kid got from Karen Feinstein's phone, that kind of thing."

"What are we talking about?"

"Logistical. Support."

"What kind of support?"

McNeal had drawn up a list of items—including the real-time GPS data chart from Andrew Forbes's cell phone to be sent to his number. He also requested a vehicle to be ready at a specific location. He handed it to Luigi. "I also need one of your guys as a driver. The most reliable. The best driver."

Luigi looked over the list. "Damn, is that all?"

"Five million should cover it."

"Damn right it will."

"But this is about trust. I trust you. Some may say I'm stupid . . . Maybe I am."

"You've come to me with a problem. You're asking to pay for services at an astronomical rate. I'm not going to argue with you. And I'm going to take you at your word."

McNeal stared into the dark red wine.

"You're crazy, you do know that."

McNeal said nothing.

"I don't mean that literally. I'm just saying, you know . . ."

McNeal finished his glass of wine just before Luigi topped it off again. "How do you know this place isn't bugged?"

"I told you, it's swept twice a day. No cell phones from my crew allowed in here."

McNeal was quiet as he anticipated the hours that lay ahead.

"It isn't easy being in your position, I understand that, Jack. When do you want this?"

"It has to be before Peter's funeral. So, I want it in forty-eight hours. That is if I live that long."

"That's a big ask."

McNeal shrugged.

"So, what exactly are you planning?" McNeal stared at Luigi. "You're really going to do this?"

"I'll guess we'll know soon enough."

Forty-Five

It was just past midnight.

Forbes had sat glued to the TV for most of the day after his visit to his lawyer. He was seriously freaked out by the coverage. He crunched on cashew nuts and washed them down with Diet Coke. He gave a half-formed thought to whether Karen Feinstein would ever emerge from the coma. It was a possibility. But the longer she languished in that state, the better for him.

He also knew that if the Secret Service or the FBI or the cops wanted to talk with him, he would insist on Iverson being there. He would also deny everything.

It wasn't a bad mantra. *Anything negative happens, say, "I didn't do it. It wasn't me."* The President pulled the same trick all the time. When a reporter asked him why he had said or done something, he denied he had said or done such a thing. Even when he was presented with evidence, he just brushed it off.

His cell phone rang. The caller ID said it was from his publisher.

"Andrew, it's Guy. Have you seen the news?" he slurred.

Forbes grinned. "Yeah, I just heard about it," he lied. "I'm in shock. How awful."

"You're all over the front page with the President. With the host, too, only hours before she was found in a coma? I'm sorry I sound a bit wired. I've been at a book reception, and I just got back and I couldn't sleep, when I got this notification from the *New York Times* on my phone. This is insane."

"It's very sad news."

"Yeah, of course, it's sad. But these pictures and the fact that she is close to death—my God, we need to know everything about what happened last night in minute detail. This could be a tremendous blow-by-blow insight into who she mingled with as we try to capture the mood of last night."

"I can do that."

"Fantastic. Did you speak to her? The coma woman, I mean."

"Yeah, I spoke to her. She was a lovely lady."

"We need to use that photo in the book. Put it on the inside cover."

"Yeah?"

"Sure. Places you right at the heart of things. Love it. Talk about scandal and intrigue."

"I guess."

"I also think we need at least a chapter on that party," he said.

"You don't think that's in bad taste?"

"Are you kidding me? This is exactly the sort of rare glimpse into your life that readers will definitely want. Oh my God, absolutely yes. Was she overdosing? Pills? Xanax? Did she use cocaine?"

"I have literally no idea."

"Of course you don't."

Forbes smirked. "It's terrible what happened," he drawled. "I don't know if I'd feel comfortable talking about all that."

"With all due respect, Andrew, let the readers decide. They want and demand an exclusive insight into your life."

"Isn't it a bit exploitative?"

"Are you kidding me? If the reader is forking over thirty dollars for a brand-new hardcover book, trust me, they want the juiciest and sexiest and most shocking revelations. They want intrigue. They want to devour as much detail as possible. Champagne? What kind? Rosé. Brut. Was she guzzling vintage Cristal? Moët? And what about the wallpaper? What celebrities were there? We need to know everything. Did she seem under the influence?"

Forbes felt as if he had entered a parallel universe. And he was loving it. So, too, was Guy!

"How were people dressed? Was anyone doing drugs? Was anyone *not* doing drugs? Was the President eyeballing any of the girls? Or boys, I don't know. We need to fucking know, you understand?"

"I get it."

"Of course you do. Andrew, we're paying you a massive advance. But you've got to earn it. It's going to be a great book. I want to know about Karen Feinstein. She's this seemingly megasuccessful businesswoman. What did you say to her? What was she wearing? Was she drunk? Was she stoned? Was she doing lines of coke? Was she flirting with the President? Did he touch her inappropriately? Was she talking about politics? Was she gossiping about the President? Talking about his wife? I want to know everything."

Forbes laughed. "I see exactly what you're getting at. Leave it to me. I think I'll start writing down my recollections of last night."

"Do it now!"

"I've got a few things to do. But, yes, I'm going to start work on that later on, in the morning."

"That's great. The sleazier, sexier, and more decadent, the better."

"Don't worry. I'll give you all that."

A beat. "I'm just reading the *New York Times* article for a third time. What a picture! You handsome devil."

Forbes tried to snap himself back to his fake empathy. "Tragic what's happened."

"It is. But we need to draw on everything you know and everything you experienced last night. That's fantastic. Tragic, but fantastic."

Forbes stared at the TV. A *New York Times* front page flashed up on the screen. A photo of him shaking hands with the President. This was unreal. "How about I start right now."

"Get to work. I want five thousand words by the end of this week, on my desk. What do you say?"

Forbes had already been spoken to regarding the death of the chief of staff. If Feinstein died, it would pique their interest, at the very least. It might make a great section of the book if he recounted his dealings with the Secret Service. But he would deal with them and the Feds at a later date. Iverson had that all under control.

As it stood, the FBI wouldn't have their chat with Karen Feinstein now. At least not for a while, if she was lucky enough to pull through.

He couldn't believe what he had done. Part of him was shocked at how easy it had been. Ridiculously easy. Part of him was excited. It turned him on. Killing as an aphrodisiac. Who knew? He wondered if he could do it again. The thought of that excited him also.

Forbes got up and stared out the windows. The buzz of the Upper East Side. Cabs. People. Late-night New York. The bustle of the city. He loved it. Far better than the grind of the White House.

He closed his eyes and began to imagine Feinstein lying in the hospital bed, attached to a machine helping her breathe. He had caused it. *What the hell was he?* His mind retreated to the very beginning, to Feinstein handing him the gun to kill the honey trap woman. He hadn't foreseen that. How could he have? He hadn't had a choice. It was either kill or be killed. He was surrounded by masked men, the woman hog-tied, writhing on the ground.

Feinstein wasn't bluffing. He would have been killed if he hadn't pulled the trigger. He knew he was in over his head.

He could understand Feinstein's rationale. It was to give him some skin in the game, so that she wasn't the only monster.

The photos of him with Feinstein had shattered him. A connection to her. He knew the game was up. And he was terrified it would all come out. He was the prime mover in ordering the deaths of Sophie Meyer and Caroline McNeal, in order to protect the President. The man who killed them was a psychopathic assassin, ex-CIA operative Frank Nicoletti. But it was Henry Graff who was the linchpin in putting the whole thing together. Graff was a decorated special forces soldier, an old friend of the President who loathed his socialite wife, Meyer, who had been conducting a longtime affair with the President. Graff and Feinstein developed a plan to kill Meyer, making it look like an overdose. Then a decision was made to neutralize Caroline McNeal, who was investigating the suspicious death of Meyer. And from there it had begun to spiral out of control. Wildly out of control.

Jack McNeal of NYPD Internal Affairs had started poking his nose around. He must have learned all about the chain of events from the secret files his late wife had squirreled away. And he took it to the Feds.

What a mind fuck.

Not long after, Henry Graff and Nicoletti, the hit man, had disappeared. Was this the work of Jack McNeal and his brother? He didn't know for sure. But he'd heard that Jack had been hauled in for questioning.

Feinstein's team had informed his lawyer about the reprisals on those connected to or helping Jack McNeal. A slow-burn operation to silence O'Brien, McNeal's father, and McNeal's brother, before finally dealing with the Internal Affairs detective last of all.

The problem—McNeal was still alive. In all the excitement, Forbes had forgotten one salient question: Who was going to take down Jack McNeal now?

The woman who could have ensured McNeal got killed had been taken out of the game by him! Probably permanently. He hadn't thought this through. Perhaps he should have. To be fair, he had been spooked that Feinstein could be ready to cut a deal with the Secret Service or the FBI. She had serious connections, as had Graff. That was a problem.

Forbes began to pace his apartment.

The threat from the chief of staff was gone, and Feinstein was as good as dead.

All that remained was Jack McNeal. The bastard was still around. The Secret Service and federal investigators were closing in on him. Forbes considered how long it would be until McNeal was arrested for his involvement in the death of Henry Graff. It was just a matter of time. It had to be.

Forbes knew from his own meeting with the Secret Service that they were not to be trifled with. He believed that he had definitely helped his case by neutralizing the threat of Karen Feinstein. But he was also angry with himself for not seeing the threat she had posed to him until it was almost too late. He was flattered she had fallen for his charms. But he could see now that it was just a pattern of behavior to ingratiate herself and compromise Forbes further down the line.

Fuck her!

The more he thought about what he had done, the more turned on he got. What a stone-cold maniac he was. Everything had always just been so fucking easy for him. Had landed in his lap. Opportunities. Networks. Money. It all started with his impeccable background, expensive schooling, and friends in high places. They could pull strings for him. Get him the best advice. The best of everything.

His background was the polar opposite of Feinstein's. She had grown up blue collar, and only her high intelligence and ambition had propelled her forward. She hadn't had any helping hands or networks to assist her.

Forbes was aching to know her condition. He imagined her in a hospital bed. He pondered that mental picture.

Slowly a germ of an idea began to form in his head. He shouldn't, should he? How cruel would that be? Then again, why the hell not?

Once morning arrived, Forbes headed out of his apartment, wrapped up against the icy blast of cold air, and headed over to Lenox Hill Hospital. He wore his aviator shades against the harsh glare of the winter sun. On the way, he bought some flowers at a bodega.

He felt so exhilarated entering the hospital. He took the elevator to the ICU. He saw a patient behind the glass. He took off his sunglasses and peered through the window.

Feinstein was hooked up to a ventilator, a tube down her windpipe. The machine was breathing for her.

"Do you want me to take those?" a nurse said.

"Thank you."

"I'll put them in her room later."

"This is such a shock. What's the prognosis?"

"Are you family?"

"I'm a dear friend."

The nurse gave a sympathetic look. "It's not so good."

"What do you mean?"

"I shouldn't be saying this . . ."

"Please, she's a very dear friend. I came here as soon as I heard. I've been so concerned the last few hours. I need to know."

The nurse took him aside. "I spoke to her doctor fifteen minutes ago. There is brain damage. Catastrophic."

Forbes closed his eyes, as if devastated.

"There's no way she'll survive without the machine."

Forbes feigned tears. He was rather surprised at his brilliant portrayal of sadness and devastation. His drama teacher at school had complimented him on his expressive eyes. Who knew they would come in so handy? He dabbed his tear-stained face and stared through the glass at Feinstein. The machine mechanically pumping her lungs. She was alive, but only technically.

"I'm so sorry we don't have good news for you."

"I'm just struggling to understand. I'm not a medical person. So, she won't recover from this brain damage?"

"Very sorry, but no, there's no way back for her. It's tragic."

Forbes reached out as if he were a helpless child and placed his hand on the glass. "God bless you, Karen."

The nurse fought back tears of her own.

Karen Feinstein was, for all intents and purposes, dead.

Forty-Six

It had been a long, dark night of the soul for Jack McNeal. The sun finally came up. Still he sat and digested what he had ended up with. He had lost everything. He delved deep into his innermost thoughts, fears, and remnants of what was left of his humanity. But he had already resigned himself to his actions.

He would never find peace. He knew that. He would always be yearning for the son whose life had been taken. The wife who had left him and was then killed, found floating in the Potomac. He wished with all his might that he had been there to protect her. He cursed himself again and again. He loathed who he had become. He was being devoured by the vengeance he sought. Hour after hour, day after day. No good had come of it. He wished he could turn the clock back.

Then he thought of his tough brother, Peter, and how he had met his end. The bastards were playing games. Sick, demented games. An eye for an eye. Biblical justice. But was it any different from the blood justice he and Peter had meted out to Graff and Nicoletti?

He thought of Peter's family. His children. Their incalculable loss. Grieving. Despair. The breadwinner was gone. His widow would get his police pension. He didn't know if Peter had taken out any insurance policies. He doubted it, as Peter and his family had been struggling to get by. Jack had offered to give him whatever he could. But Peter, a proud man, had refused any handouts from his brother. Peter drank heavily, and his poor wife had been left to try and make do the best she could.

Jack wanted to talk to her in case something happened to him. He didn't have any family. No son. No wife. No brother. No father. He had no one. His brother's family was his only remaining connection to that life.

He locked up his apartment. He headed down to the parking garage and drove out of Manhattan on a bone-chilling morning down to Muriel's house in New Jersey. It was on a modest street in a nice, tidy, safe area. He realized he was turning up out of the blue.

McNeal knocked on the door, and his sister-in-law hugged him tight, weeping hard.

"Oh, Jack, I've been trying to call you," she said. "I feel like I'm going out of my mind."

"I wanted to come out yesterday, but I had to meet with a lawyer and stuff, tying up business before I came out here."

Muriel showed him inside. The kids were with her mother, inconsolable. "Jack, I don't understand it. Peter wouldn't do that. He wouldn't leave us. He just wouldn't leave us!"

"I know."

"The police say it might be related to some gangster he put away a few years back who's been released."

McNeal shook his head. "I don't know. It's terrible. Devastating. I can't begin to imagine what you're going through."

Muriel sat down and lit up a cigarette. "I don't know what I'm going to do. I don't know how I can stay in this house."

"Did Peter have insurance? What about the Police Benevolent Association? Have you contacted the NYPD Operations Unit?"

"They've been in touch. They're very nice. I just don't know how I'm going to cope. I've got enough for the next year. The pension will take a while to get organized. There's a small insurance policy. But how long does that last? I'm thirty-two, Jack. Thirty-fucking-two and a widow."

McNeal bowed his head.

"Listen to me ranting. You've lost your father and brother too. I'm sorry . . ."

"Forget it. Listen, I'll tell you why I'm here. I want to help you and the kids out. That's what Peter would have wanted."

"You don't have to do that, Jack. You've got a lot on your mind."

"Listen to me. Caroline left me money in her will. A lot of money."

"What?"

"I want to do this. Check your bank account now, will you?"

"My bank account? Why?"

"Just do it."

She reached over and picked up her cell phone. She logged on to her bank online. She scanned the screen before covering her mouth with her hand. "Jack, what is this? Seriously?"

McNeal sat still.

"Ten million dollars? Seriously? This is insane. I don't deserve this."

"You deserve everything."

McNeal handed her a key and a business card for his lawyer.

"Jack, you're scaring me."

"First, the card is for my personal lawyer. He is now your lawyer. Available anytime, day or night, whatever you need."

"Are you serious?"

McNeal went on. "The key is for a safe-deposit box, Chase Bank, Hudson Street, Manhattan. This will open a box. The contents are for you. And don't worry, I spoke with the manager. They'll be expecting you."

"Jack, have you lost your mind! I can't take this."

"It's too late. It's yours."

Muriel began to cry. "Nobody has ever done anything nice for me. Your brother, sorry, I loved him. But things have been tight. Oh God, I want him back!"

Jack hugged her tight. "I'm so, so sorry."

"Why is he gone?"

"Listen to me. You need to focus. You've got a long time to grieve for Peter. But now, you don't have to worry about money. Ever again. It's for you. But also, importantly, the kids. Make sure they get whatever they need. Do you hear me?"

"Sure, I hear you."

"They need things. You'll need to pay for college."

Muriel closed her eyes. "I want him to come back. I just want him back."

Then she began to cry, sobbing uncontrollably.

Forty-Seven

McNeal took the long drive back to Manhattan. He was glad to have cleared the decks ahead of what he was planning. The well-being of Peter's family was paramount. Whatever was about to happen, he knew they would be free to live their lives without any financial burdens.

His cell phone rang.

"Jack?" The voice of Luigi. "How are you?"

"I'm okay. How are things on your end?"

"We're all set. Made a few calls. Got a team in place. I think we can help you."

"Perfect."

"Listen, the reason I'm calling is we have some information."

"I'm listening."

"You can't go back to your apartment."

"Why?"

"Got a couple of my guys not far from your apartment, keeping an eye on things for you. A couple of FBI vehicles have been outside the last thirty minutes."

"Seriously?"

"Dead serious. Don't go home. They'll pick you up."

The gears in McNeal's mind began turning.

"One more thing. I have been handed some very good intel on your situation."

"From who?"

"Remember I told you about the superbright kid helping us?"

"Yeah."

"Well, the kid has the cell phone number for your Woodcutter pal and just accessed all the fucking messages and calls."

McNeal's heart skipped a beat. "Are we sure this is the same guy?"

"I asked him the same thing. He checked the location and date of birth of the person who owned the cell phone, and they all match. It's Woodcutter. He's going for a jog first thing tomorrow morning. Six a.m., in Central Park."

McNeal made a mental note. "Six in the morning . . . You said you have the vehicle and the clothing I requested?"

"You ask, Luigi delivers. Didn't I say that? Did I or did I not promise you?"

McNeal realized he was smiling at the crazy fuck. "You did indeed."

"Jack, you able to do this business?"

McNeal slowed down as the driver up ahead braked suddenly. "I'll know when the time comes."

"Fair enough. Listen, if I was you, and I had this information on a guy I wanted out of the way, at that time of day, I would think that the jog was perfect. My guys will be able to track him on the phone too."

McNeal already had a picture in his head. "I'm trusting you, Luigi. I'm trusting you to keep your word. I know what kind of man you are. I know your record. But I'm putting that aside. You said you were a man of your word. And I'm taking that at face value."

"So am I. Listen, I'm done talking. There's an apartment we have never used. For emergencies. Why don't you just use that now?"

McNeal's senses were alert. This could be a trap. He was trying to see the angles. "Where is it?"

"East Sixty-Seventh Street. I'll text the address and pass code. Real quiet."

McNeal wondered if he was getting set up to get shot by Luigi. "You're not fucking with me, are you?"

"Don't ever say that. Don't ever joke about such things. I loved Peter. We grew up together. And I want to do what I can."

McNeal shot his eyes to his rearview mirror and saw a motorcycle. It was four cars behind him, two people riding it. His gaze was drawn to the bike. And the passenger. "Send me the address."

"The apartment has just been stocked up. We've got clothes for you, new cell phone, whatever you want to wear. And the fridge is full. Parking garage right next to it."

"Why are you doing this, Luigi?"

"People like me don't forget where we came from. A lot of people do. But I don't. And neither did Peter. You're the same. Sometimes, like family, you might not like them, but you stick together. And especially when the bad times come knocking."

McNeal peered at his side mirror. The motorcycle was still visible. And now it was only two cars back.

Forty-Eight

The operative was riding a Moto Guzzi, Ramirez sitting behind him. He was no more than twenty yards from McNeal's car.

The crash helmet's earpiece buzzed.

"Talk to me." The voice of Tom Steele.

"We got a visual. Two cars ahead. I think we have him in a perfect spot. We got this. I repeat: we got this."

"Where exactly?"

"Holland Tunnel."

"Listen, we got a problem. I can't green-light this."

"What are you talking about?"

"The boss is in the hospital."

"What?"

"Don't you read the fucking papers or watch the news?"

"Fuck no."

"She overdosed; that's what they're saying."

The operative shook his head to figure out if he had heard correctly. "Say that again."

"The media is saying she overdosed."

"Copy that. So, who issues the green light now?"

"I'm trying to determine that. I haven't got the authority. It might be a member of her advisory committee."

"We have him in our sights!"

"Copy that. But we do not—repeat: do not—have a green light. There is a protocol in place, and the protocol determines who gives the green light."

"Copy that. So, what's the plan?"

"Stick with him. Find out where he goes. Report back."

"I'm within reach. Let's do him in the tunnel."

"That's a high-risk operation. It's watch-and-wait for now."

"Copy that."

"I promise, we will neutralize him."

"When?"

"That's not your concern. Find out where he goes. I will get the authorization."

"Copy that."

The operative felt the adrenaline coursing through his veins. He felt strangely deflated. "You heard that, Ramirez?"

"Copy that," she said. "Stick close."

The earpiece buzzed—Steele on the line. "One more thing."

"What's that?"

"While you and Ramirez are waiting for the green light, there's a small piece of intelligence required."

"Where?"

"Not far. It'll be later tonight. In New York. Details will be forthcoming."

Forty-Nine

The motorcycle disappeared from McNeal's rearview mirror when he hit Manhattan. He let his shoulders relax in case he was just being paranoid. But he was glad to get to the safe house. The fifth-floor apartment was painted white with solid hardwood floors. Black-and-white photos of old New York lined the walls. The Brooklyn Bridge. The Empire State Building. Rockefeller Plaza. Very tasteful. High-end gut renovation.

McNeal looked around. He understood with startling clarity that he was now working alongside the mob. The realization crashed through his head like a concrete block. It felt unreal. It *was* unreal. But the reality was that Jack McNeal was using a Mafia safe house on the Upper East Side of Manhattan. He pieced together how it had all gotten so crazy. He was being devoured. Hour by hour. Day by day. It was like there was nothing he could do to extricate himself. The problem was that he was too far gone. Too far down the line to give a shit anymore.

He took a look around the apartment as he got familiarized with his temporary home. It was all so new. The furnishings paid for in blood. How many people had been killed or tortured to make the money to buy a place like this on prime East Side real estate?

He appreciated the impeccable and spacious apartment. He shot his eyes around the room, checking subtly if there were spy cameras fitted in the light fittings, lamps, or smoke detectors.

McNeal headed into the kitchen. A pristine iPhone was on the white quartz countertop, still in its packaging. He opened up the box and took out the phone. Then he slid in the new nano-SIM card and powered it up.

A few moments later, a message came through. It had a new number for Luigi. He called it.

"You up and running?"

"I'm in."

"How you feeling?"

McNeal felt sick to the bottom of his stomach. "I'm alright."

"It's okay to be nervous. We all get that. It's natural. You know how it is, right? You've done this before."

"Done what before?"

"You know, whacked a guy."

McNeal realized it was the stone-cold truth. He had killed before. He could see that he was going to kill again. In cold blood. Why couldn't he have trusted the police and the Feds to investigate? He should have just dealt with it in a legal and lawful framework. It was all too late now.

The more he thought about the path he had taken, the less he cared. He was beyond the pale. No good was going to come of what he was going to do. Just like no good had come from avenging his wife.

McNeal thought back to how he had dealt with that situation. He had done the right thing at the beginning, acting in a legal and responsible manner. He had passed a compelling dossier to the Feds that his late wife had assembled. He often thought about what the outcome would have been if the Feds had acted on it. But they hadn't. They had either sat on it or buried it.

He would never know.

"You still there?" The harsh voice of Luigi snapped McNeal back to reality.

"Can you get the guy who accessed Woodcutter's phone to call me?"

"Not an option."

"Why not?"

"He's paranoid about his digital fingerprints being all over this. He could text you whatever you wanted."

"Guess it'll have to do."

"I'll get on it. You'll be hearing from him in the next hour."

"Luigi, one more thing. I'm going to ask you one final time. You're not fucking with me, are you?"

"No, I'm not. This is a special favor. I did one for you and your brother before. This is my final favor. Take it or leave it. Your choice."

McNeal considered the chance he had signed his own death warrant.

"Your choice. You can walk away and get back to your life. But is that really what you want to do?"

"I don't know what I want to do."

Luigi let his silence stretch out before saying evenly, "If you don't want to continue, you need to let me know right now."

McNeal closed his eyes. "I'm too far down the line. I'm going to do whatever it takes."

"Keep your cell phone charged. You'll be hearing more about the arrangements as this gets underway."

"In the meantime?"

"Relax. Kick back. And say a nice prayer for Peter and your father, God rest their souls."

Fifty

It was just after midnight when they entered the hospital.

The operative and Ramirez wore masks, white coats, and hospital ID lanyards as they strode down a corridor in Lenox Hill Hospital. The decision to begin a damage limitation operation had been authorized. He read the text. He reread it. None of it made sense.

He triple-checked the order from Tom Steele, the acting operations director of FeinSolutions. The decision had been made by the nonexecutive chairman of the firm, William Garner, who had won the unanimous backing of the senior management team, Steele included.

The operative never expected this task being assigned. Never in a million years. He was one of the most trusted operatives who had been hired by FeinSolutions. He worked as and when required. His surveillance of Jack McNeal and his role in the executions of Finn O'Brien and Peter McNeal were all part of the service. It always went to the highest bidder. And that was, invariably, Karen Feinstein's company. She paid top dollar.

But that all changed when Karen became incapacitated. A shadow operation was activated.

The operative gave thought to if he should refuse to carry out the order. It did cross his mind. On reflection, he knew that would be the last move he ever made. In his line of work, you handled your business or you were out of business.

He had only been told about the operation two hours earlier. He had discussed it with Ramirez. She was fine with it.

His breathing was steady, despite the mask. He hated wearing the damn thing. But in the circumstances, it was perfect cover.

The operation was taking a new direction, and he had been tasked with carrying out the orders. That's what he did, no matter the personal risk. That's why he was paid a small fortune. To deliver results. To deliver messages. To make sure the operation succeeded, no matter the cost.

He approached the pretty nurse on the desk. He tapped a manila file to get her attention.

"Dr. Garcia from Neurology. What's the latest on Karen Feinstein, Nurse Chong?"

Chong looked up from the computer screen. "Ah . . . Dr. Garcia, I don't have any note with regard to neurology. Is this something new?"

"The head of Neurology, Dr. Shah, is looking for me to oversee the figures on her file."

"Dr. Shah, of course. Is there a specific problem?"

"I don't know. Probably routine. You know how it is. What are her latest numbers?"

Chong turned her computer screen and shook her head. "Numbers haven't moved for twelve hours."

"Let me see the file, and I'll give the patient the once-over. He's looking for an overview of the eye movements, a couple of other tests."

Chong's phone rang, and she handed over the file, slightly distracted. She covered the mouthpiece. "If you hand it back after the examination, that'll be great."

The operative took the file, careful to thank the ICU nurse. He and Ramirez headed into the room where Karen Feinstein lay. She had been intubated, a machine breathing for her. He took out his penlight and pulled back her eyelids. He shone it into the pupil. No dilation. Good. He looked across at Ramirez, who pretended to consult the file.

He bent down beside Feinstein and checked her other eye. No dilation.

Ramirez surreptitiously muted the ventilator's alarm so it wouldn't alert nurses for a couple of minutes if there was a sudden change in the patient's condition. Then she tapped a few buttons and reset the ventilator's alarms, disabling them for sixty minutes.

The operative waited until Ramirez had shut the blinds and locked the door from the inside. He lifted up Feinstein's head and took out one of the starched white pillows. He held it tightly. Then he pressed it softly onto her face and the tube into her throat. Then harder and harder.

A few twitches, slight convulsions as if she was, on a very primitive level, trying to fight for life, but he pressed down even harder.

Ramirez held Feinstein's feet tight together.

The operative kept up the pressure for a full minute. Her vital signs flatlined, but no audio alarm. Perfect.

He carefully lifted her head and slid the pillow back into its position. The operative stroked her hair back into place. Her face waxy and pale. The tube down her throat had moved. He adjusted it back into the center of her mouth and stared down at her. It was like she was sleeping. It was ironic. The woman who had authorized dozens of killings across the world would die at the hands of one of her most trusted operatives.

The operative felt nothing. He turned and nodded at Ramirez. She opened the blinds and unlocked the door, and they carefully left the room, then shut the door quietly behind them.

The ICU nurse was still stuck on the phone as they left the file on her desk. "That was quick," she said.

The operative winked. "No change. The measurements are as indicated."

The nurse looked relieved. "Thanks."

The operative and Ramirez walked out of the ICU and took the elevator to the basement. They went out a rear entrance to a waiting ambulance.

They climbed in the back, and the vehicle pulled slowly away.

Karen Feinstein was dead.

Fifty-One

It was 1:03 a.m. The minutes crawled by. McNeal tried watching TV. Flicking between channels. Inane game shows. Late-night horror flicks. Talk shows. More and more bullshit. He switched to the news channels.

He switched it off.

He tried to kill time. He showered. He put on a T-shirt and the jeans Luigi had supplied. Everything fit.

The cell phone Luigi had supplied him with vibrated on the table. It was the first text from the kid who was working for Luigi's crew.

The message said simply, Target has set alarm on phone for 5:01 am. More to follow . . .

McNeal knew it was just a matter of hours. He googled the name *Andrew Forbes*. A photo in the *Times* of a clean-cut, good-looking young man standing beside the President. *The personal assistant*, the press called him. At one time, Forbes carried bags and made sure all the little things behind the scenes were attended to.

This was the man who had put in motion the death of his wife, presumably Sophie Meyer as well. This was where it all started. This young man, a son of privilege, his father a seriously wealthy and reclusive investor. It seemed incredible to McNeal that this young man—who had his whole life ahead of him—had ordered people killed, just to protect the President's reputation.

But who was he to talk? Look at him. A killer. A disgrace to the uniform and to law enforcement. He had investigated cops for wrongdoing, most for doing nothing like he had done. Mostly alcoholic cops, burned-out cops, or just broke cops.

He was far, far worse than anyone he had put away or gotten thrown off the force.

The buzzer rang, and he snapped out of his dark thoughts. He checked the video intercom.

"Pizza!"

McNeal sensed something was wrong. "I didn't order any pizza."

"Courtesy of Luigi."

McNeal buzzed the kid in.

"There you go, man." A huge pizza with four bottles of spring water. "A gift from Luigi."

McNeal tipped him fifty bucks.

"Thanks, man."

The kid left the building. McNeal wolfed down the food, having not eaten since breakfast. It was nearly three in the morning when he received a text from Luigi. Car on level 3 of parking garage from 04:20 a.m. Use stairwell.

Just over an hour away.

His heart beat faster. He still had time to bail.

Half an hour later, a man arrived at his door, as McNeal had arranged. The man was inked all over his hands and neck. He was a tattooist.

"You a friend of Luigi?" McNeal said.

"Yeah, sort of. He's a regular guy."

McNeal didn't want to get into a discussion. He just sat, looking away, as the needle was inserted into his skin. Slowly, excruciatingly, a triangular three-dot tattoo was inked on his left hand. "How long will this last?"

"It's a special ink. Will disappear in three months."

Twenty minutes later, it was done.

The man left.

McNeal was satisfied. He washed his hands in antibacterial soap. The three-dot tattoo was still there. He was laying a trail for a reason.

He sat down on a chair in the living room, staring at the walls.

Just after three, he changed into the hooded black tracksuit top and pants, black beanie, black Asics running shoes, Nike thermal running hood, and discreet earbuds to receive instructions. Then he took the unlicensed Beretta out of the bag. He racked the slide and placed it in the belly bag alongside the car keys and one thousand dollars in cash.

Not long now.

Fifty-Two

The alarm on Forbes's cell phone rang at 5:01 a.m.

He needed to get his bearings. He groaned and stretched, squinting as he got up. He pissed, washed his hands, and splashed cold water on his face. He put on a hooded navy Ralph Lauren tracksuit, wool gloves, white sneakers. He did five minutes of stretching exercises. Then he put in his AirPods Pro earbuds and took his cell phone in hand, Metallica's "Enter Sandman" rousing his senses. He headed out of his apartment, the street still cloaked in darkness. A yellow cab cruised past. He watched his breath turn to vapor in the freezing air.

Forbes walked toward the park and headed across the Fifth Avenue crosswalk. Waiting on the other side was Iverson.

"You all set, kid?" he said, wrapped up in a thick tracksuit, beanie hat, and gloves.

Forbes thought Iverson was in great shape. Lean. Sharp. "Let's do it."

They walked into the park under the dim streetlights. They did some more stretching exercises. A few early-morning joggers drifted past.

Forbes did some deep breathing.

"Unbelievable what happened to Feinstein," Iverson said.

"Any improvement?"

"Don't think so. Fucked up, or what?"

Forbes didn't want to get involved in a discussion about that. He would rather forget what he had done. A small part of him now loathed what he had done. But it happened.

They walked and chatted for about half a mile, about everything from the freezing weather hitting the Northeast to what an asshole the mayor was.

Forbes and Iverson reached East Drive in Central Park. A few runners and cyclists and walkers were already there. "Let's go!" They set off at a jog up the icy path snaking its way around the reservoir. It was one of Forbes's favorite spots. They ran counterclockwise, as was the norm, following the lead of all the other runners.

A few minutes later, Iverson had already dropped a yard or so back.

Forbes felt his endorphins kicking in. He felt the energy levels rise. His mood elevated. And then he began to peak. Running faster. Stronger. On and on. He turned around and shouted back at Iverson. "Keep up, Jason!"

Iverson kept a steady pace, lifting his hand to acknowledge him.

Forbes ran on harder. He loved New York in the winter.

Fifty-Three

It was still dark as McNeal adjusted his thermal ski mask and limbered up. He stretched his calves and thighs ahead of his run. His nostrils breathed in the cold air as he warmed up beside the Central Park Reservoir.

His earbuds buzzed to life.

"The kid is not alone." The voice of one of Luigi's men. "You get that?"

"What?"

"His smart-ass lawyer, Iverson, is with him."

"Appreciate the heads-up."

McNeal could've done with a heads-up earlier. But he knew that events are sometimes random. Maybe there wasn't a cell phone message. Maybe it had just been a verbal agreement to meet up for a run.

He had to roll with this. The time for brooding was over. The time for grieving was over. He needed to avenge. It was time to finish this.

He felt his belly bag and the Beretta against his skin underneath his fleece tracksuit top.

McNeal spotted them coming into view. He recognized Forbes right away. He made a mental note. Forbes wouldn't know who he was. His identity was concealed well behind the mask.

He kept on stretching. The pair ran past him.

He waited before he set off. He began slowly. Then he picked up the pace. He couldn't lose them.

His breathing grew faster as he got into his stride. He ran harder. Faster.

McNeal's breathing became more labored in the brutal cold. He ran on. In the distance he saw their silhouetted figures. But he struggled to keep a visual on them.

It wasn't long before he was losing sight of the pair. He dug deep. He ran harder and harder. Birds scattered into the dark sky as he puffed his way past.

McNeal felt as if he was living someone else's life. He thought of his father's last moments. He thought of Peter lying sprawled on their father's grave. And he thought of Caroline, her last fateful breaths on this earth. He thought of the faceless assassins that had been sent to kill his flesh and blood.

And he felt an anger, a terrible anger rise up within him.

Suddenly, up ahead, the pair stopped. Hands on hips, as if taking a short breather.

This was it.

McNeal realized he had to do it now. It was just him, Forbes, and the lawyer. The three of them. No one else around.

He slowed down and walked calmly up to Andrew Forbes, the fresh-faced, good-looking college kid who had organized the murder of McNeal's wife. And others.

Forbes turned as McNeal walked up to them. "You lost?"

McNeal stepped forward and pressed the Beretta tight up against Forbes's forehead. He stared into his confident, arrogant eyes. Fear staring back at him.

McNeal didn't hesitate. He didn't say a word. He simply pulled the trigger. A flash of light. The suppressed gunshot echoed, birds in flight. Blood on the snow. Forbes lying dead, sprawled.

McNeal turned to the lawyer.

McNeal watched as Iverson fell to his knees, trembling, sobbing. "I haven't done anything! Do you want money?"

McNeal stood over him and pointed with his left hand, three dots visible. "That was for Henry Graff and Nico." He was laying his false trail.

The lawyer nodded.

"Gimme your cell phone."

The lawyer reached into his back pocket and handed him the cell phone.

McNeal took it with his left hand. "Close your eyes, count to two hundred before you even think about moving. Understand?"

The lawyer closed his eyes tight, nodded frantically, shivering and shaking in shock.

McNeal put his gun back in the bag, along with the lawyer's cell phone. He turned and headed off the gravel path, sprinting south on East Drive. He thought he heard a distant scream.

He cut down Fifth Avenue and jogged the twenty-five blocks back to the parking garage, next to the apartment he had stayed at the night before.

He breathed hard as he bounded up the stairs to the third level.

McNeal spotted the silver Ford Explorer. He took the key fob out of the belly bag and pressed the button. The locks opened. He slid into the passenger seat. His driver pulled away slowly.

They headed onto the Queensboro Bridge. A short while later they joined the light traffic headed out of town to Queens. In particular, Willets Point, known locally as the Iron Triangle, a neighborhood in Corona near Citi Field. They found the junkyard beside Flushing Creek.

His driver navigated through the rutted, icy road.

The gates were locked behind them.

Waiting for McNeal was Luigi.

"You okay?" he asked.

McNeal nodded as he handed over the belly bag. "The gun's inside. Also the cell phone of the lawyer who was with him. I'd like all the data from that."

"Part of the deal, Jack. Leave that to me. How you feeling?"

"Numb."

Luigi nodded. "It'll pass."

McNeal followed him into an office. He was handed some clothes and a bag. He headed into a bathroom and changed out of the running gear. He put on the jeans, T-shirt, thick coat, and new sneakers. He applied concealer on his three-dot tattoo.

Luigi handed him a bag. "It's got your fake passport."

"I'm going to Florida."

"You never know how it goes down there. You might have to leave the country. Just in case. New cell phone. I'll tidy up any loose ends."

"You got your money?"

Luigi nodded. "Every dime."

"I don't know what to say."

"You don't have to say anything." Luigi hugged him tight. "I don't suppose you'll feel better for doing this. But I admire you for doing what you did. Takes a lot of guts."

McNeal bowed his head. "You might get some heat."

Luigi patted him on the back. "I know how to deal with heat. Don't worry about me. Take care of yourself."

Fifty-Four

It was a short drive to JFK as he checked in for his flight down to Miami.

McNeal felt paranoid as he was scrutinized by airport security staff. He checked his luggage, but kept his carry-on over his shoulder. He waited in a bar with a cold beer before he boarded his half-empty flight.

He felt wired. He blocked out distractions and the drone of the engines with Springsteen on his headphones. He nodded off. Then it was touchdown in Miami. It was high seventies while New York was still freezing.

He took a cab to South Beach and checked in to the Ritz-Carlton. He wanted a sanctuary. A place to hide. A place to be undisturbed.

He was shown to his room overlooking the ocean.

McNeal tipped the bellhop and took his second cold beer of the day out of the room's bar. He went out onto his terrace and gazed at the ocean. The sand.

He needed time to decompress. Get his head around what he'd done. What he'd become. It was midafternoon when he eventually headed down to the pool. He swam forty laps. The simple pleasure of swimming. He remembered taking Patrick swimming at the outdoor Longshore Pool in Westport. He could see his son's face, smeared in sunscreen. He lay on a lounge chair and felt himself drifting off, cocooned by the warm winter sun. He slept like a baby. He didn't dream. He didn't have nightmares.

No corpses fell past his window.

The sound of New Yorkers talking loudly nearby snapped him out of his deep sleep. Moaning about New York weather. Taxes. Crime. Dog shit. The homeless. There was no escaping them. He was one of them.

McNeal dozed off and on in the afternoon heat until the sun was low in the sky. Dark shadows spread across the poolside.

He gathered up his things and headed inside. Showered and put on fresh clothes. He headed over to Ted's Hideaway. He sat at the bar and ordered a Bud, hot wings, and fries. He knocked back his beer and finished the food in a matter of minutes.

He had been famished.

He took a few more beers, made small talk with a couple of the locals. The TV replayed highlights of the last Dolphins game.

"Another beer, my friend?" the bartender said.

"Bottle of Schlitz."

"I like it. Coming up."

The booze was quieting his mind. He was glad to be out of New York.

A woman at the end of the bar called across. "I heard your accent. Don't tell me, New York?"

McNeal nodded. He was wary.

"I'm from Brooklyn."

"Nice to meet you. Staten Island."

McNeal drank his beer.

The woman looked at the bartender. "You want to change the channel?"

The bartender pressed the remote.

The huge TV showed breaking news on Fox.

McNeal stared at the screen.

The reporter said, "And the big news coming out of New York tonight is the murder early today of the President's former body man, Andrew Forbes. The young man was gunned down just before dawn in Central Park as he was jogging with his lawyer. Police sources believe the wanted man has a three-dot tattoo in a triangular shape on his left hand, perhaps indicating his connection to gang culture. Sources are speculating that Forbes's execution-style killing might have been a case of mistaken identity. But the shocking development comes hot on the heels of the death of presidential fundraiser and New York businesswoman Karen Feinstein. It is believed she took her own life ahead of an FBI investigation into her company's illicit activities."

McNeal felt numb. Not happy. Just numb.

The Brooklyn woman said, "That's terrible. I jog in the park once a week."

McNeal said nothing.

"New York is crazier than it's been for a while," she said. "Don't get me wrong, it's always a little bit crazy, but a good kind of crazy, right? But recently, I don't know, it's gotten pretty fucked up again."

McNeal nodded and finished the beer. He thanked the bartender. He stopped off at the Deuce dive bar on Fourteenth Street, an old favorite of Peter's when they were down on vacation.

He had a couple of beers and walked toward Ocean Drive. Past Lummus Park and onto the beach, down to the water's edge. He sat down, waves crashing onto the sand.

McNeal felt empty. He hadn't found solace in his vengeance. He was just alone. So very alone.

His thoughts returned, as they often did, to his dead son. Killed by McNeal's former partner, a drunken, psychotic cop. Patrick had been dead for eight long years. Jack yearned for him. More than anything, even more than his wife, his brother, his father, it was his son he missed.

He hadn't been the same since Patrick had died. He traced it back to where it all began. A slow descent into a living hell. Work. Interviewing fucked-up cops. Unable to sleep. More fucked-up cops. Listening to alcoholic cops justify their actions. The nightmares. His wife gone, then murdered. He tracked down and killed Graff and Nicoletti. Then the rest of his family is killed, one by one. He, in turn, killed Forbes.

The more he thought about it, the more he realized he had lost not only his moral center, but the remnants of what made him human. He had lost his soul or lost his mind.

No wife. No brother. No father. No son. A killer. A cold-blooded killer. Nothing more, nothing less.

McNeal knew he was still in the crosshairs of the Feds. They hadn't just forgotten about Henry Graff's death. They would be building a case against him and his dead brother. But what did they really have?

He stared at the shimmering moonlight on the water. The waves crashed onto the sand.

His mind lingered on the killing of Andrew Forbes. The split second as he stood there. The eyes staring at him as if puzzled, not comprehending what was about to happen. Before his mind could process it, Forbes was lying dead, blood on the frosty ground.

He wondered if he should have left the country. But that wasn't him. He wasn't going to hide away.

He was an American. He would live as an American, and he would die as an American, unbowed and unapologetic, still a free man.

Fifty-Five

The weeks rolled into months as McNeal hunkered down in plain sight in Florida.

He swam every day. He walked. He sat and drank coffee at sidewalk cafés, people-watching on the beach. He ambled around the Art Deco district enjoying the warmth and vibes. Up north, everyone was still wrapped up against the cold. His colleagues in Internal Affairs were probably dealing with the usual backlog of cases building up. That wasn't his problem.

From time to time, he checked in on Muriel to see how she was holding up. She would occasionally break down, missing her husband. Her soulmate. She thanked Jack for allowing her the luxury of never again having to worry about how to make ends meet. But that wouldn't bring her husband back.

He called his psychologist once or twice. She asked when he was coming back to "civilization."

The more he hung out in the sun, the more his world began to slow down and the more he felt inclined to move down to the Sunshine State for good. In many of the cities, it was like being in New York, except with fantastic weather. You couldn't move in Boca Raton or South Beach or Naples without hearing voices that sounded like the five boroughs. And in Key West, it was ridiculous.

He didn't blame them. Life was good if you had a few bucks to spare in Florida. It was a perfect place to retire. Sun, sea, and sanctuary from brutal northeastern winters. He felt healthier. Less crazed. He had time to breathe. Time to think.

McNeal went out marlin fishing on a few occasions. Mostly with only the boat owner for company. A few beers, sitting out on the deep blue waters, hoping for a bite. Hoping for peace. He finally learned to switch off.

It was late summer when he arrived back in Manhattan. He felt able to go on, for the first time in a long time, despite losing everything that mattered to him. He caught a cab back to his apartment. He half expected the Feds, the NYPD, or the Secret Service to be waiting for him. But there was none of that.

His doorman gave him a pile of mail.

"You enjoy your vacation, Mr. McNeal? I missed you, man."

"Very nice, Rico. You and your family got any plans this year?"

"My wife wants to see her family in Puerto Rico. She gets so homesick. She doesn't like Brownsville."

"It's a tough part of town. Any chance of a move?"

Rico gave a sad smile. "I'd love to move. I can't afford to move. We're trying to save up enough for a $30,000 deposit for a one-bedroom apartment in the East Village."

McNeal took out his cell phone. "Tell me your bank details."

"What?"

"Give it to me. I might be able to help you out."

"I don't want your charity, man."

"Who said anything about charity? We all need a helping hand. You've helped me so many times, picking up packages and letters and bullshit like that."

"I feel embarrassed."

"Give me the details. I might be able to help you out a little."

Rico reluctantly gave him his bank details.

McNeal noted the numbers and wired the money directly. A few moments later, the money had been transferred. "Hopefully that gets you a little closer to your goal."

Rico just stared at him. "I don't know what to say."

"How about, *Nice to have you back*."

"Very nice to have you back, Jack."

McNeal had no idea why he had acted so rashly. He figured it was his money, inherited from his wife, and his to do with as he pleased. And he had.

Maybe it was guilt. Whatever it was, it made him feel good. For once, he felt good.

He rode the elevator and was relieved to get back to his apartment. It was all pristine. It even smelled nice. Fresh. Clean. The ghosts of the past seemed to have lifted. He knew it was a temporary thing.

He sifted through his mail. He saw the envelope with the NYPD Internal Affairs stamp on it. He opened it up. It was from Bob Buckley, asking him to come into the office. It was dated three weeks ago.

McNeal called ahead and said he would be there in under an hour. He picked out a nice navy suit from his wardrobe, his best tie, a white shirt, and black shoes and took the short walk to the Internal Affairs Bureau office. It felt weird to be back.

Buckley was on his phone, feet up on his desk, signaling for McNeal to come in. "Three weeks, sir, and we'll have it wrapped up. That's a promise. No, thank you." He slammed down the phone. "What an asshole."

McNeal stood and waited for the invitation. "Pull up a seat. Jesus Christ, look at the fucking tan. You been in the Caribbean?"

"Florida."

Buckley sat up in his seat. "How are you feeling?"

"It's been a rough spell. I needed to get away. My father and brother both dying out of the blue. I didn't feel like myself."

Buckley picked up Jack's shield and ID lanyard. "Here, these are yours."

McNeal took them, clasping his career tightly in his hands. "And that's it?"

"Suspension's over."

"Yeah?"

"A month ago, I had a visit from the FBI. A guy from the Secret Service was there too. They said the investigation into you, and links to the disappearance of Henry Graff, is over. They believe, and this is off the record, that he was killed by someone working for Karen Feinstein. They believe you and your brother were followed after you met up with him. I've also heard that the death of the President's body man might've been linked to that."

"I read about that."

"The assassin had a gang tattoo—you know, the three dots, on the triggerman's left hand. Complete fucking mess."

"Who organized the hits?"

"Honest to God, I don't think they even know. It's a mystery. It's murky stuff. Graff was ex-CIA. So was Feinstein, apparently. Feds had begun looking into her company. Tax evasion. Then she overdoses."

McNeal sat in shock. "So, I'm back."

"If you want, you're back. How does that sound?"

McNeal mused, "The backlog must be worse than ever."

"You have no idea."

McNeal let it all sink in. "This is a lot to process."

"It's been a rough time for you, Jack. And I'm so sorry about what happened and how you got dragged into all this."

McNeal nodded.

"I'm so sorry about Peter. I know you two were close. I think he must've taken it hard after your father died."

"I don't want to think about it."

"Oh, I meant to tell you, the psychologist lady, Katz, she's been bugging me to talk to you."

McNeal rolled his eyes. "She has?"

"Wants to know when you'll be back."

"What did you tell her?"

"I told her, 'Jack will be back when his head has cleared.' And she said she would like you to make an appointment as soon as you get back into the office."

"I'll think about it."

"I think you need that help, Jack. We all need help."

"Let me get my feet under the desk again. I'll see where I am then."

"Good to have you back."

Fifty-Six

A few days later, on a day off, McNeal headed out to Staten Island and laid fresh flowers on his brother's and father's graves. He remembered the terrible, indelible sight that had greeted him, his brother's bloody body crumpled by his father's headstone. But today, the sun shining, there was no sign of the hell that had erupted all those months earlier.

He walked slowly back to his car. He pulled away from the cemetery and drove all the way up to Westport, Connecticut. He headed next to the windswept cemetery where his wife was buried. He kneeled down beside her grave, setting more flowers in the metal vase. "I just want to say I love you. And I miss you, honey."

He kneeled in the warm summer breeze. Thinking of the old times. Their time together.

McNeal then laid fresh flowers on his son's grave. A sacred spot. He touched the alabaster. The boy he would never see grow up. He knew that part of him died the day his son died. That's where it had all started. His dark thoughts. The obsessions. The ghosts in his mind, haunting his existence.

"Son, I hope one day you can forgive me. For what I've done. For what I've become." He closed his eyes, and he saw his son again.

Walking toward him, arms open, as a child. "For not being there for you."

McNeal didn't want to open his eyes. He wanted to stay in that moment forever. He felt his son's warm embrace. The sound of laughter in the distance.

He opened his eyes. No one was around. He was alone.

McNeal got back in his car and took the short drive to a spot a hundred yards from Compo Beach. He saw the sparkling water in the distance. Long Island Sound looked inviting.

He took out a pair of binoculars and scanned the beach. Families playing on the sand, a few hardy souls in the sea.

McNeal scanned the rest of the beach. Then he saw them.

Under a flawless blue sky, not a cloud in sight, temperature in the low eighties, he spotted Muriel and her children, sitting on a blanket, enjoying a picnic. She handed out sandwiches as the children built sandcastles. And they were laughing. Everyone was laughing.

McNeal felt his throat grow tight. He watched them on the beach for nearly an hour. So many emotions washed over him. He felt a terrible sadness. But he also felt glad that they seemed more at peace.

He watched as Muriel and her kids packed up, making sure to pick up any napkins, and left. The family walked off Compo Beach and across the road to his and Caroline's old house, by the sea. The old, salt-blasted colonial.

His Westport home was now theirs. They owned it. And they were using it on a perfect summer day.

He took a slow drive back toward his old home.

McNeal pulled up outside the house and sat in his car. He felt as if he was trespassing in someone's life. He got out of the car and rang the bell of the grand old home.

The door flung open and kids hugged him. "Uncle Jack, you came!"

"Jack, come on in! So nice to see you again."

McNeal hugged the kids and pecked Muriel on the cheek. He listened to the kids talk excitedly about their new house. They were now in schools in Westport. Nice schools. Nice friends. Peter's family had left their old life and sad memories behind. "How's the place working out for you?"

"Jack, it's fantastic. The school's great for the kids. So much more space. I just wish . . . Well, you know, I just wish Peter was here to enjoy it."

"He would have loved you and the kids to have this kind of life. I know it. But anyway, I just wanted to know that you were all okay. That's all I wanted to know."

"We're doing okay. It was a rough few months after . . . Well, you know. But we're getting there. Slowly."

"Daddy's not coming back, Uncle Jack," Frankie, the youngest son, said.

McNeal picked him up and kissed him on the cheek. "No, he's not. But I know something."

"What's that?"

"Your daddy was a very brave man. He was a good man. And he will be looking down on you and your brother and sister and mom and be really happy that you're all together and you're doing okay. That'll make him very happy."

"I miss him, Uncle Jack. I miss my dad!"

McNeal felt tears in his eyes. "We all miss him. And we'll never forget him, what do you say?"

Little Frankie nodded sadly and went to his mom, hugging her apron.

"A long road ahead," she said. "But we'll get there."

It was the same for him too. "I know you will."

About the Author

J. B. Turner is a former journalist and the author of the Jon Reznick series of political thrillers (*Hard Road, Hard Kill, Hard Wired, Hard Way, Hard Fall, Hard Hit, Hard Shot, Hard Target, Hard Vengeance,* and *Hard Fire*), the American Ghost series of black-ops thrillers (*Rogue, Reckoning,* and *Requiem*), the Deborah Jones crime thrillers (*Miami Requiem* and *Dark Waters*), and the Jack McNeal action thrillers (*No Way Back* and *Long Way Home*). He has a keen interest in geopolitics and lives in Scotland with his wife and two children.

Follow the Author on Amazon

If you enjoyed this book, follow J. B. Turner on Amazon to be notified when the author releases a new book!
To do this, please follow these instructions:

Desktop:

1) Search for the author's name on Amazon or in the Amazon app.
2) Click on the author's name to arrive on his Amazon page.
3) Click the "Follow" button.

Mobile and Tablet:

1) Search for the author's name on Amazon or in the Amazon app.
2) Click on one of the author's books.
3) Click on the author's name to arrive on his Amazon page.
4) Click the "Follow" button.

Kindle eReader and Kindle App:

If you enjoyed this book on a Kindle eReader or in the Kindle app, you will find the author's "Follow" button after the last page.